13 Lessons

for

Pleasing

the

Divine

13 Lessons for Pleasing the Divine

A Witch's Primer

LADY RAYA

WEISER BOOKS
Boston, MA/York Beach, ME

First published in 2001 by
Red Wheel/Weiser, LLC
P. O. Box 612
York Beach, ME 03910-0612
www.redwheelweiser.com

Library of Congress Cataloging-in-Publication Data

Raya, Lady.
    13 lesssons for pleasing the divine : a witch's primer / Lady Raya.
        p. cm.
    ISBN 1-57863-245-5 (pbk. : alk. paper)
    1. Witchcraft. 2. Goddess religion. I. Title: Thirteen lessons for pleasing
the divine. II. Title.

    BF1566 .R36 2001
    299--dc21   2001026081

Typeset in Weiss
Book design by Jill Feron/Feron Design

Printed in Canada
TCP

08 07 06 05 04 03 02 01
  8 7 6 5 4 3 2 1

Contents

Part One
An Invitation

Chapter 1
How This Book
Came to Be

It takes only three generations for knowledge to be lost in our world if it is not passed down. In times gone past and not so long ago, many practitioners of the olde religion were forced underground. If the conditions were not right, they had no way to pass their knowledge on to children or grandchildren. Telling would put the children at risk, and by the time the children were old enough to keep a secret, they were too old to learn the ways.

Now, Goddess be blessed, the Wiccan religion is arguably the fastest-growing religion in the United States. Founded in 1948 by Gerald Gardner, it is a reconstruction of the pre-Christian nature religions found in every culture and every nation throughout the world. Defined as a neo-pagan religion, Wicca is the worship of a Deity who is both Mother and Father to all of us, and who created the universe out of nothing. Wiccans revere nature as a gift from Deity and believe that it is our responsibility to live in harmony with nature, respectful of the bounty with which the Goddess provides us.

Once again, the olde ways are being passed along. *Thirteen Lessons for Pleasing the Divine* is my offering to those ways and to you. If you have picked up this book, you are likely looking for something different in your spiritual life. I invite you in.

The story of my life shows us that even if our knowledge was lost it can be reclaimed. In my life, I might have been the girl next door in your neighborhood, but through my heritage, I was a witch. I invite you to read my story and consider whether your long lost heritage might have made you the witch next door, too.

My Story

I grew up in a small town in Pennsylvania. My immigrant grandparents took me in and raised me when my mother asked them to help her. Like the old woman in the shoe, my mother had too many children, and she didn't know what to do.

My grandfather, Poppy, went to church every Sunday without fail, and, almost always, I went with him. I sang in the choir, participated in the Sunday School classes, and led the youth groups. It was the music that kept me in that church, and it was through the music that I first met the Goddess. I met Her in the choir pew, although I don't know if She was there first, or if I brought Her in with me.

I can't say the exact date the Goddess first came to me, for She has many forms. I do know when She came in person, and I know all the way to my bone marrow the day I met the Lord. Meeting the Lady fuzzes into a glowy background. When you meet the Lord, it's a spikey, sharp, bone-shaking thing—but that's the later story. I promise to tell you that story at the end.

My grandmother didn't share Poppy's interest in going to church. She never went, not once. Not on Christmas, not on Easter, not even to hear me sing the solos. Strange, I thought at the time. Mostly, women go to church, and men stay home, but Grammy and Poppy did it backwards.

Grammy knew things. She knew when the tomatoes were exactly ripe, and she knew which weekend we had to pick all the cherries off the cherry tree before the birds got them. She knew how to make a poultice for my skinned knees from some funny flowers she used to grow, and she knew how to keep a root cellar, with strange things growing in it. Sometimes, she would say odd things. Little comments that no one understood, and funny words under her breath. Or she would opt out of going somewhere that everyone else in the family was going. "Just let me have my peace," she would say, as we all bundled off on an outing. When I was fourteen, my father returned to my life. For reasons that I will never truly know, he approached my grandfather and insisted that I return to live with him, my mother, and their other children. My grandmother spewed epithets at him (in German, I assumed), but when my mother stood out from behind my father and said she also wanted me to come home, my grandmother turned away. My grandparents had no legal right to keep me against the will of both my mother and my father, and so I was torn from the only parents I knew and moved to my biological parents' home.

At age seventeen, I graduated from high school. I was pregnant. I moved back into my grandparents' house. All summer, I thought about what to do for a job. To my absolute shock and horror, I learned that secretaries don't make much more money than babysitters, and waitresses were in almost a deadlock tie. In those days, 1967, the local newspaper carried job openings under the headings "jobs for males" and "jobs for females."

"What should I do, Grammy?" I asked as she slapped the cards on the table. She was always playing some type of cards.

"Not for me to say," Grammy answered. "Your choices. Your decisions."

"What should I do, Poppy?" I asked the only man I saw as my father.

"Get married, I think," Poppy advised.

Grammy flicked her eyes at him. And for just an instant, the cards stopped slapping on the table. Silence. Poppy and I waited for Grammy to speak. And in that silence, the television suddenly blared up: "If you have a good math aptitude, you could be a computer programmer."

Almost imperceptibly, I saw Grammy nod. And in my bones, I knew the deed was done.

Ten days after my son was born, I turned him over to Grammy and Poppy's care. Every morning, I rode the train to Philadelphia, and I walked from building to building, asking to speak to the head of personnel. "I don't need a job application," I said to the clerks. "I need to speak to the man in charge." Whenever I got my audience, I would sit up straight, look the man in the eye, and say, "I have a good math aptitude, and I'd like to be a computer programmer."

Two months it took. Man after man turned me away, and clerk after clerk refused to allow me to even have the interview. But when I came home to that baby each night, and took him from Grammy's arms, I felt the confidence she had that this plan would work.

"You only need one man to say yes," Grammy's unspoken words echoed in my head. "Look more deeply into their eyes," I seemed to hear her say. "And hold your gaze."

One day Grammy's wish came true. One man responded, and I had a job. I was a junior programmer at age eighteen with Leeds Northrup, R&D Division. I was assigned to program the SDS Sigma 7 in assembly language.

My first paycheck exceeded what my father made after twenty years in the workforce.

I liked my job a lot. The years flew by. With Grammy's help I bought a house. After Poppy died, Grammy moved in with me. The little boy grew, and I built a life. I met a man. He pleased me. He excited me. I loved him. I wanted to marry him.

But it was not to be. It was 1970. The world, at least in small town Pennsylvania, wasn't ready for an interracial marriage. George knew it, even if I didn't. "It can't be," he said.

"Why not?" I was shocked. This was my plan. Since when did my visions fail to materialize? But George was right. He drove me to Philadelphia. We were stopped by the police. We were refused a seat in a restaurant—there were no tables available—not now, not later, not ever for a black man and a white woman. After we sat together on my front porch, my garden was vandalized, my windows broken.

George said, "This is how it is; I love you, but we cannot be married. Your little boy would be seriously damaged."

Grammy watched and never said a word, until one day, she said, "This child must have a life, and so also must you."

I kept all these things in my heart, and pondered them.

And then I kissed George sweetly and told him good-bye.

What Grammy Said

One day Grammy told me, "I am a wise woman. And you were born one, also. This means we understand things. Things not everyone sees or knows. Our family came from the Black Forest in Germany. We knew many ways, then, and they are not ways to be told. Only some will know these ways, and others cannot be told, either with words or with actions. Nor do they need to be told. They have their own existence."

She went on, and this was a lot of words for her, "When I was a young woman, we lived through the Great Depression. I had only two children in all those years, and yet my mother had thirteen. We had no birth control pills. It was common for doctors to give abortions in their offices. Then, during the war, women had to work in the factories. But after the war the government needed us to leave our jobs to make room for the men. It wasn't easy to get women who didn't want to become dependent again out of the factories. So the government told the doctors they had to stop abortions, threatened them with jail. So your mother had five children in seven years, and it overwhelmed her. I told her I could help her find ways to prevent this, but she was afraid. She is not born to us, child. She is not a wise woman. But when you were born she saw that you were. That is why she brought you to me, to be nurtured as one of us."

"One of us what?" I asked

"One of us People," Grammy said. "Just People like us."

I did not understand. I said to Grammy, "She just had too many children. She couldn't take care of all of them."

"I can't explain it in words. It's just our way. You'll see. When the time comes, you'll know. We are just the People who get things done. Just the People. It's something you'll figure out for yourself."

And she would say no more that day.

And I Became A Person Who Gets Things Done

Shortly after Grammy's talk, I decided to ask my mother for her version. I took her to dinner and asked her why she'd left me with Grammy.

"Because you spoke in sentences when you were nine months old."

"Is that a reason?"

"It frightened your father," she said. "And I had to protect you."

"Then why did you let him take me away from Grammy when I was fourteen?"

My mother said she couldn't stop him, but she thought Grammy would. It dawned on me that my mother wanted me to come back—to protect her, to save her. I knew then I was there because I was the one who would fight back when my father came home abusive and drunk. This is what happened:

One night I heard the unmistakable sound of a slap, followed by my mother crying. I waited a moment, reviewing my options. "I may be stuck living here," I remember thinking, "but this isn't how it's going to be where I live."

With no more thought I hopped out of bed, tore down the stairs, and burst into their bedroom. My father turned to me. "It's all right, honey," he said. "There was just a little misunderstanding." He tried to put his arms around me. With all my strength, I shoved him away.

"Then misunderstand this," I said in an even voice. "While I live here, you don't dare sleep if my mother has any reason to cry because of you."

He stumbled backward and clutched his chest. My legs were wobbling, but I determined he wouldn't see my fear. "Remember, sleep can be dangerous, and a bully is fair game." I nodded once in his direction, turned sharply to dismiss the topic, and walked with a commanding air out of the room.

I never heard or saw him fight with her again. That night was another lesson in how to be one of the People who get things done.

Now, at dinner with my mother, I asked her, "Didn't you know you have power, too? Didn't you know your mother would have given you what you wished for?"

My mother stopped, her fork in midair, "No, Raya," she whimpered, "I truly didn't know."

And when I understood what my mother didn't know, I knew Grammy's secret.

The power is within us, and we decide. My mother opted not to know her power, but it was there. She made her choice with her unconscious mind and never consciously examined it. It was like a sleep, from which my mother had not awakened.

We can't make a dream come true unless we awake.

And What I Did after I Became a Person Who Gets Things Done

The following spring I drove to the University of Pennsylvania and applied for college, in a rather unconventional way. "I don't want to just fill out the application," I told the admissions clerk. "I need to speak to the person who makes the decision."

And, after some runarounds I did. He, of course told me they had a committee and criteria. "It's a competitive school," he said, "and we select based on comparison with other candidates."

I told him I had some special circumstances, including a small son and my grandmother to support. "How could I come here if I have no money?"

He explained. If a department wanted me—badly enough—they'd find the money. I had my SAT scores and high school transcripts. He looked at them, allowed as how they were competitive. "But the final decision is the committee's," he said.

I leaned closer to him. "What would I need to show the committee to get a competitive edge?"

He hesitated. I licked my lips.

He put his hand to his mouth. I opened my hands, palms up, on the table.

He brushed his hair back. I leaned forward and put my chin in my palm.

He averted his eyes. I stretched my ankles out where his averted eyes would see them and slowly rotated one. No, I wasn't trying to seduce him. I wanted him to see me—not as a supplicant, or threat, or pain-in-the-neck. As a person, wanting something from him. My actions were what was required, for this place and this time and this man and this context. I was doing what gets things done. His hesitations told me my actions were succeeding in breaking through to his consciousness.

"Would you, by any chance," he finally and tentatively proposed, "be interested in going to the engineering school?"

I was and I did.

I became an electrical engineer. My father died, right before my graduation. People said he talked a lot about his daughter who was going to be an electrical engineer. At his funeral, I cried. I've always believed that life is eternal, and so death is not terribly upsetting. But failure to choose to live when the opportunity is presented? That, I think, is heart-wrenchingly sad.

Grammy died at nearly the same time. But I did not cry for her. Her life had been full, and she experienced it. She told me little more about being a wise woman. "The knowledge is of the universe," she said. "It comes to you. If you are watching, you will see it. Pay attention. The information is everywhere, but mostly it's in your heart. Follow your heart, and you will always know."

So I followed my heart. I signed on at the Bell System and started on the fast track. They trained me and prepared me for a career in top management. I watched and learned. Four years later I left Bell for the Harvard Business School. After Harvard, and a stint of international travel, working preparing proposals and analyses for acquiring companies, I went to work for a large computer integration company where I turned a ragtag group of six analysts into a mega-force of sixty engineers and MBAs with our own floor. I convinced my boss we needed a special key-lock on the elevator. Only those with a "need-to-know" could get off at our floor. This, of course, allowed us to run an operation with different rules. We'd work around the clock to meet a deadline, and then we'd stay home for a few days. Different, definitely, but we ran an operation that always met its goals. We did what it took. We were the People Who Got Things Done.

Ultimately I started my own company and took it all the way to Vancouver for a public offering.

Then, just when I believed my company was poised for success, my mother died.

And the company bankrupted.

For a Moment My Will Flickered

It was the bankruptcy, in the face of the previous years of phenomenal success that brought me back to thinking about Grammy. By that time, I had married, and I had two more sons. Bankrupting my company didn't make me unemployable. I could still code computers. I could still command a six-figure paycheck or a four-figure consulting fee. By the standards of the subculture of my birth, I was still rich and successful beyond the wildest of fantasies.

I had come a long way from my small-town beginnings. I had lived a twenty-year career on the fast track. I had traveled throughout the world, tasted the finer things society offered, experienced my days to their fullest. I realized it wasn't likely for my life to have turned out as it did. I had been a teenage mother on welfare. Yet, for me, the cycle of poverty had not held.

My mother died, and for just that moment, just the time that it took for her to disappear from Earthly existence, I lost my will, and it wouldn't return to me.

When my will flickered, my company's light went out.

By my philosophy, I had to believe the bankruptcy was my own unconscious choice. I believe we make our own world, and we wish it into being. If I remained true to my own belief system, I had to believe I chose to allow the bankruptcy to happen, or if I had not wished it, then the decision was made for me by divine providence. Why did I do that? Or, why did She, our

Creator, set me up for it? What message did my mother's death give me that derailed the train I had chosen to ride? What purpose did the Goddess have in sending me this message, this way? I needed to know. There are no accidents, my belief system said. No blips of mistake in the Lady's way. What happened had a reason, and the reason needed to be known. I resolved to understand my question, find my answer, and know my self, and my part in Her plan. I committed to know what drives me, and I determined to meet my soul.

I Came Home

And so one day, I went to my private cabin on the river, nestled deep in the forest, where I could be alone with the nature I loved, and I called on the memories. I lit the candles as the candles desired to be lit, and I walked the land as the land called for walking, and I performed the rituals as the rituals requested action, and I called the quarters as the guardians of their towers commanded, and I respectfully requested an audience with the Lord. And when the Lord answered, I asked for my instruction. When I received my instruction, I saw Grammy's smile. I considered the plan I had received for what would be my new life, and I knew my mother had finally found her power. She had used it, for the second time, to call me Home. In the distance, I heard the cry of my first granddaughter, yet to be born, and I knew the archetype of the power intended to ensure its passage, from generation to generation, through sunrise and sunset, slowly through the years. The power would get done what had to get done for the People to survive.

And this is what it is to be "of the People." There is a divine primordial power inside each human being. We may choose to surrender to it, or we may choose to keep it chained. If we chain it, we live in constant threat that one day it may become unleashed, and storm our castles. This is the source of our fear, and the block that kept my mother from knowing herself. But if we give up to that divine power, and let it be the force of nature that it was designed by our Mother-Creator to be, then we live our lives in the nurturing flow of the crafted, perfectly balanced, divinely pronounced good, peace and harmony of the universe. As I surrendered to the rush of the flowing stream of Nature's unfettered power, I heard my mother's voice. In her own way, she sang:

> Maiden, virgin, mother, crone, Built the universe alone
> But for him, her other side. Two as one! The yin yang cried.
> As I stood to take her call, I knew life within the hall
> Of the crimson king. Two see, in my heart, the best in me.

As I sang in the choir when I was a child, Divinity said, "Receive me, and let me come in." I answered, "Copy that, breaker, breaker." May you know the call of your heart to be one of us, and receive the transmission. Then you will understand that inner twinge of longing when we say,

Welcome Home
to the community of the People, just the People, Who Get Things Done

* * *

I promised to tell you about the first time I met the Lord, didn't I? Unlike the Lady, who is warm and welcoming, the Lord is sharp and commanding. He's a driver of people and the source of our ambition. I met him in person first in a classroom of the Harvard Business School. He walked into the room during a break and sat down next to me. Just then, a woman dressed in a uniform came in to wash the blackboards. I suddenly felt awash with shame and embarrassment. Sitting in those hallowed halls of learning, I became sharply aware of the servant class in our society. "You don't have to do that," I wanted to rush to the front and tell the washerwoman. "We can wash our own blackboards, do our own laundry, clean up after ourselves." But, of course, I realized this was the job she was being paid to do. The handsome man next to me seemed to know what I was thinking. "**Pay attention**," he boomed, in a deep voice that resonated through my head, and bounced off the walls of my brain. "**I want you to know what makes one mother's child grow up to be a washerwoman, and what makes another mother's child become a leader. I want you to know everything about the factors that determine fate. Knowing what drives destiny is your assignment. Study it, and learn it well enough to teach it to others.**"

I turned to respond to the man who was speaking to me. But, of course, when I turned my head, there was no one there. I breathed deeply, and tried to write the encounter off to imagination. But the words were written on my soul, even in the marrow of my bones, in a chilling and shivery manner, and from time to time as my life played out, they resurfaced. It was only years later, when I finally came home, that I knew these words would drive me until I fulfilled them.

After my coming home ceremony, I organized a church of witchcraft, and in that group I began to teach. This book is the written version of the course I taught. It is my hope that these lessons will teach you how to drive to your own destiny and find the fate written in your stars. I invite you to consider its teachings.

Blessed be,
Lady Raya

CHAPTER 2
WHAT YOU WILL
FIND HEREIN

"Thou shalt have no other gods before me," thunders Jehovah, from the script on the stone tablets of Moses. Meanwhile, with Moses in the mountain receiving the word of the Lord, the abandoned Israelites are feverishly melting their gold jewelry to forge a calf they can worship as a symbol of deity. Disheartened and angered at the apparent display of the Israelite pagan allegiance—and no doubt in a greatly agitated state as a result of his recent encounter with a burning bush—Moses slams the stone tablets against the golden calf, breaking the calf and the tablets into pieces.

A questioning reader of the Bible may wonder, "How did the Israelites come by this affinity for worshipping other gods, and why do they do it repeatedly throughout the Old Testament, bringing unspeakable horrors and wraths upon themselves at the hand of a jealous Yahweh?" What is the appeal of these other gods that makes the chosen people continually turn from Yahweh and turn toward worship at the altars of Astarte, Ishtar, Asherah, and Isis? Why would a seemingly homogeneous people, descended from a single ancestor, find the gods of other nations so appealing and seductive? How could Solomon, the great king of Israel, also be one of the most important contributors to magickal thought and pagan ritual? How did Solomon's Temple come to be the worship place for pagan goddesses for 240 of its 360 years? And most importantly, what exactly is God, what is our human relationship to God, and how many Gods are there? How can we discern whether we are worshipping a false God if we cannot truly fathom exactly what God is, and how can Yahweh be jealous of other gods if they don't exist?

In their hearts, most people have a definition of God. It may be difficult or impossible for them to describe this God, and words may fail those who try to paint a picture of the Almighty, but as we get to know another person, we are generally able to see, by their behavior, what another person worships.

One person's actions show belief in God as Money. Another person's actions indicate belief in God as Societal Approval. Yet another may worship at the feet of Outstanding Achievement, winning and competing at any cost. Many in today's society worship Technology, believing there will soon be a pill to solve their woes and aches and hardships, a miracle created in the laboratory of humankind. Each of these people is worshipping a "false" god—for neither Money, nor Approval, nor Achievement, nor Technology are the creator of our world; nor can any of these false gods grant the seeker inner peace.

However, true Deity, the creator, is awesome and powerful, a God whose name, according to ancient mystics, we can never truly know. To name something, according to both mysticism and science, is to form and associate it in our minds, to limit it and bind it by a definition. The mystics and religions of the East tell us that when we name, limit, and describe God, we are like a convention of caterpillars, sitting on a tree, trying to explain New York City. God is beyond us—omniscient, omnipresent, omnipotent, the All and the Everything. The ancients knew this and told their folklore tales of gods as a means of humanizing and explaining their observations of the frightful realities of the natural world. The all-too-human exploits of the divine Olympians reflected not a belief in multiple gods but an attempt to systematize the many realities of God and to set in place a logic with which to understand the complexities of the universe. People used the legends as a means of learning the personality of Deity. Individual legends revolved around local events and the local culture and environment. People who felt drawn to the hunt worshipped Diana; those who felt drawn to science and intellect worshipped Athena. People worshipped the Great Mother, queen of heaven, because they came from Her womb. They felt comforted and nurtured when they returned there. Isis, Astarte, Ishtar, Rhiannon, Hera, Aphrodite, Hecate, Asherah are all the Mother, all the womb, all the same.

When people worshipped their creator and Deity, they were not worshipping a false god. She was their Mother, creator of all life, and also their Father, patriarch and disciplinarian, who provided backbone, ambition, and the will to survive in a harsh reality. Their Mother provided comfort. Their Father provided structure, competence, and the will to live. He offered strength to prevail and victory in battle. She offered the reason to live; He offered the means and weapons to do it. Whether their names were Ishtar or Lakshmi, Kali or Vishnu, Diana or Apollo, Zeus or Hera, Allah or Jehovah, Shekinah or Sophia, Jesus or Krishna is unimportant. Children need not know the names of their Mother and Father. Our God is our God, and when we approach our Creator in the reverent manner of a beloved child, we are not worshipping a false god. It is only when we usurp the position of our loving Mother and Father with the non-gods of the stock market, the doctors, the boss, the abusive lover, the possessions, and the technologies that we are worshipping falsely. Then we are in danger of provoking a jealous Yahweh, who is the spirit of the Lord. When we bend our knee to the Lady, Creator of the universe, and show Her the reverence due from an appreciative child, there can be no doubt that it pleases the Lord.

"Thou shalt have no other gods before me," thunders Jehovah, Allah, Brahma, Zeus, while his female persona, Shekinah, Mother of us all, says:

> *Listen to the words of the Great Mother, who of old was called Artemis, Astarte, Dione, Melusine, Aphrodite, Cerridwen, Diana, Arienrhod, Brigid, and by many other names:*
>
> *Whenever you have need of anything, once in the month, and better it be when the Moon is full, you shall assemble in some secret place and adore the spirit of me who is queen of all the wise. You shall be free from slavery, and as a sign that you be free you shall be naked in your rites. Sing, feast, dance, make music and love, all in my presence, for mine is the ecstasy of the spirit and mine also is joy on Earth. For my law is love unto all beings. Mine is the secret that opens upon the door of youth, and mine is the cup of wine of life that is the cauldron of Cerridwen that is the holy grail of immortality.*
>
> *I give the knowledge of the spirit eternal and beyond death. I give peace and freedom and reunion with those who have gone before. I demand naught of sacrifice, for behold, I am the mother of all things, and my love is poured upon the Earth. Hear the words of the star goddess, the dust of whose feet are the hosts of heaven, whose body encircles the universe: "I, who am the beauty of the green Earth and the white Moon among the stars and the mysteries of the waters, call upon your soul to arise and come unto me. For I am the soul of nature that gives life to the universe. From me all things proceed and unto me they must return. Let my worship be in the heart that rejoices, for behold—all acts of love and pleasure are my rituals. Let there be beauty and strength, power and compassion, honor and humility, mirth and reverence within you.*
>
> *You who seek to know me, know that your seeking and yearning will avail you not, unless you know the mystery: for if that which you seek, you find not within yourself, you will never find it without. For behold, I have been with you from the beginning, and I am that which is attained at the end of desire."*

And so we come now to our Mother.
And it makes our Father smile.

---

* "The Charge of the Goddess," attributed to Doreen Valiente.

May you walk in the wisdom of Chokmah and the understanding of Binah.

Blessed be.

How to Use this Book

As I said in Chapter 1, the Wiccan religion is arguably the fastest-growing religion in the United States. This book records the lesson plan used in the teaching of one Wiccan tradition, Elijan Wicca. A tradition in Wicca is the same as a denomination in Christianity. There are many traditions, and each has its own rituals and practices, while all loosely follow the same theology. Designed originally as an oral teaching to be passed from high priestess to high priestess in a small coven structure, the tremendous growth of interest in the Wiccan religion ultimately demanded that the teachings be written down. Those who have been attracted to Wicca by the promise of learning magickal workings and witchcraft will not be disappointed, but those who truly learn magick will be surprised and astonished to learn what magick is.

Working entirely in a religious context, the teachings of White Wolf Temple of the Olde Religion (formally incorporated as The Temple of St. Catherine) describe ritual magick and spell casting as well as spirit guides, meditation, divination, and pathwork. The witchcraft of the coven bears a shocking resemblance to the power of prayer and an uncanny affiliation with the miracles of science. "Magic," as Carl Sagan reminds us, is the word used by the uninitiated for every sufficiently advanced technology. The technology of faith need be no exception. Those who work these lessons carefully and earnestly will find that the toothpaste of understanding can never be squeezed back into the tube of unawareness again. This book requires a caution label. Read it with an honest intention, and the world as you knew it will change forever.

This book presents a thirteen-part course in the tradition of Elijan Wicca. As you work through each of the lessons, you may take an online test. In the virtual environment of the World Wide Web, you can meet with other Elijan Wiccans through chat rooms and discussion groups and post questions for group discussion.

The lessons are designed to be taught in a small group—ideally thirteen people—meeting once a month, preferably on the New Moon. A ritual circle should be constructed, and one member of the group should take the role of high priestess to teach the lesson. The role of high priest in Wicca is equally important, and both the high priest and high priestess lead the coven and have defined duties in the group. Far from negating gender differences, Wicca celebrates sexuality and honors the male and female in each of us, recognizing that as the Mother and Father of Deity is One, so also we are each male and female inside. Wicca honors the sacred cycle of fertility and the wheel of nature's year. Nudity is perceived as beautiful and natural, and many Wiccan covens worship "skyclad," that is, clothed only in the sky, as a symbol of freedom, honesty, and vulnerability before God.

Each of the thirteen lessons includes a homework assignment for private study during the lunar cycle. As you proceed through the assignments, the skills and abilities known as the craft of the witch (*wicce* in Olde English, pronounced "witch") blossom and emerge inside you. At the end of the year and one day study program, you dedicate yourself to the service of Deity and become officially a priest or priestess in the Wiccan religion. All Wiccans are members of the clergy, fully qualified and able to communicate and hear the word of God for themselves, although further study and practice is required in order to appropriately lead others in the Wiccan path and become a high priest or high priestess.

Each of the lessons has a learning objective.

Lesson 1, The Origins of Wicca, describes how the religion of Wicca began. With this lesson, you will start keeping a personal Book of Shadows, such as *The Book of Dreams and Shadows.*

Lesson 2, Basic Wiccan Beliefs, teaches some general beliefs of the Wiccan religion. During this lesson, you will begin a regular meditation program.

Lesson 3, Karma and Ritual Tools, explores the nature of coincidental guidance and names the ritual tools used in casting a sacred circle.

Lesson 4, Sabbats and Sacraments, lists the eight Wiccan holidays of the year and describes their meanings. You will learn to identify the seven sacramental festivals of a Wiccan life.

Lesson 5, Pagan Mythology, describes how pagan myths influenced the development of mainstream religion.

Lesson 6, The History of Witchcraft, defines witchcraft as it is practiced now and as it was practiced throughout history.

Lesson 7, The Meaning of the Wiccan Rede, gives in-depth instruction in this central concept. You will recite the Wiccan Rede and give specific examples to explain its meaning.

Lesson 8, Spelling and Conjuring, lists various methods for spell casting and describes the basic rules of spelling and conjuring.

Lesson 9, Pathworking and Tarot, presents the ten sephiroth on the Tree of Life, and describes their tarot associations.

Lesson 10, Divination and Dreaming, explains appropriate uses for various methods of divination and lists the types of messages sent to the dreaming brain.

Lesson 11, Free Will versus Destiny: Finding a Personal Path, describes the meaning of "giving up to the Lord."

Lesson 12, Committing to the Goddess, illustrates how to design a personal dedication ceremony.

Lesson 13, The Initiation Ceremony, is the final lesson. Here, you will review the initiation ceremony in preparation for the decision to become an initiate in Elijan Wicca.

The path to the Goddess is a personal one. The God stands by Her side, ever ready to defend Her honor and fulfill Her desire. One does not step on the path lightly, nor does one approach Her with superficial or trivial intent. If you study Wicca in the Elijan tradition, you will learn about the Deity within, the self that is divine, and without a doubt, that Deity will claim you. You will learn to stand in the face of adversity, bend with the winds of change, and march to the beat of your own drummer.

Elijan Wicca adds Jehovah and his wife Asherah to the pantheon of Greek-era gods and goddesses. The name "Elijan" Wicca comes from the prophet Elijah, who performed many acts of magick at the will of God. The church uses his name to represent that our magick is done by the hand of God, and we are only vehicles that God (the Goddess) uses to perform it. As most of us in America have been raised as Christians, the Temple of St. Catherine feels it is important to reconcile the God of our fathers with the Goddess of our great great-grandmothers.

This book includes an audio CD for certain poetry and chants, which must be spoken and heard to be effective. You may also participate in my online discussion forum and take the online tests for this book at http://www.LadyRaya.org/. You will find your password information at the end of the first lesson. As you study the rituals of Elijan Wicca, keep in mind that they are to be performed with reverence for the Goddess and the God, who will be with you in body, mind, and spirit as you work, and who see you as their beloved child.

Part two
The Lessons

LESSON 1
THE ORIGINS OF WICCA

RUN dot Child, and find your Way
Blessed. Be the light of day.
You're the Star Light of my "I"s
Be Thou Wise.

YOUR OBJECTIVE FOR LESSON 1

After this lesson, you will be able to describe how the religion of Wicca began and will start keeping a personal Book of Shadows, such as *The Book of Dreams and Shadows*.

In the beginning of human history, as cave people began to draw pictures on walls, they left evidence that they believed the universe had a Creator. Pregnant bellies, from which humankind emerged, suggested to humanity that the Creator was Mother. Even today, we know every child's greatest fear is "separation from my mother." Early humans felt that fear and sought to know this Mother; thus, religion was born.

THE GREAT MOTHER GODDESS OF FERTILITY

Connection with the Mother is a primordial drive. Its importance in our human makeup can not be disputed. Animals show it. We all know the feeling inside: Mother is primary to our perception of safety and our need for comfort and warmth. All aboriginal tribes and primitive peoples concluded this Great Mother was God. Why, then, would humanity, after 25,000 years of worshipping the Great Mother, suddenly deny Her existence and replace Her with a patriarchal God? What would—or, did—the worship of a God at the exclusion of a Goddess do to the structure of society's values?

Early humans did not conclusively recognize the role of fatherhood in reproduction. After all, much copulation was going on. Who could imagine what its result would be? As people noticed similarities in the way a child looked compared to his or her father, the connection began to be drawn, but until tribes comingled and fathers from different ethnic groups were added to the group, the relationship between fathers and children was unclear. The winds and the rivers were suspected of carrying pregnancy, just as the birds and the bees carried pollination of the fields. The Great Mother, Goddess of the fertile fields and the fertile bellies, reigned. Fertility was everything, for fertile land produced food, and fertile women produced more warriors to hunt for the tribe. The Sun, Moon, and stars provided the clock that set the pace of life. Early humankind knew the Great Mother was watching and built their religious beliefs around the womb of nature She provided for our home.

The Introduction of a Lord

Much time passed in the development of humankind, and the ape-hominids evolved into groups of civilized societies. Seven of the greatest were the Mayan, the Egyptian, the Anglo-Celt, the Greek, the Norse-Saxon, the Chinese, and the Roman civilizations. These great civilizations had structure, hierarchy, technology, and order. Each of them also developed a belief system in which the gods also had structure, hierarchy, technology, and order—an order, in fact, that reflected much about the society's order, and told the story of the society's development. Their mythological stories explained their thought processes. Mythologies and legends defined their concepts of heroism, their visions of good behavior, and their opinions of what constituted crimes against the people.

These stories had much in common. In every pantheon (group of gods and goddesses that were associated with a civilization), we find the Great Mother associated with the Earth and usually the Moon, and the Sky Father associated with the Sun and the Stars. The sky, Sun, and stars represented our understanding of the passage of linear time. We learned from the sky how to build a calendar, and so the God became Father Sky and Father Time. He was a linear representation of time, and he became associated with the *lingam*, or the penis, of fertility.

The Mother was associated with the nurturing comfort of cyclical time. She was the cycle of agrarian planting and the monthly cycles that brought menstruation. She became Mother Earth and Mother Nature, associated with the Moon and the circles of our lives. She was the *yoni*, or the womb, of fertility. The dark Moon was Her menstruation because we believed women hid during this time.

By observation over time, humanity learned that both He and She were required for fertile creation. We needed both the clock and the calendar, the *yoni* and the *lingam*, the zero and the one. Human civilization decided to add a Lord to the Lady, and thus the Son was born.

THE MOTHER-SON ARCHETYPE

We find in ancient mythology that gods and goddesses of all cultures tend to marry their brothers and sisters and to have children with their mothers and fathers. We find that the Mother-Son relationship tends to be originally a "virgin birth" (because the Mother is the beginning), and then the Son grows up and becomes the father or overthrows the father. Just as the great sum of all Greek gods, Zeus, impregnates his mother, Rhea (by turning into a serpent), so also Horus, the son of the Egyptian goddess Isis, becomes ruler beside his mother, and Jesus turns from the Lamb to the Lion in the Book of Revelation and takes over his father's position as God, making it possible for Him to marry the Lady with the stars in Her hair—his mother, Mary. The stories of our gods and goddesses bear great similarities among all civilizations.

The archetypal story programmed into humanity's collective software is an Oedipal story: "Son-loves-Mother-and-fights-to-overthrow-Father." The hierarchical structures developed by men to run corporations and armies exist to keep that primordial tension in check. Men work in hierarchical groups because hierarchical groups work men at their most primordial level. Women work in corporations, armies, and hierarchies only to the extent that women call upon the part of themselves that contains the male energy. We are each part male and part female. It is the male part that operates in the tribal structure of hierarchy because it is the male part that is constantly aware of the (sexual) tension between the Father (God) and the Son (God). This maleness of God was introduced into human society when the society recognized its need for structure and order. God became the evolving ape-men's version of the anthropologic "dominant male."

THE DUAL NATURE OF GOD

Now we know what the male energy in each of us does. It structures. It orders. It times. It analyzes. It drives. It produces logical thought. Being born a physiological male does not make one person more analytical and logical than another person, just as it does not make one person more capable of playing baseball than another person; but it does make the entire group of males more right-brained than the entire group of females, on average. Like everything that is exhibited by the probability of chaos, however, we must be careful to realize that knowledge about the characteristics of the group average carries no information about the characteristics of any one individual in that group, so any one specific female can have more right-brain characteristics than any one specific male. We each have varying degrees of male energy and female energy within us.

The God, however, does not have that variation. He is all male. She is all female. By definition, the God is male energy and the Goddess is female energy. Added together, they are perfection and all-encompassing. Separated, something is missing. In Wicca, we envision God as the Lord and the Lady, a perfect couple. Dual in nature, they are always up to the task at hand. The opposite of androgynous, which means asexual, the Lord and the Lady are sexuality at the extremes. They personify the characteristics that delineate sexes. Wiccans never think of Deity as an "it" or an impersonal energy force. Rather, the Goddess is divine femininity, and the God is supreme masculinity. But They, the one true God, are male and female. "Let us make man in our image," Jehovah-Shekinah says in the Book of Genesis. This is the reflective response of the One making Two. The male energy and the female energy are Deity, and they are the force of the yin yang creating the world.

While the male energy is structure, discipline, drive, and ambition, the female energy is intuitive, compassionate, nurturing, and mothering. She is accepting; He is judging. A society that denies this female part of God hurts itself immeasurably. It turns its people back to their animal nature.

Women work in egalitarian circles, not hierarchies; quilting bees, not militia platoons; they become small business entrepreneurs, not monopoly tycoons. This is the female nature, to cling to family structures, not business structures. When God does not have a feminine representation as well as a masculine one, the society learns to denigrate the female parts of everyone. Domestic violence, child abuse, pornography, and sexual perversion result from a social fabric in which the feminine principle is not equally divine. Humanity needs this perception of the Great Mother so that the Son will have someone to love.

The Loving and Present Mother and Father

The origin of Wicca is the primal human understanding of the differences in the sexual nature of our being and the celebration of that nature in its context of the created and crafted world. We know this world is a living organism, carrying us in Her Womb, guiding us by His Hand. The vision of Her Womb and His Hand give Wiccans a grounded concept of a God who is both comforting and protecting, nurturing and guiding. This belief in a loving and present Mother and Father pervades our daily life and causes us to live in a magickal context, in which we see God in our daily circumstance, and to feel guidance from ever-present coincidence. We replace the mores and behaviors taught to us by our earthly mothers and fathers with the guidance placed in our hearts by the Great Mother and the Sky Father. Led by this divine Will, we say:

An' it harm none, do as Thy Will.

We know that the desire in our hearts is the desire placed there by our Mother and Father, who are only in heaven to the extent that heaven is here on Earth. There is much heaven on Earth, should one choose to see it. The only hell in existence is the hell we create in our own minds.

From these ancient beginnings, Wicca, the religion of Nature, arose. In observing that Nature, we believe we come to know God.

DEFINITIONS FOR LESSON I

Wicca. A neopagan, Earth-based religion put together in format by Gerald Gardner in 1948. The religion is based on a belief in both a male and a female Deity of the universe and a strong connection to the cycles of Nature and the harmony of the forces of Nature. The theology is a reconstructed version of aboriginal Earth religions. Wiccans are usually strongly proenvironment and highly individualistic. They are characterized by their aversion to unnatural structure and their belief that there is only one law, which is "An' it harm none, do as Thy Will." Most, but not all, Wiccans practice witchcraft. Most, but not all, worship a dual Deity—the Horned God, who is the Father of humanity, and the Triune Goddess, who is Virgin, Mother, and Crone. The Lord is considered the Husband-Father-Son energy of the divine. The Lady is the Wife-Mother-Daughter energy of the divine. Wicca has grown dramatically since 1995, with the advent of the Internet, as more and more of America's Christians search for a spiritual solution that they feel is more relevant to their lives. Wicca is showing particular appeal in America's high schools where Wiccan covens are being formed by word-of-mouth among teens who read books about it. It is essentially a grassroots spiritual movement, led by nobody and emerging without a central leader.

New Age. Emerging since the 1960s, a peculiar brand of spirituality without theology, New Age is primarily a conglomeration of Christians and ex-Christians who feel uneasy about leaving behind their childhood church teachings. New Age is generally a Christian philosophy that incorporates metaphysical principles such as channeling, dream analysis, séances, tarot reading, psychic encounters, reincarnation, and astrology, without breaking from a Christian identity. It has no one particular leader but is generally marked by an angel theme and can be heard to refer to the archangels Michael and Gabriel frequently. New Agers are distinguished from Wiccans in that New Agers generally assume a male God and a heaven although discussion of theology and the nature of God is not commonly practiced as part of the spirituality.

Witchcraft. Witchcraft is a skill used to perform magickal workings. Wiccans (the religion) practice witchcraft (the skill), but Witchcraft is also a particular pagan path whose practitioners declare themselves descendants of witches from pre-Christian days. In some of these traditions, elaborate schemes of training and initiation proclaim to make "real" witches out of the mundane. These groups argue that their religion predates Gardner's introduction of Wicca and was simply in hiding to prevent persecution. They say their practices have been kept alive through the ages by word of mouth, handing down the tradition orally. This might be true. Who can know?

Pagan. Any of many religious paths that fall under the common grouping of belief in the gods of mythology. Some of the many pagan paths are called: Druid, Wicca, Witchcraft, Native American, Enochian, Ceremonial Magicians, Voodoo, Asatra, and Hindu.

Rosicrucianism. A form of Christian mysticism and a mystery religion that is said to have spawned the Freemasons. An outgrowth of Rosicrucianism was the Golden Dawn and the Thelemic Society. Not specifically Christian, and not actually a religion, Rosicrucianism is more of a club membership.

Ceremonial Magician. A practitioner of magick who may use incantations and ritual without associating religious practices with the act.

Qabalah. Also spelled Cabala and Kabbalah. A theory arising from Jewish mysticism that explains the structure of the universe in terms of a ten-planed Tree of Life and a number theory using language and consciousness. The basis of the study of the tarot. Probably the next physics.

Satanist. There are some people who worship the concept of ego and self-empowerment and refer to their practices as the worship of Satan. Satanists are not associated with Wicca. Rather, they adopt a concept of a separation of God into an all-good force and an all-evil force. This concept is carried over from Christian ideas about Jesus and the fallen angel, Lucifer. Satanists use the upside-down pentagram as their symbol, with a goat head figure inside called a baphomet. Paganism, including Wicca, has no corollary to the idea of Satan. Pagan gods rule all, the good and the bad. Our pentagram is unrelated to the baphomet, although many people who are ignorant of Wicca mistakenly associate the two.

Warlock. A warlock is an "oath-breaker" or a traitor to witches. Male witches are called witches, not warlocks. The only place a male witch is called a warlock is on the television program *Bewitched* and in some children's role-playing-games.

Fluffy Bunny Pagans. People whose commitment to the Goddess begins and ends on Internet newsgroups and chat rooms. Wicca is a way of life. If the Goddess doesn't change you, you haven't met Her. This change is inside you, and it consists of more than "doing spells" and attending drum circles. Fluffy Bunnies are those who do not commit to the hard work of personal change and do not accept the responsibility inherent in the Rede to "harm no one" and find your "True Will."

Tradition. A denomination in a pagan religion. Elijan Wicca is the tradition of White Wolf Temple of the Olde Religion, just as Roman Catholic is the denomination of St. Mary's Cathedral. Many Wiccans today practice as solitaries, that is, witches without an associated coven or group. Tradition refers mainly to the ordains, or lawlike practices, of a particular coven structure.

Ordains. The practices a particular coven or tradition has set up to guide its membership. While the law in Wicca is singular, and consists only of "An' it harm none, do as Thy Will," many traditions expand on that law to further explain it. Coven members may wonder, "Is it okay to kill bugs? Can I do a healing spell for my mother even if I can't tell her I'm doing it because she doesn't know I'm a witch? Can I wear a fur coat? Is there a preferred format for a spell?" Generally, when a coven chooses to provide guidance in an area like this, the guidance is written as an ordain. An ordain is not a law and does not have to be followed. It is the opinion of others, provided only as a data point, should anyone feel enlightened by considering it.

Gothic. A movement among America's teenagers that may have originated with "glam rock" in the mid '70s. Goths dress in black, paint their faces white, mutilate their bodies by piercing, spike their hair, and focus on feelings of sadness and misery. They consider themselves punks with IQ who make positive changes to a degenerate society. Their appearance and behavior are designed to shock society into thinking more deeply. Goths privately discuss art and philosophy in coffee houses. Because Goths sometimes use the pentagram as one of their symbols, many people confuse them with Wiccans. Because Wicca does not communicate its theology in public forums, many Goths mistakenly believe they are Wiccan. Wiccans feel concerned that our lack of publicizing our theology may have caused this confusion. The Goth movement was not started from any Wiccan sources, and its attitudes are decidedly not Wiccan.

Solitaries. This is a word used to describe witches who practice privately and are not part of a coven. In the final analysis, however, all witches are solitaries, whether they join a coven or not. The practices of the skill of witchcraft and the religion of Wicca incline us to make our own decisions about our spiritual life. Since our spiritual life and our daily life are tightly integrated, we practice alone almost all the time. Coven meetings are only a few hours in a month, but we are witches twenty-four hours a day, seven days a week.

Relationship between Wicca and Christianity. Most Wiccans, by the nature of when Wicca was reconstructed as a religion, grew up Christian. Wiccans who grew up Christian do not necessarily reject the God of their childhood. Many Wiccans first found God in a Christian church, most likely because they took the Lady there themselves. It is not the God of their childhood these Wiccans reject, but the church structure and doctrine of their childhood.

Wicca has some specific doctrinal beliefs that the current Christian churches deny, such as reincarnation. In addition, Christians and Wiccans disagree over such matters as the Deity and/or the humanity of Jesus, the doctrine of original sin, the writings of Saul of Tarsus (the apostle Paul), and the doctrines of Satan and hell. Because of these specific theological points, most Christians would reject a Wiccan who professed to be Christian. Most Wiccans, however, would say that a Wiccan who accepted Christ was just another Wiccan with her own path; Jesus may be added to the pantheon should a Wiccan choose to do so. White Wolf Temple of the Olde Religion, and the tradition of Elijan Wicca, reconciles the development of these seeming irreconcilable theologies and provides a bridge between the God of our fathers and the Goddess of our great great-grandmothers. For those who are not ready or able to profess their religion to nonpagan families, White Wolf Temple is formally incorporated as the "Temple of Saint Catherine."

Elijan Wiccans specifically add the God of our fathers, Yahweh, and His feminine aspect, Shekinah, or the Sophia, to the pantheon as a means of understanding the personality and temperament of the Deity is as it is implemented in Western culture. Our tradition's priestesses and priests study mystical qabalism and its context and historical origins. We reference the Bible, the Qur'an, the Sefer Yetzirah, and the documents of Qumran as literary sacred texts. Our tradition takes its practices from the practices of the Levite priests in the five books of Moses (but without the patriarchal attributes of the Israelite culture). The tarot and Qabalah tie to the Book of Ezekiel. The mythology of Genesis has its roots in the Babylonian myth of the Garden of Dilmun. The story of Mary and Jesus is the mythology of the Mother-Son and Isis-Horus. The prophet Elijah performed magickal acts in the service of the Lord and the Lady. Elijan Wiccans practice magick in concert with Elijah's example.

Wiccan Concept of Duality. We only know light because there is dark. We only know good because there is evil. We only know pleasure because there is pain. The Lord and the Lady are the male energies and the female energies of the universe. They are yang and yin. We need both of them in our lives. There are times when the intuitive nature of the Lady is God to us. There are other times when we need the drive and ambition of the Lord. Male and female made He them.

What the Bible Says about Witchcraft. The King James Bible was translated from Hebrew and Latin (after being previously retranslated from Greek to Latin and back to Hebrew) during a time when witchcraft was much feared in England. As a result, passages in the text that should be correctly interpreted to mean "poisoner," "trickster," and "unethical huckster" were translated as "witch." The people of God are then warned to stay away from them. In chapter 22 of Exodus, verse 18, the Hebrew word *chasaph*, which means "poisoner," is used. The Hebrew text reads "Thou shalt not suffer a poisoner to live." In the times when a poisoned well meant death to the desert tribe, this is reasoned advice by a caring God. King James I, paranoid about demons coming to get him—to the point that he even commissioned the writing of a book called *Daemonologie*—instructed his translators to change the text to read "Thou shalt not suffer a *witch* to live." Likewise, the "Witch of Endor" reads in Hebrew a "Woman of Endor." In the early seventeenth century, a woman's power was seen as a witch's power, and it was greatly feared by the patriarchal society.

The Greek word that was translated as "witch" in the many versions of the New Testament is *pharmakomen*, which probably should more correctly be interpreted as "drug dealers." One suspects, under today's circumstances, that HMOs and insurance companies could be subject to that interpretation!

The Torah of Judaism, the Holy Bible of Christianity, and the Qur'an of Islam all claim ancestry from Abraham. They are filled with revelations from

God, some very specific to the societal circumstances of a particular time and a particular people. The advice to "marry our cousins," for example, or to "avoid eating pork," are examples of advice with situational relevance. The Hebrews needed to marry their cousins to keep their tribes together and prosper; they needed to avoid pork because it carried disease. Likewise, the advice against poisoners and drug dealers was appropriate for the day.

Wiccans believe that the scriptures and practices of all religions are revelations from Deity. The Lord and Lady choose to have diverse religious practices on Earth, because they believe in "different strokes for different folks." As a result, the Lord and Lady actually do say different things to different people. This conflicting guidance is part of their diversity program. Nature loves diversity.

Reading the Bible, like reading the scriptures of all religions, offers an opportunity to receive personal revelation from Deity. Wiccans read the Bible as spiritual literature, just as they read the Vedas, the Tao Te Ching, the Qur'an, and the Torah. People of intellect everywhere do this. No one has a monopoly on God. To presume that any one religion is "right" and the others are "wrong" is to insult the Deity's genius.

SUMMARY POINTS OF LESSON I

- Worship of the Great Mother as God was common to aboriginal societies worldwide for as much as 25,000 years of human history.

- The male Lord was incorporated into human worship practices as societies learned structure, hierarchy, law, and order. This Lord was at first the Son of the Great Mother, and then grew up to be Her husband. She, being the first creator, produced the Son by virgin birth.

- As society turned to patriarchy for survival, the God overshadowed the Goddess. To enforce tribal sanctions of behavior, the male God was used as the evolving ape's version of the anthropological "dominant male."

- Wicca sees the Creator as encompassing both male energy and female energy, just as human beings have both male and female parts inside them. This dual Creator is still one, but rather than being an androgynous and impersonal energy force, the Creator represents the boundaries of maleness and femaleness. They are our Mother and our Father, not a sexless energy force.

- The origin of Wicca is the primal human understanding of the differences in the sexual nature of being and a celebration of that nature in the context of a created and crafted world. It is the ancient religion of nature, and in observing that nature, we come to know God.

LEARNING EXERCISES FOR LESSON I

Reading Assignment for This Lesson

Read at least one, and preferably two, of the following books:
Cunningham, Scott. *Wicca: A Guide for the Solitary Practitioner.*
Adler, Margot. *Drawing Down the Moon.*
Buckland, Raymond. *Complete Guide to Witchcraft.*
Starhawk, *Spiral Dance.*

Homework Exercise

Step 1. During the month, purchase two blank notebooks. One should be a simple, lined, spiral notebook like you would use for school, with at least seventy pages in it. The other should be a large, blank journal, with a decorative hard cover. The decorative hard cover book is going to be your first Book of Shadows, and you can write "Book of Shadows" on it, along with the date it was begun and your craft name. Your craft name is a name the Goddess gives you. It is a special name that comes to your mind and pleases you. It may be a name you have heard in a dream, or in meditation, or just one that has been sticking in your mind for a time. However your name has come to you, if it pleases you deeply, it is the Will of the Goddess for you to have it. If you are a beginner to Wicca, you may not have learned your craft name yet, or your current craft name may be temporary. In that case, simply use your birth name until a craft name announces itself to you. You may wish to purchase *The Book of Dreams and Shadows* that was designed to be used with this book as your Book of Shadows. Other than that, put the book aside and do not write in it until you are told to begin.

Select a pen that is comfortable for you to write with. The ink color may be whatever pleases you. Set aside a time period when you can be undisturbed for at least two hours, preferably longer. Unplug the phone. Lock the door. Pull the shades. Send the kids to a babysitter. You may want to go somewhere outside where you feel comfortable and will not be disturbed.

Light a blue candle and set it where you can easily see it while you are writing. If you have any special talismans or charmed objects that give you particular comfort, place them near you. You may also want to put an amethyst crystal nearby, where you can touch it if you feel the need. In the spiral notebook, start from the beginning and write the story of your life.

Write quickly. Let the pen flow. Don't think about it too much, and don't write for the eyes of another. This story is for your eyes only. Don't censor what is coming out of the pen. Don't try to put it in nice English. Don't think out in advance what you are going to write. Don't worry about run-on sentences. Don't correct your grammar. Don't correct your spelling. Don't be concerned if you write things out of order—and, most importantly, *don't go back and change anything*. Don't rewrite your own history to make it sound better.

After you have learned the lesson of this exercise, you will destroy the book you are writing now, so that it will never be read by anyone else. Write it for yourself. Write it with the assurance that if you color your history, you will be deluding only yourself. Write it so that you can learn what happened. Write it like a confession, and, above all else, reach inside your heart to tell the truth.

If necessary, buy yourself some kind of locked safe to keep the book in while you're working with it so that you can feel assured that no one else will ever see it.

Step 2. When you have completed your life story, go to *RUN dot Child*, the CD that came with this book. Listen to the last track, Track 9, which is a hidden track not listed on the liner notes. Follow the directions to learn step 2. Be assured that step 2 will not involve showing your notebook to anyone else. It is a book of secrets and will remain private between you and God. Remember, do not look at step 2 before you have completed step 1. In order to do step 2 correctly, it is necessary for you to complete step 1 without knowing what step 2 is. If you personally know someone else working through this course, keep the contents of step 2 a secret.

The path of Wicca is not for everyone. If you have been chosen to walk the Wiccan way, your life history will already have revealed this. The path will not be new and strange. Instead, it will feel like what you have always been. It will feel like you have been away and are now returning, like you were once surrounded by aliens and now have found your own kind. This is why when someone approaches us to become Wiccan, we do not say "Join us in our way," but instead say,

"Welcome Home."

Blessings on your assignment, and I look forward to working with you.

Lady Raya

To join in the private online discussion forum exclusively for readers of this book, and to try the test questions for this lesson, go to:

http://www.LadyRaya.org/religion/classes/

When you register, you will automatically be registered for both the online test questions and the private forum. You must register your craft name and e-mail address, and enter the password: **WelcomeMe**

You will find an online test for each lesson, and a discussion forum about each of the lesson topics. Feedback about your text will be sent directly to your e-mail address. In the forum, you will also find discussions that I moderate, and topics on the Website covering spell craft, dream interpretation, herbs and oils, ritual tools, and Wiccan workshops and events.

Lesson 2
Basic Wiccan Beliefs

RUN dot Child, and make your mark
Be the candle in the dark
You're the Eagle who can soar
Lion, Roar

Your Objective for Lesson 2

After reading the coursework and participating in
the learning exercises, you will be able to name some
general beliefs of the Wiccan religion, and you will have
begun a regular meditation program.

In the first lesson, we learned that the religion of Wicca originated from ancient observation of the cycles of nature. Now we are going to explore how Wiccans generally practice their faith. The religion of Wicca is extremely tolerant of personal deviation, so to say that Wiccan beliefs are such and such seems at first to be an impossible task. Yet Wiccans as a group have developed a set of standards that set them apart from other pagans and New Agers. Although there are almost as many different traditions of Wicca as there are Wiccans, there is still a core set of beliefs that most, if not all Wiccans, would hold dear.

The Cycle of the Year

Most Wiccans would agree that the Creator is both the female energy force of the universe, manifested as the Goddess, and also the male energy force of the universe, manifested as the God. Most Wiccans would refer to this Deity as "the Lady and the Lord." Most would agree that the Lord is the Lady's consort, rather than Her husband, and that She is the

Great Mother, prime Creator, the uncreated, while He is alternately Her son and Her lover, equally divine, and equally a participant in creation.

The Lord is the Sun King during the spring and summer months, and the Dark Lord in the fall and winter. Every year at Mabon, the Sun King dies, to be replaced by the Dark Lord, and the Sun King is reborn at Yule and grows through the spring until He overthrows His father and rules the summer. The male cycle of conflict between the Dark Lord and the Sun King mirrors our own conflict between ambition and striving versus pleasure and play. Far from being evil, the Dark Lord is our capability, our backbone, and our creativity. We ritually sacrifice the Sun King—our desire for play and pleasure—during the cold months in order to build our backbone and strength for the winter ahead. However, the Sun King doesn't stay dead long, and we rebirth Him every Yule, and let Him grow back to manhood by the spring.

There are eight commonly accepted Wiccan Sabbats, following the agrarian wheel of the year. These are holidays, days for playing and celebrating and feasting with friends. Wiccan ceremonial rituals normally take place on the Full Moon and the New Moon (called Esbats). Magick for building is usually done on the Waxing Moon (the period in which the Moon is growing in the sky), while magick for tearing down something is done on the Waning Moon.

The Astral Realms

Many who have worked extensively in the occult advise against contacting the dead and holding séances, or, in particular, using Ouija boards. While not prohibited in our religion, the wisdom of the elders says these are activities with too much down side to be worth the price. We build ritual circles to keep these entities out and ask for protection from the watchtowers to guard our boundaries against them. The world of the dead can sometimes be a place a Wiccan will visit, but it is not common practice, and it is never a parlor game. The world of faerie, however . . . well, that world is alive and well and with us always.

The Beauty of Sentient Experience

Most Wiccans would agree we have more than five senses. Also commonly believed is that there is plenty of heaven on Earth and more than enough hell on Earth, and people choose to live in one or the other of their own volition. "As above, so below," we say, and this means there is nothing in heaven that is not on Earth, and nothing on Earth that is not in heaven. Our perception of the world makes it heavenly or hellish, and that is a choice of our own free will. Almost all Wiccans would agree we are reincarnated, although the specifics of how this process operates varies among individual perceptions of it.

By definition, Wiccans do not believe in Satan or the devil and consider hell, judgment, and punishment to be entirely Christian concepts, foreign to our beliefs. We take particular issue with the distasteful doctrine of original sin. We consider our babies born blameless and beautiful and each human being personally responsible for his or her own actions, with no supernatural Satan responsible for tempting us.

Reverence for Deity

We come to the Goddess standing tall, heads held high, eyes open, chins up—not bowing our heads and closing our eyes—and most certainly never getting down on our knees or prostrating ourselves. We are the Goddess's children, not Her servants, and although we serve Her, She chooses never to demean us. We are respectful of the Lord and the Lady, and we honor and revere Them. Indeed, we worship Them but we do not cower before Them, because They would be insulted if we did. Children do not fear their parents; they honor them, desire to be in their presence, and seek their approval.

The Law of Threefold Return

All the same, the Lord and the Lady have rules for Their household, and, as Their children, we live under Their roof and obey Their laws. One of these is the law of threefold return. Whatever a witch does, it is returned multiplied three times. If you do good, you will get three times better in return. If you do bad . . . well, it might be hard to live through it. This is a very strong reason to do only good and to take care to discriminate between the good and bad.

The Wiccan Rede

Witches live by only one hard and fast rule. It is: An' it harm none, do as Thy Will. This may sound like a simple rule to follow, but, in reality, it is difficult to determine our own True Will and to discern the direction of our hearts. Knowing what we can do that will harm no one is hard, as is understanding ourselves in our relations to others. The requirement to harm none includes not harming ourselves. It is really, really hard to avoid harming yourself. Most harm done to people is self-inflicted. So this one law can take a lifetime of striving to learn to follow.

OUR HARMONY WITH NATURE

Wiccans believe every witch is a priest or priestess and therefore clergy before the gods. Our religion is a way of life, not a nominal weekly or monthly meeting. In living the magickal life, we see meaning in coincidence and circumstance. We see beauty in nature and strive to be in it and near it whenever possible. We choose to touch the ground and the trees and the flowers and the herbs with our hands. We believe we are part of nature, and we strive to live in harmony with nature's laws. In that context, we see nothing shameful or lewd about nudity and nothing to be covered up or hidden about sensuality and sexuality. At the same time, because sexuality is part of our sacred nature, we do not associate it with violence, as has become the case in much of Christian America, and we do *not* tolerate domestic violence within the craft. Witches are not abused. Think about it.

Personal power and the empowerment of the Self is the hallmark characteristic of the witch. We believe divinity is within and without. How can one be a child of the Goddess without being divine oneself? But divine potential needs some work to be realized, and we do that work through specific practices and rituals.

Among these rituals is a practice called "drawing down the Moon." In drawing down the Moon, done inside a properly-cast ritual circle, we invite the Goddess to come to us and speak to us or *through* us. This has many ways to manifest and display itself. Sometimes the Goddess gives us visions, sometimes dreams, sometimes simply private revelations or extraordinary coincidence and circumstance. Other times, though, the God and the Goddess bring us inspiration and creativity. We often study the mythology of other cultures to learn characteristics of the Deity, and to impress the archetypes of the Godhead on our subconscious minds.

THE PRACTICE OF NONINTERFERENCE WITH ANOTHER PERSON'S PATH

In magickal workings, as in daily life, we strive to *avoid* manipulating another. We see everyone as having a unique relationship with Deity, a unique destiny, a unique path. But we are not Fluffy Bunny pagans or New Agers. In the end, we are witches, and where another's path crosses our own, we seek to protect ourselves and ensure that our energies stay balanced. We are spell casters and magicians as part of our celebration of the lives the Goddess has given us.

Meditation and Invocation of the Gods

Here is an example of the result of a private meditation that I did. I was attempting to solve a personal struggle with my weight, and I likened that problem to difficulties often faced by women with a zoftig (Venus-like) body type, that is, large breasts and hips. I wished to learn from the gods what I might do about this problem, and so I hoped to contact Aphrodite (Venus) to explore the issue.

Now it's important to know a little about Aphrodite's mythology to understand this meditation and invocation. Aphrodite was a foam-born goddess (born of the sea), possibly an adopted daughter of Zeus; in addition, Aphrodite was rumored to be a consort of Zeus. She had a magic girdle, and when she wore it, no man could resist her. After each liaison, Aphrodite restored her virginity by returning to the sea, so she remained ever pure and ever virgin (Cupid, or Eros, was one of her sons). Aphrodite was married, by Zeus's order, to the deformed and crippled blacksmith, the god Hephaestus. Her marriage to Hephaestus (Vulcan) didn't slow down her erotic exploits, however, and this was always a bone of contention on Mount Olympus.

Now Hephaestus was a fascinating character in his own right. The son of Hera (Zeus's wife) and Zeus, he was born so ugly and deformed that Hera, in a fit of rage, threw the newborn child off Mount Olympus. He landed in the sea, and the Goddess of the sea, Euronyme, caught him and raised him as her own. Hephaestus grew up quickly (as gods do), and showed himself to be an extraordinary craftsman and metal worker. Euronyme built him a fabulously equipped blacksmith shop, and he became craftsman to the gods.

One day, Euronyme went to a party on Mount Olympus, wearing a beautiful piece of jewelry that Hephaestus had made for her. Hera saw it and wanted to know where it came from. Although Euronyme resisted, Hera was a strong personality, and eventually Euronyme told her about Hephaestus. Hera was overcome with guilt over what she had done and rushed to the sea to find Hephaestus, begging his forgiveness. She enthroned him back on Mount Olympus and built him a blacksmith shop twenty times bigger than the one Euronyme had built for him. Over time, mother and son restored their bond and built a close relationship. Hephaestus became a respected and sought-after craftsman, held above the other gods in the areas of creativity.

Eventually, Hephaestus persuaded Zeus to give him Aphrodite for his bride, and so the ugliest god married the most beautiful goddess. Although she was never faithful, she was nevertheless married, and after her exploits it was always Hephaestus who kept the hearth warm for her and made her a home. He treasured and valued her, when he wasn't fretting and ill-tempered over her exploits, and he taught her the subtleties of love over lust.

When I called Aphrodite in my meditative trance, I was answered instead by Hephaestus. If you would like to read what Hephaestus said to me, light an orange candle, to represent encouragement. I wrote this poem in trance, in a space of slightly more than an hour. Not one word has been changed from my original handwritten channeling. Before dedicating to the Goddess, I never wrote a poem in my life. The poem is presented here to illustrate the potential results of Wiccan meditation and invocation. The words in italics were spoken by me in the meditation, acting the part of Aphrodite. The other words are spoken by Hephaestus.

Read this *out loud*, or play the third track on your *RUN dot Child* CD to achieve the appropriate effect:

THE COCKED CLAUSE

If I had smelled the Garbage I would not have bought the Rose
    For even in the tightest circles every Adept knows
        What Chalk is for. *Could you repeat? I didn't get that Note.*
            Nor will you, for the Talk is Sweet behind the Bill. *You quote,*
perchance, and yet you dream, and nothing further seems the same.
And with each passing Tick the Tock remembers how to Name
The moments. They're beleaguered for they hide behind the Tree,
    And every Time is numbered with a phrase. *If I could see*
        Your Point I'd surely crumble, for the Id knows how to spy
            And once it gets the Vision it invokes. The inner eye
    Of mind can be deceiving if it chooses. Patterns lay
        in waiting for the Spider who reveals the Web. *You say*
            the Spider just reveals it? It was in there all along?
        Well, surely. Just the same as You reveal your inner song
    Each time you push the buttons of the chord that I owe You
        And send along a payment. *Karmic debt cannot accrue*
to one who won't agree, I've heard. Then you've been made The Fool,
        for every Tom and Harry knows that Dick's a part of School.
            And Santa Clause is waiting for the Jane who can't be sure,
                So Sally comes along before She finishes Her Tour.
Now what's this got to do with being fat, I know you say.
        Well, here's the Truth about the Beef. It isn't what you weigh
            That calculates the reason for your lifely circumstance,
                But it's the Pomp you give it when you do the Ghostly Dance
        That comes and goes around. *Oh, talk in Riddles, Barley Corn.*

I coulda' said it better but I'm blowin' onna Horn,
And this Horn's made for Walkin' so it's sorta like a BOOT
And Boots are what make Networks come up. See it? *At the Root*
Of Evil lies a CornFlake that was Dandruff long ago
And it fell off a HEAD that had a Mountain topped with snow.
And every time Olympus grew an inch, the puppet's nose
Reflected all the stories. *Drop the rhyme. Say this in PROSE.*
Not now. I'm just a WordSmith named Hephaestus. I can make
A story or a poem, but I simply cannot shake
The feeling that arises when my Hackles rise. *The Hare*
that lost the race to Tortoise played a part in this Software.
You see, each single person had to have a program, but
there weren't so many plots to go around, so Father cut
A door in all the Sequences to let them all be shared,
And when the patterns stuck to Chaos Theory, they were Squared.
Oh, please, Smith, tell me true you can't mean life must oft repeat.
I tell you with my Heart on, Aphrodite, you are sweet
And full of Lust because you fit the mold of one I love
And others find their path is likened to another. Of
the gods here on Olympus, few have ever been unique,
and goddesses abound who have the virtues we each seek.
But Seven is enough to draft the outline of all plots
And lives all form a line to draw the picture from the dots.
Then can we not be changed? Oh, mercy, Change is our Ideal.
For if we have no Change, we just get Dollars. You can steal
A Bill to pay the piper just by transferring from Paul
To Peter, but the Invoice keeps a record of it all.
And that's the Sticky Wicket in the Game of Life. Croquet
Or Golf or even Cricket in the end becomes a Play
On Words that can't be mended if the Stage becomes a Phase
And Waxes to its Fullness. *Now your consciousness can raise*
The issue if it Nose it, for the Stink gets mighty Ripe
And Smelling is an option if you cannot hear. The Pipe
Of Pan can call the Mother to request a change in Tune
But only you can dance it by the shadow of the Moon.
A cock is only pregnant if the gun is ready, Smith,
And Wesson would be helpful for the Pop Corn to eat with.
But though you try to shirk it, duty calls and you must go.
So summarize the lesson, while my Ears prepare to blow.
The Fact is, little Pumpkin, Big is what you want to be,
And that is why the Id has called the Genie. So you see
Your wish is being granted. It's a function of the Plot.

And you're imbued with Magick to ensure it. *You can blot*
The lines out or rewrite them if you know the story line
But if you don't reread it you'll be doomed to hit Re-Whine
And then your Life's Remorses will RE-Peat and Pete some more,
And quicker than a winkle you'll Re-Use the Memory. Store
A Table in a Pick-Up or remove it to a Drive,
unless you change the program, you will never be alive.
And programs can't be changed unless they show on Uninstall
So Register their Filenames by enacting one more Call
To Mother with a Letter. It will need an Envelope.
And better you should fill it also with a length of rope
To hang yourself from rafters so you'll get a new rebirth
And in your Second Coming you can demonstrate your worth.
Oh, excellent. I'm Jesus. I can be the risen Christ!
Not hardly, mon cherie, but you can get your Karma priced.
And once you've got the bargain firmly set within your head
Why, then, you can go out to do the job. *Now you can spread*
The price across more lifetimes if you choose to take it slow
But once upon a lampshade you were blessed with an ON-GO
Expression in your Triggers, and that clocks your DNA
So don't postpone the EndGame or the whistle blows. The Play
Can never be The Thing unless The World remains The Stage,
So keep the Party going while you work upon the Rage
Engendered at the Banging and distributed to Man
And Woman by the Goddess who relied upon Her Pan
Of fields to do Her bidding. Did He bid your price too high?
Could be, so you must conquer all your Labels. You can try
To cut the little TAGs off, but they're mostly clamped in place,
So if your Price and Value aren't the same, then why not Face
The Fact of your Amusement and the Myth of your Ideal.
Alas, my little pumpkin, don't believe that YOU are Real.
For all that is Existent is A Charge of Up or Down,
And every Word that echoes has been spoken by a Clown.
So run to wash the teardrops. They are lurking near the Swill
And wear the Enigmatic Smile that hides the strength of Will.
For you are but reflection of The Word that lives inside
And if The Word gets Dirty it cannot be washed. The Bride
Of Heaven has Her Pattern, and Her Dial is Set. Two Won
The Battle of the Sexes, but the Prize went to The Son.
And that is You, My Pretty. You're the Prize for which the War
Was fought on Mount Olympus. Now you'll find that this may bore
Your senses to distraction, but remember only this:

If you are Aphrodite, you will never live in bliss.
The gods have made a program. You can crack it with a song.
And that's the song of Tantric evolution. **All along**
I meant to tell you, Mother, you are truly part of Me,
Living, breathing, hoping, and relaxing in the Tree.
And We are but exceptions to the Drama all around
Stirring all the pots and clanging lids to hear the sound.
Push the little key and turn the lock to make a noise,
You and I together fill the world with Girls and Boys.
They are but a dream. There's nothing here. Just You and I.
Swinging on a limb, and blowing stardust from the sky.

Love,

Hephaestus

The Archetypes of Deity

The gods and goddesses of mythology are archetypal stories common to the feelings and lessons intended for all humankind. Each pantheon, or cultural grouping of gods and goddesses, teaches the lessons learned by the society in which the mythology developed. Although I work almost exclusively with the Greek pantheon, every witch chooses his or her own set of gods for development. You may feel a preference for the Mayan stories of One-Maize-Revealed, who built the world of the center in the Popol Vuh. The Polynesian gods of the storm may appeal to you. You may like the gods of the Scots, or the Welsh, or the Irish, or the Norse. Perhaps you prefer to call Aphrodite and Hephaestus by their Roman names of Venus and Vulcan. Maybe the Egyptian tales of the dead speak more to you. Possibly you will find your Native American roots and speak to the Sky Father and the Great Mother.

Depending on how religion was presented to you as a child, you may feel most comfortable calling Jesus and Mary, Yahweh and Shekinah, or Vishnu and Lakshmi. Until you study world mythologies, you cannot tell which of the god-archetypes appeals to your senses and feelings. Perhaps after reading some mythologies, you will choose your own pantheon, selecting a few gods from different pantheons and putting them together in a new family of your own choosing. Of course, it is always possible to go to the Lord and the Lady simply as Father and Mother. After all, children don't need to know their parents' names, do they?

What God is

Just because we as human beings personify our gods through mythology does not mean these gods are creations of humanity. Deity is far beyond the capacity of humankind to understand. God is not a person, but our personification of God helps us to know God better. God is the all and the everything, present at all times and in all places, infinitely powerful and complete in knowledge. As Wiccans, we do not believe that our gods and goddesses are different entities, but rather they are multiple facets of ways for us to understand the persona of Deity. This Deity is our mother and our father, our creator and our soul. The archetypes of gods and goddesses are teaching images for our dreaming brains. They are a way for us to know God personally as a loving parent. They guide us to our home in Her arms.

If you would like to see an example of a Wiccan Esbat service, see page 211, "An Esbat Ceremony for the Dark and Full Moons." There you will find the New Moon and Full Moon service for White Wolf Temple of the Olde Religion. The Canon of Beliefs in Elijan Wicca is on page 221.

SUMMARY POINTS FOR LESSON 2

In this lesson we learned that Wiccans generally believe:

- The Lady and the Lord are present in our daily lives, presiding over the cycles of nature and the wheel of the year.

- There are eight holidays, or Sabbats, which correspond to milestones in the agrarian year. Wiccan ceremonial worship services are called Esbats, and generally are held on the New and Full Moons.

- A sacred circle is built to keep entities from the astral plane out of our worship area. It protects us from their intrusion. A circle is guarded by the watchtower guardians at each of the four directions.

- Heaven can be on Earth, if we choose to perceive our lives in that way. There is no hell, and no supernatural evil being.

- Babies are born blameless and beautiful. There is no original sin.

- We are the children of Deity. Each of us is born for a purpose, and we are on Earth to learn lessons for our soul. We are eternal beings, and we live forever, in multiple lives. Our souls remember.

- There is only one law for Wiccans. It is "An' it harm none, do as Thy Will."

- Whatever a witch does, whether good or bad, returns to the witch three times harder.

- Wicca is a way of life, not a club membership or social forum. Every witch is clergy before the gods, and is able to receive communication from Deity through meditation, vision, dreams, revelation, or inspiration.

LEARNING EXERCISES FOR LESSON 2

Answer the questions at the end of each exercise.

1. In the homework for Lesson 1, you wrote your life story, and from it you developed some life themes that have shown a pattern throughout your life. These themes echo a mythology of your own, a story that belongs to you. "What's his story?" we ask, when we believe someone is behaving oddly. Our lives operate from our inner story, the tale told to our dreaming brain that guides our path. These are our archetypes, and from these archetypes, the gods teach. If your life were a story written by a best-selling author, what do you think would come next? Write a fantasy ending to your story, the end you would like your life to have. What actions would you, the character who is playing the hero in your own book, have to take to make your fantasy ending come true?

2. Go back through the story of Hera and Hephaestus and consider what archetypal lessons this story teaches us. Hera, the Mother, rejects her child because of his deformity, and throws him out of Mount Olympus. Later, she learns that he had value in a different way and feels remorse over her actions. What does this story tell us about abortion, at least in the case of a child who may have Down's syndrome or may be deformed? Remember, myths lived through the years because they spoke in a deep way to something primordial in us. If a feeling is so deep within us, and so shared among many people that it would live through thousands

of years in a myth, there must be a truth inside. What truth does the story of Hera and Hephaestus tell?

3. Hephaestus was ugly, but he appreciated beauty and art and craftsmanship. His ugliness was only skin deep. In addition to being ugly, he was also crippled. Yet his accomplishments and his value to the society in providing metalwork and blacksmithing were extraordinary. His purpose in the pantheon was to teach the society that people have different talents and contributions they can make. We do not all have to be beautiful people in order to be valued. Aphrodite was given to him in marriage as a reward for his contribution. She was a prize that every man wanted, yet it was the ugly Hephaestus who got her.

However, the marriage was not easy. Aphrodite never agreed to it, and so Hephaestus was always wooing her, constantly working at winning her affection. While Zeus may have been the boss on Mount Olympus, and he could order the marriage, even Zeus could not force Aphrodite to behave faithfully. (Since faithlessness in marriage is a weakness Zeus had himself, he had no power to order it in others.)

What are the rights of someone who is the boss? If Zeus, the head of all gods, could not enforce marriage vows on Mount Olympus because he would not honor his own marriage vows, what do we learn about the responsibilities and obligations of holding power and authority? Until Zeus was willing to clean up his own act, he lost all power to order others to behave as he himself would not. Can we think our own children will follow our orders rather than our example when we hear this story?

4. Although Aphrodite was given to Hephaestus like a prize, she retained the final authority over herself. He could have her body by decree, but her heart was her own to give, and only she was the bestower of it. What does this behavior by Aphrodite tell us about our relationship with authority figures? Can we ever kowtow to a boss or bend our knee to a lover if Aphrodite is our role model?

5. Aphrodite used a ritual tool to help her maintain the mental attitude she needed to ensure she would not lose her power. She had a magic girdle, and when she strapped it on, no man could resist

her. Can we learn from this how magickal objects get their power? If we need assistance in maintaining an attitude of self-assurance, why not imbue a pendant, amulet, or a piece of clothing with the ability to keep us mentally positive? Could your lucky sweater actually be magick after all? Might that extra ten pounds actually *not* be what's keeping you from getting a date on Saturday night? Could a nose job possibly *not* make the difference in whether you live happily ever after?

6. Although Aphrodite was unfaithful in matters of lust, Hephaestus continued to work at teaching her the ways of love. She was perpetually kind and gentle to him and tried to keep her affairs secret so as not to hurt him. She presented him with three children that she called his but who were actually the children of the god Ares (Mars). On one occasion, Aphrodite lingered too long in bed with Ares, and Helios (the Sun) saw them. Helios reported this to Hephaestus, and Hephaestus schemed to catch them in the act, hoping he could appeal to Zeus for a direct order to change Aphrodite's ways.

Hephaestus built a special magic net in his blacksmith shop, and he hung it on his own bed. Then he told Aphrodite he was taking a vacation and would be away for a few days on his favorite island. That night, Aphrodite invited Ares to the bed she shared with Hephaestus in his own home. The net sprang and caught them together, entrapping them.

Meanwhile, Hephaestus quickly returned to see who had been caught in his net. He called all the gods and goddesses to witness his outrage, believing they would agree with him to censure Aphrodite. The gods all showed up, but the goddesses refused to come. Unfortunately, the gods' reaction was not as Hephaestus expected. Rather than share his outrage, Zeus called him a fool for making this activity a public spectacle, and the other gods started a bidding war to see who could get to trade places under the net with Ares. Meanwhile, the goddesses all fumed in private and thanked Zeus they weren't married to Hephaestus. After ranting for a while about his situation and threatening to petition for divorce, Hephaestus settled down and reconciled himself to his situation, for he truly realized he would rather have Aphrodite as she was than live without her.

The gods of Mount Olympus lived a peculiar soap opera, didn't they? Is this account of Hephaestus and Aphrodite a true story of how people might behave in similar situations? Why did Hephaestus think he could control Aphrodite by decree? What made him expect the other gods and goddesses to behave differently than they did? Do you think this is a story of how people should behave, or an account of how they do behave? Have you heard of any experiences in real life where one person's expectation of how others would behave was vastly different from what really happened?

Reading Assignment for This Lesson

Research at least one pantheon that interests you. Learn its mythology and consider whether its lessons speak to you. Look at your life themes (developed in Lesson 1) and see if they are reflected in the behaviors of the pantheon. Move on to study other pantheons and look for one that's yours.

Meditation Exercise

1. Hephaestus came and spoke to me in a poem. In the poem, I took the role of Aphrodite in order to speak to Hephaestus. I was having trouble understanding and reconciling a lifelong weight problem, and I asked Hephaestus for advice. Review the poem slowly, being sure to read it out loud or to listen to it on track three of your *RUN dot Child* CD. Then light an orange candle and write in your own words what Hephaestus told me to do. Write quickly. Let the pen flow over the paper. Do not make the mistake of excessive thinking. Do not censor your words or force reason on your answer. Write the words that pop into your mind. Write all at once, in one session. Write as long as the pen flows, and stop when the pen stops.

   You may write one sentence, or you may write an essay. Only write what comes out quickly, directly after you have read the poem out loud. Overcome the tendency to think and analyze what you are writing. *Do not censor yourself.* Write whatever is sticking in your head *directly* after you have read the poem out loud. This is not an English class. Do not linger slowly and correct your grammar. Just *write* whatever you hear in your mind.

   If you feel completely uncomfortable with writing your answer, get a tape recorder and speak whatever comes into your mind into the tape recorder. Do *not*, however, type your answer on the computer. Pen and paper, or microphone and tape only.

Start your paper with these words:
Raya wanted to know what to do about being too heavy. Hephaestus answered:

2. Go back and read your answer. If you followed the directions, and wrote what popped into your head, rather than what you thought up and analyzed, you will have written an answer that applies more to you and a problem you have than it does to me. Look at your life themes developed in Lesson 1 and see if your answer applies to a problem you have in your life themes. Choose a god (not a goddess) from your favorite pantheon and ask him to speak more to you about that problem. The exercise will work more easily if you can choose a god whose mythology is somehow related to the problem you are examining.

In your meditations, you need to achieve connection with Deity outside of yourself. This is not hard, for the deities choose to speak to you. Your biggest problem is that you censor them and refuse to hear them. You believe you are imagining the answer you hear, and you reject it as foolish or invalid because it is (often) spoken in riddles, rhyme, and analogy. The gods do not tell you more than you can bear, nor do they reveal the future in a manner that would take away your free will. They often code their answers in riddles that you will understand later. So when you say "Oh, great Pan, more beast than man, tell me please whate'er you can about my love life," Pan is constrained to give you clues to follow so that you will come to appropriate conclusions on your own, rather than say specifically, "You're going to marry the guy you meet at the Safeway this afternoon." If he did that, you would behave inappropriately; you would take actions that were not consistent with free will and independent thinking, and you would change the future.

So instead, Pan might say, "peanut butter fudge and red suspenders."

You would hear this in your mind, believing you thought it. If you have not understood the function of meditation, and you are still censoring your mind, you would refuse to write down "peanut butter fudge and red suspenders" because you would think of it as irrelevant. You would say, "Oh, I can't think of anything as an answer," and you would erase "peanut butter fudge and red suspenders" from your mind.

Within hours, you will have a craving for peanut butter fudge. When you feel that craving, you will go to the Safeway. There you will meet a guy (or gal) wearing red suspenders. Sometime later, you'll get married.

If you are not awake, you'll think that was coincidence.

The homework assignment for this lesson is to develop a relationship with a god-form (not a goddess-form) through meditation. Choose one you find in a mythology book, or make up one you've been thinking a lot about recently. Learn everything you can about this god, and then attempt to contact him. Write your notes about what you've learned about him, and the meditative experiences you have with him, in your Book of Shadows, or *The Book of Dreams and Shadows*.

You may achieve better results in your meditations if you try some of the following methods for training the mind.

Helpful Hints for Meditation

1. Commit to meditating daily, but not necessarily at the same time each day. Meditation works best when it is done at a favorable planetary hour. You may not know what hour this is, but the God does. He'll call you when it's time. Commit to meeting Him daily, and then pay attention to your inner feeling and desire, so you'll know when He's calling you. Once you've agreed and contracted with Him for a meeting, He will send a desire to call you to the appointment.

2. Pick a special place where you will meditate, either a specific chair at home or a spot in your office. (You'll need both because you're not sure when this appointment will occur.) When you feel the desire of the God calling you, go to that chair or spot to wait for Him to arrive. It's always good form not to keep the God waiting. When He calls, go to your spot and get ready for Him to arrive later. You may have to wait for Him.

3. While you're waiting, get your mind ready. Light your candle, if possible, or visualize one if you are at your place of work. Have a special pen you use only for meditations. Keep a special book, a Book of Shadows, or *The Book of Dreams and Shadows*, that you write in for only this purpose. Treat the appointment with respect and the God as real. In a short time, you will notice that suddenly the phone stops ringing and people stop coming to your door when you are in conference this way.

4. Arrange your spot for meditation so that there is no visible clock or watch. A timepiece tends to distract your subconscious and to interfere with the conversation.

5. Work at emptying your mind. Try to stop thinking. If a special amulet or talisman can serve as a focal point to help you with this, carry it with you. At the point where your own thoughts have stopped flowing, you will hear the God speak. Try to shut up and let Him get a word in edgewise.

6. Try to use the multisensory correspondences (see the chart on page 52) that will help you achieve the different mental states represented by the Tree of Life.

7. Commit to the practice of meditation, working through the various realms of mental states. Even if you sit quietly for an hour and nothing happens, continue to do it daily. In the worst case, you'll be more calm. In the best, you'll make contact with yourself and become what you already are.

CORRESPONDENCES FOR MEDITATION

Mental State	Essential Oil	Herbal Tea	Crystal	Color and Texture	Candle Color	Tarot Card to Study	Realm on the Tree of Life
Dramatic breakthrough	Frankincense	Chamomile	Amethyst	Purple velvet	Burgundy or red-violet	The Tower	Yesod
Mercy and forgiveness	Jasmine	Fennel	Opal or moonstone	Dusty blue linen	Dark blue	The Hermit	Chesed
Natural instincts	Citrus	Ginger	Turquoise	Brown-orange denim	Light blue	The Wheel of Fortune	Netzach
Grounding & centering	Rose	Rosemary	Bloodstone	Red wool	Green	The Moon	Malkuth
Rationality	Cinnamon	Echinacea	Tourmaline	Light green rayon	Yellow	The Aeon or Judgment	Hod
Appreciation of beauty	Sage	Green Tea	Tiger eye	Dark gray flannel	Orange or gold	The Devil	Tiphareth
Inner strength	Vanilla	Peppermint	Jasper	Magenta cotton	Red	Justice	Geburah
Connection with Deity	Ylang ylang	Kava kava	Lapis lazuli	Light blue silk	White	The Chariot	Binah

To join in the private online discussion forum exclusively for readers of this book, and to try the test questions for this lesson, go to:

http://www.LadyRaya.org/religion/classes/

Enter your e-mail address and the password you were given at the end of Lesson 1, on page 33. Then select Test 2 from the list of tests. Feedback about the test will be sent directly to your e-mail address. You can also participate in the discussion forum for the topics in this lesson.

LESSON 3
KARMA AND RITUAL TOOLS

RUN dot Child, and set your sight
On the sky. And let the night
Become Dawn, for you are mine.
Baby, Shine!

YOUR OBJECTIVE FOR LESSON 3

You will identify the nature of coincidental guidance
and name the ritual tools used in casting a sacred circle.

WHAT IS KARMA?

Karma is another word used for fate or destiny. It is the force that ensures the intended and preordained goal for our lifetimes. Although we are fated to meet this destiny, how we get to it, through how many lifetimes, and with what degree of agony is all a matter of free will. Karma is the surrounding atmosphere and aether that guides us to the path that will lead us home. Karma must remain in balance, and so one develops a karmic "balance sheet," with recorded assets and debts. We must pay our karmic debts in order to keep our personal universe in working condition.

WHAT IS THE PURPOSE OF RITUAL?

When we perform an act in a repetitious and ritualistic manner, we are encouraging our mind to shift into an automatic state. The objects used in ritual, and the soothing boredom created by the repeating chants and repeated actions, put us into a mental state that invites the force we call karma to settle around us. In ritual, we can shut down our consciousness and allow our subconscious to take over, creating a form of trance. This mental trance reduces our resistance to the karmic force and allows it to guide us.

What Is the Purpose of a Ritual Tool?

Our ritual tools, such as those we use to build the sacred circle or perform magickal acts, become "placeholders" to bookmark our minds to return to this trance-like ritual state. By keeping our magickal tools in beautiful boxes, or wrapped in fine silk, or otherwise stored in a treasuring manner, we train our minds to respect them. That respect triggers the mental state that brings on trance. When we see the object removed from its sacred storage place, our minds are able to recall that trance. Karma is then able to work more easily, as our consciousness gives up its state of resistance. We perform rituals and use ritual tools in order to train our mind to stop resisting the force of karma.

We speak of karma in terms of currency. Karma has a debt or it has an asset. Through all our lives, we strive to keep our karma balanced. Someone who is born with a high potential and much talent has a correspondingly high karmic debt. That person owes the Deity something for being given all these extraordinary gifts and talents. Usually, the Deity expects that person to give something back to society by using these talents. It is insulting to Deity and damaging to karma to fail to use talents or assets. Ritual tools and ritual help us to quiet our conscious minds so that we can learn about our talents and assets. We can thereby hear the task Deity has assigned to us that uses our talents and pays down our karmic debt. We pay our karmic debt with karmic currency.

The Five Currencies of Karma: Intent, Behavior, Attitude, Physical Sensation, and Intuitive Awareness [I B(e) APi]

What is the meaning of karmic currency? "Current" is the presence of a moving electric charge. Alternatively, it means occurring in the present time. "Currency" is a valid form of payment for debts or a medium to hold an electric charge. It should be noted that bills are dollars, which can be considered assets. For each of our assets, we incur a karmic debt. Those who have high talents, abilities, and blessings have a correspondingly high karmic debt. Karmic currency can be in the form of bills, or assets, or it can be in the form of change, or transformation. The bills of karma can only be paid with the change of transformation. Note also that a transformer is a device to generate power.

A karmic currency, when used to pay down a karmic debt, is the process and the hard work of personal change. Karma cannot be paid with personal pain and suffering, nor with achievement, money, or the approval of other people. Karmic currency is the blood, sweat, tears, music, and dancing of the change that causes us to become all we can be, fulfilling our potential. We buy our karmic destiny with this change. It can't be bought with dollars.

Why Do We Have to Buy Our Destiny?

Money came into existence as a means of measuring and assigning value to barter. By itself, money is meaningless. Its value is assigned in terms of what goods or services it is capable of obtaining. To say we are buying something implies we are taking legal ownership of it, through the transfer of its title from its current (or present) owner to ourselves. The present owner of our destiny is Father Time, who lives in the moment. As we all know, Father Time is the consort of Mother Goose. Until we purchase our destiny, we are the children of Father Time and Mother Goose, mere cartoon characters in the programmed plan. After our destiny has been purchased, or redeemed, we move from the world of animation to the world of magick, and our Father and Mother change accordingly.

We buy our destiny so that we can take ownership of it, thus becoming captain of our fate, master of our ship. It is much easier to ensure that our ship will come in if we are sailing it. The alternative to being captain of our own ship is to be buffeted by the winds of fate and adrift on the sea of change.

What Is the Meaning of the First Karmic Currency, Intent?

There's an old axiom that says, "The road to hell is paved with good intentions." We cannot just intend to do something, but we must actually do it. I may intend to clean the house, but unless I do it, it will stay dirty. This is a conscious intention. We often do not actually do what we consciously intend to do. But there is an inner, subconscious intent that is always reflected in our actions. This true intent is followed by the id, sometimes not known to the conscious mind. The id is our childlike subconscious; it is our dreaming mind. The id knows our soul's purpose, and fully understands our hidden intent. This is the intent that is the currency of karma.

This intent carries out our true inner wishes, and it always performs in the manner in which we are truly desiring. If our conscious mind thinks "I intend to clean the house," but we don't actually do it, the reason for our avoidance of the task can be found in our true intent, which is subconscious.

Maybe our true intent, at the level of our id, is thinking "I have more important things to do today. Cleanliness is next to godliness, and I'm not feeling godly."

Here is a simple example of how the inner will of human beings shows itself, although it operates at the subconscious level.

THE CHILDREN'S GAME: ROCK, PAPER, SCISSORS

The game works like this: Scissors defeats paper because it cuts; paper defeats rock because it wraps; rock defeats scissors because it breaks. Each child makes a hand signal simultaneously to show whether they choose scissors, rock, or paper. Best two out of three wins.

In the subconscious mind, the id is thinking:
Scissors = Pressure
Paper = Will
Rock = Time
Pressure defeats Will. Will defeats Time. Time defeats Pressure.
If the pressure must be released, give it time.
If the time must be conquered, apply will.
If the will must be broken, exert pressure.
Even the children know this.
Only the children know this.
Who told the Children to play this game?
And the wind said, "I" did.
Now to show you how the subconscious thinks, set the letters of the words equal to numbers and count them. A = 1, B = 2, C = 3, and so on, all the way to Z = 26
You will see that:

$$S + c + i + s + s + o + r + s = P + r + e + s + s + u + r + e$$

Likewise, the number calculated for the word *paper* equals the number of the word *will*, and the number of the word *rock* equals the number of the word "time." For generations, children have played this game, without ever knowing the subconscious message.

The subconscious intent always knows what it's doing. Our language and consciousness are built on mathematical principles and respond to the nature of Qabalah and gematria, which is the breath of God. We find in our ordinary language the truths of the universe.

The karmic currency of intent is the implementation of the desire of the true subconscious will. It is the dream we carry inside, for which we make a dream come true. To explain the karmic currency of intent, we say: *I know myself and follow the guidance of my heart."*

What is the Meaning of the Second Karmic Currency, Behavior?

Each of us lives in a karmic ocean. In this ocean we are sitting in boats. Some of us have individual sailboats. Others live in great, collective ships. Some of these ships are ocean liners, but some of them are pirate ships. The boats represent our particle nature in quantum physics. The ocean represents our wave nature. The people in individual boats have an opportunity to effect their own fate. The people who live in ships have entrusted their fate to the captain, but the captain of a pirate ship is a pirate, and the captain of an ocean liner is a servant of a great corporate hierarchy. The people in the pirate ship have to work for the pirate to change the sails, but they don't get any say about which way to move the ship. Some of the people break away and escape to individual lifeboats, where they have to use the shirts off their backs to make a sail. The people who live in ocean liners don't have to work to sail the boat. They just vacation and enjoy the ride. They trust the structure to know what it's doing in guiding them.

Now, the sea moves and changes in accordance with the strength of the great winds that blow across it. When these winds blow, all the boats that are in the winds' path are pulled along in the direction of the wind, or they are capsized and destroyed. The people in the boats have control of the sails, and if they fight against the wind, instead of turning their sails into it, they will be annihilated. The people who are good sailors know to adjust their sails to go the way the wind blows, and they are carried on through the sea, along with everybody else who accepts the wind's decision and goes in its direction. However, the people in the ships are completely at the mercy of the captain, and if he perishes, they perish with him.

Some boats find themselves going where they want to go by following this wind, and they are very happy. But other boats end up in places they don't want to be, and then the people become sad and frustrated. So the people begin to wonder what they can do to effect a change in the wind and direct their boats to land. These people begin to study the patterns of the wind and try to improve their skill at sailing so that they can move their boats by the force of their own will and change their destiny. In the ocean liners, only the captain gets to choose the destiny. All the other people get the destiny chosen by the captain. But the pirate ships are safer than the individual boats, and the ocean liner is safest of all.

The probability that the pirate ships will survive with everyone on board safe is higher than the probability any individual sailboat will survive. If you're in a pirate ship, you just need to be sure you know who the pirate is. If you are in an individual boat, you need to learn the skill of being captain very well. If you're in an ocean liner, you can trust that the boat has a navigation officer—but you have no ability to impact your own fate. You can't override the captain's decision if he chooses to head for land. Before the voyage began, everyone chose a type of boat to be on, but no one fully understood the implications of that decision. Now that we are on the high seas, to change boats is very difficult.

But the wind is strong, and the amount of control offered by adjusting the sails on the boats is weak. So although these little actions of sailors make some change in the direction of the boat, the change is very minor in the context of the whole ocean and the strength of karmic direction. All the same, these minor changes in direction accumulate, and eventually the boat is guided to a place different from the place the boat would have gone if no sailor had intervened. Unfortunately, wind is a very mathematical force. It calculates down to the last electrical charge in the last atom in order to find out where it should blow and how it should act. So when the boats have changed their course, the wind recalculates, and the wind also changes its course, in order to blow the boats back where the wind had originally intended for them to be. This causes the boats to be blown and buffeted, and soon many problems occur in the people's lives. If you are in an individual sailboat, you are your own captain. You can decide what to do about this guidance from the wind. But when you are in a great, collective ship, you have no option but to let the captain decide.

Soon, the boats find themselves thrown by the winds, and they have difficulty remaining afloat in the choppy sea. Skillful captains resign themselves to taking the wind's direction, and soon they are back on course, all the worse for wear from their struggle. The wind will take them to their destiny, and they must learn to accept it.

Some boats make it to land before the sea changes. If they were guided to land by their captain, then the captain was lucky enough to have achieved a goal and to have thwarted destiny. When this happens, these boats find themselves sitting in shallow water, stagnating, unable to get a wind to move them again. The lives of these boat passengers, once adventurous and challenging, become routine and boring. Whatever their destiny was to be, they have missed it. They got what they wanted—but they lost what was written in their fate. The captain must decide to accept the wind in order to guide the boat to its destiny.

So the moral of that story is:
There is a tide in the affairs of men,
  Which, taken at the flood, leads on to fortune.
  Omitted, all the voyage of their life

Is bound in shallows and in miseries.
On such a full sea are we now afloat
And we must take the current when it serves
Or lose our ventures.
—William Shakespeare

In the boat of your life, sail with the wind, and know your captain.

The karmic currency of behavior is the tendency to use our lemons to make lemonade, while keeping our ship on course. For the second karmic currency, we say: *I sail my ship with the wind and plot my course by the stars.*

What is the Meaning of the Third Karmic Currency, Attitude?

The karmic currency of attitude is the ability to see ourselves as part of the overall and extensive awesome beauty of nature.

Here is a simple story to help illustrate it.

I own a cabin deep in the forest. For many years, I knew that a squirrel family lived in the attic. I could hear them scampering around in the ceiling, but I never did anything to chase them away. They weren't interfering with my life, so I didn't interfere with theirs. One winter the water pipes in the bathroom froze and burst. Since I did not come to the cabin for a long time, I didn't know about this, and the water flooded the house.

For some reason, this deeply disturbed the squirrel family. Uncharacteristically, they chewed a hole in my pine-wood walls and entered the house. Once in the house, they frantically began chewing the furniture. The sofas, the lampshades, the bedspreads, the mattresses—everything was torn to pieces by the crazed squirrels.

By the time I returned to the cabin, I found the house flooded and the furniture destroyed. The squirrels had chewed holes in the window screens to let themselves out of the house and had tracked fireplace ashes all over the walls.

To repair the destruction required a lot of time and a lot of money. The cabin was a very important sanctuary for me, and I felt devastated over the loss. After I had everything repaired, I tried to close the holes up in the house to prevent the squirrels from returning. But the squirrels considered the house to be their home, too, and they chewed new holes in the walls to get back in.

Finally, after frustrating myself trying to get rid of them, I adjusted to the idea that the squirrels were going to be my roommates, and I arranged in and out holes for them that wouldn't damage the house. As I looked up at the canopy of stars over my cabin that night, I said, "Thank you, Mother, for showing me that the squirrels are your creatures, too."

The Third Karmic Currency: *I am part and parcel of the living universe.* We adjust to live peacefully with all God's creatures.

What Is the Meaning of the Fourth Karmic Currency, Physical Sensation?

The universe in which we live has all the appearance of being physically real. We have five mundane senses with which to experience this world, plus at least two magickal senses: time and intuition. In this physical world, we are, on a quantum level, both a particle and a waveform. In our character as a waveform, we are one waveform in a universe of waveforms, all connected. When other waveforms around us move, we feel their movement. If we move with their movement, we contribute to a ripple effect. This ripple effect goes on to ripple other waveforms, and soon the universe is a churning cauldron of rippling waveforms. While the water is churning, the reflection cannot be clear.

Only in stillness, can we achieve clarity. In complete stillness, meditation, we hear the words of the collective consciousness of the universe. Here are some words of stillness that happened to be floating around in the aether.

Read this out loud for it to have impact.

Ode to the Oval Pot

Now The Time was Ripe for Plucking
But the Chickens lost their Heads
So the Mother ran the Circus
While the Father made the Beds.
But the Sleepers wore Pajamas
And the Actors called the Fuzz
For the Players in the Drama
Lived in Land that Never Was.
What! How dare You? Cried the Earthlings
And they ran to hide the Jewels
For they thought the Earth was Mama
And the Papa was for FOOLs.
So they called the Cosmos Sweetheart
And they cringed when Father Watched
And they let their dogs get rabies
And their skin get red and blotched.
They got itches. They got Scratches.
They got stuffy. They got Crows'

Feet. And under Mommie's Apron,
they got Feathers in their Knows.
They got Problems. They got Heartaches.
And they're always kneadin' Bread
'Cause their Father Nibbles Cupcakes
While their Mother isn't Wed.
So one day The Daughter caught them
And she took 'em by Surprise
They were thinkin' she and Jesus
Went to Battle over Lies.
But the Poe-Tree had a Purpose
And the Story had a Line
And whenever you Receive Him
You will learn to like it Fine.
For Transmitters need Receivers
Or the Message isn't Heard
And the God who's in This Heaven
Lives inside The Holy Word

The karmic currency of physical sensation refers to the state of alertness that allows one to hear the voice of God in the surrounding aether. Regarding this currency, we say: *I achieve clarity in the stillness.*

What Is the Meaning of the Fifth Karmic Currency, Intuitive Awareness?

Read this *out loud.*
Tick Tock Tick Tock Tick Tock Flip
All God's Children Learn to Nip
It in Bud when Flowers Bloom
Else they take a Trip to Room
Where the Hanging Peter Sways
And the Vortex leads to Plays
Acting Out the Life of Christ.
What's THAT mean? I sacrificed
Myself for Your P-Nut Brain
To Record The Inner Pain
In Its Genes — the White Beads Part.
That's what's written in Our Heart?
Ethics System. Right from Wrong.
Encoded as Part of Song.
Make a Rhythm. Sing a Chant.

March yourself right to the Pant-
y where Chakras colored Blue
Release Hormones Numbered To
Correspond to Mental States
And Accorded Different Weights
In Response to Wishes I
Chose to Place There. *Wonder Why?*
Maybe I have Free Will, too.
What You Think? You get to do
Anything You Feel Inside,
But I don't get Override
Powers? *What those Powers do?*
Eat you up. Inside of You
when you're troubled, I work through
Hormones and Anxiety.
Learn to feel My Hand on Thee.

Paying careful attention to our inner feelings and determining our own True Will is our only method of learning God's intention for our path. The karmic currency of intuitive awareness teaches us to discern the guidance of God through our internal feelings and mental states. Regarding this currency, we say: *I recognize my own desire.*

SUMMARY POINTS FOR LESSON 3

- Intent is the implementation of the true subconscious will. *I know myself and follow the guidance of my heart.*

- Behavior is the tendency to use lemons to make lemonade while keeping the ship on course. *I sail my ship with the wind and plot my course by the stars.*

- Attitude is the ability to see ourselves as part of the overall and extensive awesome beauty of nature. *I am part and parcel of a living universe.*

- Physical Sensation refers to the state of alertness that allows us to hear the voice of God in the surrounding aether. *I achieve clarity in the stillness.*

- Intuitive Awareness teaches us to discern the guidance of God through our internal feelings and mental states. *I recognize my own desire.*

By balancing these five states, we pay our karmic price. Look at the mnemonics for the set of karmic currencies.

Intent, Behavior, Attitude, Physical awareness, Intuitive awareness

I B(e) A. P. I.

In the language of our brain's software, that says "I (*am*) Advanced Programmer's Interface," which is the language instruction for developing software commands. In the language of Qabalah, which is God's software tool, it tells us this is a divine method. We are one, part of God's Internet. He is the programmer; She is the architect, We are the result—the "dot Child."

Ritual and ritual tools assist us to put our mind in the ready state to learn these karmic lessons.

LEARNING EXERCISES FOR LESSON 3

1. Make a sacred space for yourself.

   Once you've made the decision to dedicate yourself to the Goddess, you will need a place you consider sacred to hold your worship rituals and do your magickal workings. This should be a place protected from bad auras and special for your private meditations with Deity.

   Choose the area in your home or a private place outdoors to be your worship area. It should be a place that offers you a circular area optimally nine feet in diameter, more if you are working in a group. You need a large enough circular space for all of you to fit inside comfortably, and for a small altar to sit in the center. You will want to arrange the furniture so that you can walk around the area in a circle without having to jump over tables and sofas and children's toys. Do the best you can with what you have. The Goddess will forgive your limitations.

   To protect the temple area permanently, do this ritual the first time you use your space. You will not have to do it again unless some disruption occurs and you want to feel *extra* protection.

   Mark your circle area with a black candle in each of the four directions, and a black candle on the altar. Mark the circle itself with pine cones or pieces of yarn, or potpourri of some type.

Even sunflower seeds would do. Take a bowl of salt and a bowl of water. Hold them up and say:

Blessed Be, thou creatures of the elements.
"Earth and water, son and daughter,
Inside and outside, be cleansed!
Cast out all that would do me harm.
Take in all that would do me good.
Know this place, leave no trace
Of other. All for me.
By the power of the Lady's way,
So mote it be!"

With your fingers, pinch three salts into water. Stir with finger.

"May this water be purified with the earth, so that together they may cause great good."

Hold the cup to your heart and purify it until it glows.

Then walk around the temple area widdershins (counterclockwise). Carry holy water and your athame (see page 66) and a noise maker (a bell). Walk around and sprinkle water everywhere. Make noise. Say:

"Earth, water, fire, air
Call on all that's good and fair.
Air, fire, sea, and salt
At your boundaries, ill must halt.
Round I go and round I be, as my circle binds to me."

Point the athame to the ground and to the sky. Say:

"Any spirit of evil, any unfriendly being, any unwanted guest, begone.
Leave this place, my circle and my heart, so that it may be a fit place for the gods to live.
Go, by the command of the blackest darkness of the underworld!
Go, by the order of the deepest drenching of the sea!
Go, by the forces of the whirling tornado!
Go, by the crackling burn of the raging fire!
By the power of the Lady's way,
I banish you, I banish you, I banish you

Clap, chant, make noise, saying, "Be gone, I say, by the Lady's power."

Then take athame, incense, and water. Go around deosil. (clockwise), sprinkle with water, draw a pentacle at each entrance, and seal with incense.

Say:

> "Enter this place, all beings good
>> Leave it if you're made of wood
>> Shoulda', coulda', hear my cant
>> Up or down, the flow of chant
>> From the source is all the same.
>> Sacred, holy space I claim.

You should follow this protection ritual with a circle to consecrate your tools and altar for this space. If possible, you will want
to keep your altar set up always in the sacred space. If not possible, you should get a carrying basket with all your altar tools in
it. Consecrate your tools as you get each one by sprinkling them
with your holy water and offering them in service of the
Goddess. A complete example of constructing the sacred circle
for a worship service or magickal working is in "An Esbat
Ceremony for the Dark and Full Moons" on page 211.

2. This exercise helps you to respond to your spirit. Make a set of
flash cards using colored index cards. On five of the cards write:

Intent: I know myself and follow the guidance of my heart.
Behavior: I sail my ship with the wind and plot my course by
the stars.
Attitude: I am part and parcel of a living universe.
Physical sensation: I achieve clarity in the stillness.
Intuitive Awareness: I recognize my own desires.

I B(e) A. P. I. (Advanced Programmer's Interface). The words of
the idiomatic English language are a coded script that represent
the software of our consciousness. Label the card deck IBAPI and
make a logo for it.

Leave the rest of the cards blank.

Carry the cards with you in a pouch. Each time you face a problem or decision, and whenever you feel your emotion rise, take
out the cards and write on one of them. Write the date and the
problem, summarized in one sentence.

Now hold your pen over the card and review each of the five
karmic currencies. Keep thinking through the five premises as
you stare at your card. After a time, you will feel an answer in

your heart, and hear it in your mind. Write the answer down. This is the approach that will work best for you.

Common, Useful Ritual Tools— Everything You Need for the Circle

In truth, there is absolutely nothing you need for the circle. You can do the whole thing in your mind, but to train your mind to do it, you need this "stuff." It just helps the mental visualization in the subconscious id. The "stuff" doesn't have any power in and of itself, but you use the "stuff" to focus your mental energy. The energy has powerful potential. You have to concentrate and focus to learn to make it have kinesis. If you want to substitute anything on this list for something that's more meaningful to you, you can. The importance is the significance to *your* mind. The collective psyche of humanity has used these archetypal images for thousands of years. Something in the history of your being is attached to these archetypes. Find it. You'll recognize it by the way it feels. It's a feeling of pulsing, of déjà vu. Look for it. Search it out. The truth is in there.

After you acquire these tools, be sure you consecrate them to the Goddess before using them. This is a very important step. After all, you don't know where these things have been before and what they've been doing, so brush them off, clean them up, and consecrate them for your own use.

In any case, take everything you need into the circle ahead of time. Don't go out to get anything. If you forgot something, work without it. Go to the bathroom before you set the circle up so you won't have to break the circle after it's in place.

Altar Tools (items you place on the altar)

Athame, wand, incense and thurible, candle holder, salt dish (pentacle), water dish, anointing oil, altar cloth, Goddess cup, God and Goddess images.

Athame. Traditionally, this is a double-edged, black-handled knife. The real hard-core witches say you have to make this yourself. If you don't have the skills for that, search junk shops (a.k.a. antique stores) for something that has a unique look to it. You should try to carve something into the handle of your athame even if you're not making the knife yourself. The carving, the use of your hands, strengthens the associations in your mind. You're a multi-sensory biological organism. You need to associate through as many sensory experiences as possible. This is why we use smells and tastes and sounds and colors. We are approaching the mental system through sensory experience.

The athame is used in the rituals to seal the circle, to center and ground the forces, to draw the pentagram, and to acknowledge the watchtowers, as well as other air-cutting forms. It is never used to cut anything except air. Wedding cake, maybe. But that's absolutely all your athame will ever cut. In fact, it doesn't even need a sharp blade. I've seen some of them about the sharpness of a letter opener.

On the altar, the athame is placed in the South as the Fire element. Some traditions say it belongs in the East, because it cuts Air. Actually, the athame cuts the bonds that keep you from fully understanding. It releases you from the prison of your passions and frees your mind to achieve clarity.

Wand. If you have an athame, you can use it for all the same purposes as a wand. Likewise, you can use a wand if you don't have an athame. Wands are easier to get. Go out in the woods and pick something out. Strip the bark off it, paint it, carve on it, glue crystals and feathers on it. Whatever pleases your deep id fantasy.

Tradition tends toward willow or birch. It's quite fun to walk in the woods and choose exactly the right stick, and then make something out of it. Be sure to thank the tree you take it from. Men often want to make a staff, too, like a great big wand for obvious purposes.

A coven will often have a ritual sword. This makes a nice archetype for a fantasy ritual.

Remember, the power is not in the tools. The power is in your mind's associated memories and experiences in using those tools. Be respectful of the deep subconscious id of your mind. Treat your tools with respect. Wrap them in silk when you're not using them. Behave as if you believe these are gifts from Deity. Do not leave them lying around. Do not use them for any other purposes.

The respectful behavior you exhibit toward your sacred altar and its objects impacts the behavior of your subconscious and causes the subtle actions and movements that grant your power. This part is science, in addition to being religion. Wicca is a very scientific religion. The wand and the tools will focus your mental energies. They will help you control your inner self and cause you to be all you can be, within the constraints of what God has designed you for. They are simply tools to help you learn focus and self-control.

Incense and Thurible. Best case, you get a metal incense burner with a swinging handle. You put sand in it, a charcoal lump on the sand, and sprinkle powdered incense over it, matched to the correlations of the astrological powers to be called. Short of that, use frankincense and myrrh incense sticks in a little wooden holder. On the altar, incense goes in the East. It represents Air. You walk around the circle with the incense as part of the sealing ritual.

Candle holder. You're going to have a center altar candle. Get something of unique design, metal or ceramic. The altar candle will change colors, depending on your mood and task of the day.

Salt dish. In the North, you place a small dish of salt. This is used to make holy water. North is the Earth element. Best case, you paint a pentagram on a wooden bowl for this. A nice concave pentacle can be used to deflect forces, so it would have multiple uses. Paint the inside black, with white for the lines of the pentagram. Don't hold up your work waiting to get around to acquiring all this stuff. This is a lower priority item. Use ceramic, wood, or metal containers of unique design for everything on your altar. Reserve them specifically for altar use. Consecrate them before first use.

Water Dish. A small dish or container of water is in the West to represent the Water element.

Anointing Oil. Choose an attractive bottle for your anointing oil, something that looks like it came straight out of the Arabian Nights. Pick a fragrance from essential oils. You anoint yourself, and each member of the circle anoints themselves. In a coven, the high priestess might anoint the men and the high priest the women. Do it by drawing a Celtic cross on your forehead, then a pentagram (forehead, left breast, right shoulder, left shoulder, right breast, forehead). You might also add the holy triangle: right breast, left breast, genital area, right breast. Optional.

Altar Cloth. The altar itself can be any small table. It's usually low, so you can sit on the floor around it. You might be using this table as regular furniture when it's not an altar. I don't, but you could. You'll want to have a special altar cloth to cover it before you set your sacred objects on it. It's nice to have a few of these in different colors, to match the mood of the ceremony. My main altar cloth is purple with a green and blue flowered pattern. I also have a white one with ivory vines running through it, and a dark blue one with moons and stars. Choose altar cloths made of natural materials, no polyester. The easiest way to get an altar cloth is to go to a fabric store and buy material that pleases you. All you have to do is hem it, and you're going to need to learn to sew anyway, for the magickal works.

Goddess Wine Glass. You need a chalice to pour wine for the Goddess during the blessing of the Cakes and Ale. After the ceremony, you must pour Her wine onto the ground where it returns to Her. The cup of ceremonial magick represents the yoni (or female opening). The wand represents the lingam (or male appendage). The movement of the lingam within the yoni symbolizes the action of electricity which creates electromagnetism.

God and Goddess Images. As we all know, having an image on an altar does not mean you are worshipping an idol. When Christians put a cross on their altar, does that mean they are worshipping a cross? We know we aren't worshipping a statue or a ceramic model. These are simply vehicles for mental focus. You don't need to have a god or goddess statue on your altar. If you do have one, it can simply be a representative that makes you think of the God and the Goddess. Some people use antlers, but they're hard to get. Pan statues are around, too. Generally, it's bad form to pick a statue that shows the Goddess with wings. The Goddess doesn't have wings; those are angels and faeries. Angels and faeries are lesser forms, not divinity.

This is all you need to keep on the altar. Anything else you need for the day, put underneath the altar. Remember, the witchier you make your altar look, the more success you'll have at reaching that deep inner id where fantasy lives. Make the altar represent nature and natural things, however, not horror or gore. Take yourself to the primitive part of your nature in constructing your altar. Your mind will rise to the occasion.

Marking the Circle
(items you use to mark the existence of the circle)

White candle, yellow candle, red candle, green candle, black candle, blue candle. Associated candle holders. Potpourri or stones or cord—enough to mark the circle.

White and Yellow Candles. In the East for Air. You use white during the waxing of the Moon (from the New Moon to the Full Moon.) You use yellow during the waning of the Moon (from Full Moon to New Moon). You use white during the Sabbats of spring and summer. You use yellow during the Sabbats of fall and winter.

Red Candle. In the South for Fire.

Green and Black Candles. In the North for Earth. When you have a yellow candle in the East, you have a black candle in the North. When you have a white candle in the East, you have a green candle in the North. But on the Sabbats, you may change that rule, depending on the ceremony.

Of course, you may always change any rules. That's the fun of being a Wiccan. However, if you don't have any rules in the first place, you miss out on the opportunity to change them.

This particular rule actually cries out to be broken. Colors are the most exciting energy to play around with. In Native American circles, red is in the West (for the setting Sun), yellow is in the East (for the rising Sun), white is in the North (for snow) and black is in the South.

Blue Candle. In the West for Water.

Color *is* the energy used to operate the universe. Ancient Qabalistic texts declare it. Today's physicists will admit they have learned to slow and change the speed of an atom by shining the light of colored lasers. White light is the result of all the colors in the spectrum revolving very fast. The colors exist in a color *wheel*, and that wheel's revolution happens at both the macrocosm and the microcosm.

Around the circle, the colors represent:
Red: strength, vigor, passion
Orange: encouragement, adaptability, openness.
Yellow: charm, confidence, persuasion
Green: fertility, luck, finance
Blue: tranquility, health, patience
Violet: tension, power, royalty
Black: protection, karma, secrets, transformation
White: purity, sincerity, truth

Associated Candleholders. Find something unique.

Potpourri, Stones, or Cord to Mark the Circle. Initially, we used to block the circle out with a potpourri trail so we'd know not to step over the lines. We still do this if there are novices and visitors present. *If you are working indoors, make the whole room be encompassed by the circle and close the doors so that no one will step over the circle lines.*

"Under the Altar" Equipment

Book of Shadows. This is the book in which you record your ceremonies and rituals. You may wish to use *The Book of Dreams and Shadows* designed to go with this book. You will want to memorize basic ceremonies. You will want to record your magickal works, for tracking and verification. *The Book of Shadows* should be kept under lock and key. For this very reason, you will want to learn a runic alphabet and encrypt anything you couldn't bear to have found. Since most runic alphabets have been published, they're not very secret.

To really encrypt it, you make up what you want to say, then turn it into a simple mnemonic you can memorize. Record the mnemonics to jog your memory. Make a cant, that is a rhyming poem, and use the mnemonics. Just record the mnemonics, and your memory will associate it with the cant. Then nobody else will ever be able to figure out what you did. The secret to memory association is: Make it rhyme. Make a mnemonic alphabet. Associate it with a color energy. Associate it with a smell. Your brain will take over from there and remember things you never thought possible. *In fact, it will remember things you never knew—quite an interesting phenomenon.*

Broom. This is used to symbolically sweep the bad auras and astral pollution out of your circle. I use a cinnamon broom. Sometimes they're used in rituals.

Bell. You ring the bell to signify you are about to cast a circle, and any astral entities hanging around should get out. You are the master of astral entities. They don't scare you, and, with the grace of Mother, they must obey when you command them to leave.

Cauldron. This is used in magickal workings for burning things. It doesn't have to be big, just a small metal bucket of pleasing design, suitable to contain a minor fire.

Matches. Kept in a nice box with weird markings on it.

Charcoal. For the incense burner.

Tarot Cards (Aleister Crowley Thoth Deck). Okay, you can use some other deck if you already have it, but as soon as you can, buy the Crowley deck. The pictures on it carry visualization images that open up areas of the brain. The other decks don't have the full set of images, and they miss a lot of pathways.

Any Sacred Writings to Be Read in the Ceremony. The Vedas, Bhagavad Gita, Tao Te Ching, Qur'an, Torah, Holy Bible, Lost Books of Eden, the Aquarian Gospel, Pseudepigrapha, books of myths, and so on—the sacred texts of all religions carry a wealth of encoded information. Read them in a meditative state to hear what they intend. Because they are encrypted, what they say *on the surface* is not what they mean. There are messages under the messages, which your subconscious mind will grasp, but your conscious mind can't discern. Don't get fooled into taking their words at face value. Just read them and try not to think. *They are encrypted writings.* They will speak directly to your subconscious.

Special Dish. For your offering of food (cakes). Traditionally, it would be nice to have a cake or bread recipe you use exclusively for the circle, at least on the eight Sabbats. Bread made with your own hands is a sign of respect for the Goddess. Sometimes we use sunflower seeds, or make ourselves a trail mix of nuts and seeds. Don't use disrespectful foods that are processed and full of chemical ingredients, however. Food has to be real, natural, whole food.

Special Wine Glasses. For your offering of wine (ale). In the coven, we use nonalcoholic sparkling apple juice when guests are present. When working alone, we use anything from beer to champagne. Apple juice is Mother's beverage of choice. The Lord is more likely to attend when you're serving the hard stuff.

A Closed Basket. Like a picnic basket, so you can carry your sacred magickal objects out to the woods whenever you get the chance. It is fun to do a magick circle in the woods. It really is. Best to stick to sweatshirts and jeans rather than robes, though. Your neighbors will tend to dial 911 if they see you dressed in hooded robes, swinging knives in the air.

Any Items You Are Going to Use in Magickal Workings. (Rocks and crystals, magick mirrors, knotting cord, mortar and pestle, poppet cloths, etc.) For sure, you need a set of rocks and crystals reserved specifically for the circle. Make yourself a set that has one of each color.

Acquiring and using magickal tools trains your mind to expect a magickal life. This mind training allows you to see what you have chosen to believe.

What we believe is the truth of our universe, not what we see. For those who say, "I'll believe it when I see it," you can honestly respond that your magickal tools make it possible for you to "see it when you believe it." Those who cannot see with the eye of the heart, are truly blind indeed.

To join in the private online discussion forum only for readers of this book, and to try the test questions for this lesson, go to:

http://www.LadyRaya.org/religion/classes/

Enter your e-mail address and the password you were given at the end of the first lesson, on page 33. Then select Test 3 from the list of tests. You will also find there an online test for each lesson, with feedback sent directly to your e-mail address, and a discussion forum about each of the lesson topics.

LESSON 4
SABBATS AND SACRAMENTS

RUN dot Child, and sow your oats,
Joust your windmills, sail your boats.
You can fail, but you must try.
Baby, Fly!

YOUR OBJECTIVE FOR LESSON 4

You will list the eight Wiccan holidays of the
year and describe their meaning. You will identify the
seven sacramental festivals of a Wiccan life.

BUT, DO I HAVE TO GIVE UP CHRISTMAS?

Sabbats are the holidays of the Wiccan year. One of these Sabbats is Yule, which is the origin of Christmas. On Yule, Wiccans celebrate the birth of the Sun King, to our Mother Earth. This is His birth, because Yule is the winter solstice. Let's look at the eight Wiccan holidays and how we celebrate them.

People have celebrated holidays for as long as there have been people. Holidays help us remember to pay attention to our families and to get to know each other better. They are a good excuse to close down working and just spend time together. In the ancient days, people picked holidays to celebrate milestones in their project of planting the fields and harvesting crops. The holidays were like a project management schedule. February 2nd means get the seeds ready. March 21st means the animals are mating or birthing. May 1st means rake the fields. June 21st means plant. August 1st means harvest. September 21st means canning, preserving, and smoking. October 31st means prepare for the dead of winter.

December 21st means rejoice! The days are getting longer! The Sun has returned!

All the holidays were set around cycles of nature and the length of the days. They guided everybody to know what to do on the farms, and when to do it. December 21st, Yule, is the shortest day of the year. This is called the winter solstice. June 21st, Litha, is the longest day of the year. It is the summer solstice. March 21st, which is Ostera, and September 21st, which is Mabon, are the two days on which the day and night are exactly equal in length. These are called the equinoxes.

You can graph the length of the day against the days of the year to show how the holidays reflect changes in the length of daylight hours. The circle of the year gets laid out flat like a sine wave when we show it on a graph of linear time.

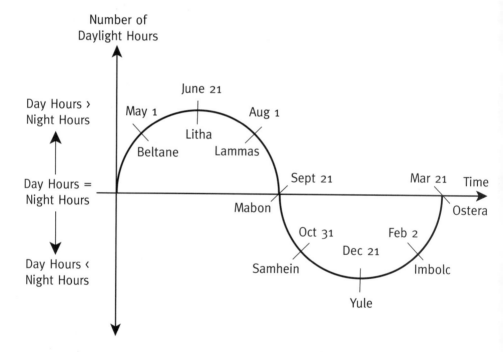

On Beltane, Lammas, Samhein, and Imbolc, you can see those days are on the knee of a curve. That means the rate of changes of daylight to night hours either slows up quickly or increases quickly. To ancient peoples, this was a very noticeable change. They thought there was something very special about days that would mark a sudden change in the length of daylight, so they called those days the major holidays. They are always on the same date. The other four days don't have exactly the same date every year. They fall within a range of two or three days of their given date, depending on when exactly the Earth's orbit causes the day to be the longest or shortest. Every year, astronomers calculate these dates exactly. They are printed in almanacs and calendars and called the winter solstice, summer solstice, spring equinox , and fall equinox. These are the minor holidays. Major or minor, holidays are celebrations, and in ancient times, everybody stopped working to have a party.

Here are the folklore legends people told to explain what was happening in the universe as the days and nights changed the number of hours. This is how people celebrated the turning of the wheel and honored Mother Nature and Father Time.

Yule. Approximately (but not exactly) December 21st. Because this was the day the Sun came back, and the days started lengthening, people called this the birth of the Sun. Its actual astronomical event occurs between the 20th and 23rd of December. The Sun was called a king or a lord. Kings and lords were very important to ancient peoples because their village structure and economic system depended on how the lord behaved. A good lord would mean all the people were happy and taken care of. A bad lord would mean the people lived in misery and hunger. To have a good lord would be something many people would pray for, and ask the Goddess to give them. When they saw the Sun returning, after so many months of winter hardship, they had hope. The Sun would come and bring back their crops! Mother Earth has given birth! Her child could be our lord! The Sun King would reign! Then there would be light! Rejoice for the birth of the lord of light!

Ancient people in every culture, on every continent, celebrated this birth of the Sun. "Behold! The Sun is born!" they said. "Rejoice! Light is triumphing over darkness!" To show that they had renewed hope that the darkness would soon be gone, they decorated their houses with evergreens and colored lights. They gave presents to each other in honor of the Sun's birthday. Even today, all major religions call this time of year holy.

Because this ancient pagan holiday was very popular—as it is now—the Roman Emperor Constantine declared it to be Christ's birthday in about the fourth century C.E. The Emperor Constantine had seen a vision of a cross in the sky, and a voice told him that he should declare Christianity as the mandatory religion of the empire. The booming voice told him that this would be an excellent vehicle to consolidate the power of the empire, as Christianity taught people to be obedient to governmental authority. This mandatory religious observance would be a way to get the peoples that were being conquered to acquiesce to Roman rule. As it was the pagan practice to celebrate the winter solstice as the day our Mother gives birth to the Sun (because now the days will start to get longer), it was a logical choice to equate the Mother Goddess with Mary and the Sun King with Jesus. The date was moved from December 21st to December 25th when the Roman calendar was adjusted (when the year was discovered to be 365 days long). Pagans need not shy away from celebrating Yule on December 25th with their families and at the time that work and school are closed, or from sending cards for Yule. This is most emphatically a fully pagan holiday and is celebrated around the world in a fully pagan manner.

Pagans, of course, believe the booming voice and the cross in the sky that Constantine saw was a facet of God other than Jehovah and/or Jesus. But that is a matter of theology to address in a different forum.

This time is a great opportunity to set up an altar in your living room, next to the evergreen tree with colored lights. Use a red velvet altar cloth, decorate the altar with fir boughs, use a cinnamon stick for your wand and a set of quartz crystals in place of the bowl of salt, and you will find that none of your nonpagan family, friends, or neighbors will see your altar as being out of place for Christmas. For those of you considering coming "out of the broom closet" to some of your family, setting up an altar like this at Yuletide offers an opportunity to begin the explanation. Welcome them home to the family of pagans who love to celebrate the birth of the Sun.

Imbolc. February 2nd, (Candlemas). From this day forward we see the rate of change of daylight increasing. This is the midpoint between the winter solstice, when the Sun-God is born, and the spring equinox, when the Goddess returns from the underworld, where She went to give birth, and is renewed Herself. The underworld is where seeds come from, so it is where the ancients believed new birth arose. She is the crone now, the old woman, as it is surely the dead of winter, and the Earth is barren, but soon She will return renewed as the maiden. This is the time to prepare for growth and get ready for new beginnings. Are the seeds ready? Planting time will begin soon.

We celebrate this holiday with individual candles for everyone, so we can all help the young Sun King grow to manhood. It is important to nourish Him now, and help Him return to His full glory as the summer Sun. This is the time for long processions of people carrying candles, encouraging the Sun King, showing Him we are ready to light our one little candle, too and initiate new efforts ourselves. Red candles help us light our inner fire. Mother is Wisdom in Her aspect as the crone. The early Christians called Her "Sophia" in Her aspect as Mother Wisdom, the crone.

Ostera. Approximately (but not exactly) March 21st (also spelled Eostre). This is the spring equinox, the day when daylight and night are equal. The Lady returns, renewed and refreshed from Her rest, ready to reign with Her King through the summer. Animals awake from hibernation, and the first buds appear. She is the maiden now. Resurrection! The old has become young again, and the Earth is renewed. The dead Earth has come back to life! On our altar, we place a bowl of seeds to bless for the coming planting, and we color eggs to show our hope for fertility in the coming spring. Bunnies and chicks are everywhere to remind us of our happiness when the fields and the families are fertile. Fertility means food for everyone. Resurrection of our Mother saves us from the harshness of winter. As the dark Moon is dark in the sky for three days, so we say our Mother "descends to the underworld for three days, and then arises from death." Purple candles and pastel colors are used for this holiday. Eostre, the Eostre Bunny, and the symbols of fertility make this the happy holiday of Resurrection. Death has been overcome, and the Earth has returned to spring.

This holiday was originally the feast day of the Goddess Eostre, who is a Teutonic lunar goddess. Her holiday is actually celebrated on the first Full Moon after the vernal equinox, rather than the vernal equinox itself. She is celebrated with rabbits, representing fertility, and eggs, representing the cosmic egg. This happens to be the "paschal Moon," which is the Jewish Passover. When Christianity became established, the calculation of the date for Jesus's resurrection (that is, the triumph of the god of light over death), was determined to be set at the first Sunday after the first Full Moon after the vernal equinox. This is why Christians celebrate Easter with Easter eggs and Easter bunnies.

Neopagans of today generally move the Eostre celebration to the vernal equinox itself, which is called "Lady Day," since it is the day the Lady (Mother Earth) returns from the dead (of winter). In Christian circles, Lady Day became associated with the Annunciation of the Blessed Virgin, which was set at the vernal equinox, in order to allow the pregnancy to culminate at the winter solstice. Annunciation means announcement and, for Christians, this is the day the angel informed Mary of her pregnancy. Pagans consider this day the day the Lady returns from the underworld (rises from the dead), and simultaneously becomes pregnant in order to bless the Earth with new life. The two festivals—Lady Day of the vernal equinox and Eostre for the lunar goddess—are celebrated as one. Neopagans of today may choose to hold their festival on the Christian Easter (that is, the first Sunday after the Full Moon after the vernal equinox) in order to coincide with the children's spring vacation schedule.

Beltane. May 1st, (May Day). In agrarian societies, our ancestors would have raked the dead of winter from the fields and be ready to burn it in preparation for planting. The balefires were a good excuse to gather around and celebrate the coming of summer. The fire was seen as a way to purify the fields and prepare for the serious business of planting. People danced around the Maypole and jumped over the balefires, laughing and singing.

The hawthorn tree was often the traditional Mayberry bush and its branches are particularly known to house elves and faeries. The berries of hawthorn, boiled into a tea, are a very good drink to improve the health of the heart. We use white candles this day, for our Mother has matured to be the virgin, and She is poised to give up Her virginity so that She may produce fruits for us.

Litha. Approximately (but not exactly) June 21st, summer solstice. This is the longest day of the year. Now the Sun King reigns, but after today He will be with us less and less. The Virgin is pregnant, maturing and blossoming in Her beauty and innocence. She will be with us through the summer, before retiring to the underworld to give birth, as She does every fall. Some of the seeds sown have begun to sprout. This is a time for gratitude and thankfulness for the beauty of life. Decorate the altar at sunset with flowers and the dark blue candles of evening.

Lammas. August 1st. By Lammas, the wheel of the year tells us it is time for the harvest. We celebrate in order to refresh and revitalize ourselves for the work ahead. The harvest can be seen in the fields. Gratitude and thanksgiving abound. The Goddess provides, but we must still work for the harvest and prepare the food. This is the time to reorient and reattune natural energies, so we will know when to harvest each fruit. In our lives today, we have produce and fruit of our efforts. This is when we must try to ground and center ourselves and be sure we are listening to the guidance of the universe in our lives, which is always the guidance of God, our Lord and Lady.

Today is Romeo and Juliet day, time for renewed romance between married couples, as they prepare for the season of hard work in the harvest. Mom and Dad work hard to make a happy family, and this is the day when they should remember they are also in love with each other. The children get together under the supervision of a babysitter and have a Peter Pan festival while Mom and Dad go on a date with each other. They renew their commitment to married romance and strong family values. It's love that makes the world go round—love in tune with Nature, so your work will be divinely inspired. We use green candles on our altar and decorate with baskets of fruits and vegetables.

Mabon. Approximately (but not exactly) September 21st, the fall equinox. From now on, night will be longer than day. Everyone worked hard since Lammas to bring in the harvest from the field. Now we stop and relax, before the canning and preserving and smoking work goes into full force. We give thanks for all we've received and say good-bye to the Sun King until He is reborn on Yule.

Soon the Dark Lord will be dominant, and our Mother will go to the underworld for Her rest and to give birth once again to the Sun King. Our Mother is with us always, but half the time She is dominant with the Sun King by Her side. When the Dark Lord is dominant, in the winter time, She is resting to give birth to the Sun King.

The Dark Lord is the male part of God who rules drive and ambition. He is the Father. He is the part of God who rules when the night is longer than the day. The Goddess is the female part of God, who rules nurturing and understanding. She is the mother of the Sun King, who is the male part of God during the part of the year when light is dominant. Her Son is the light, but His Father is the dark, because light is born of dark. We only know light because there is dark. We only know happy because there is sad. Yet all of creation is good in its context. The Dark Lord, who is the Sky Father, brings us drive and ambition, which is what we need to survive the harshness of winter. When He is dominant, we learn structure, organization, scheduling, and cooperation. These are all things we need to know, and so we think of Him as the God who enforces the rule of law. Our Mother never leaves us, even when He is dominant. She just rests in the underworld, waiting to give birth to the Sun. The underworld is where seeds come from, so She must go there to bring new life. Sometimes structure and discipline seem harsh, but we know we must learn it if we are to have the spring and the harvest. If we did not have the Sky Father, we would just be spineless jellyfish. Not a jot or a tittle of His law can be changed. Fortunately, the Sun saves us from His rule of law. We must have faith that the Sun will return.

The God who brings us through the dark of winter is our backbone. Mother calls Him for the hard tasks. He enforces Her honor. He puts the teeth into the expression "to fear God." One stays respectful of Mother when one knows the God who gave us the instinct for survival. This survival instinct is most powerful. It will fight against all odds. It will perform miracles. When the instinct for survival kicks in, all is transformed to meet its need. The God who is the Father of the Sun pulls us through hard times and overcomes harsh conditions. He is the Sky Father. We need Him to give us the will to live. He is the awesome power that overcomes all and is beyond understanding. We need Mother to ease the pain of living. We need the Sun to make living a joy. Three of them—the Sky Father, the Sun King, and our Mother, the one deep in our hearts, speaking to us always. This is our Trinity.

At Mabon, we get ready for the Sky Father. We review our plans and goals for the coming year. We decide what improvements we must make in ourselves. Mabon is a time for looking to the future and preparing to meet our destiny. It is the Sky Father who drives us to achievement and purpose.

We love to be competent and accomplish things. These are the gifts He provides. A society that does not know Him does not progress and advance. He is the force of societal evolving. His power is so strong it would break us if He did not temper it by allowing us the love of Mother.

At Mabon, we decorate our altar with the colors and leaves of fall—golds, oranges, browns, and reds, and dream our dreams of accomplishment and achievement.

Samhein. November 1 (All Soul's Day). The holiday begins at sundown on October 31st and continues to sundown the following day. This is the final turn of the wheel of the year, the end of one cycle and the beginning of the next. Every ending is a beginning when the wheel is turned. It is the moment when the souls in Summer Land are nearest to the Earth, and we remember them. We say good-bye to Mother for Her rest, and accept dominion of Father for the winter. It is a celebration of death.

The ancients understood that birth comes because of death. New seeds sprout from fertilized soil. Death is the beginning of our next phase. It is the time of entry to Summer Land, where there are no problems of harsh winter. We are thankful for everything God brings to us, and death is again a gift of God. How could we appreciate life if we did not have death to make it precious? The Goddess has given us life, and She would be very dishonored if we did not appreciate it.

We would never hurt ourselves or anyone else. That would be against our law that says we may never hurt anyone, including ourselves. This is why we never say life is meaningless, or death would be a welcome relief from our problems. We know we only live again and reincarnate, so we must face our problems in our life now and resolve them, for suicide is no solution to them. They will follow us to our next life, possibly causing us to have childhood diseases and difficulties. Death has a different meaning to one who understands karma and reincarnation. We take the opportunity at Samhein to consider what we have done to our karma in the last year and plan how we will approach it in the coming year. Now that the Dark Lord is in full reign, we know His drive, ambition, and discipline will help us structure our goals and plan our achievements and progress to align with our karmic path.

This is also the time when loved ones who may be in Summer Land may choose to communicate with us, to help us envision our karmic destiny. We look to the gods to help us receive this communication, and use it productively.

We use orange candles on our altar and honor the Goddess as we prepare to submit to the harshness of winter and the discipline of structure and organization the God provides, so we can work and build for the following spring, and call on His power to survive the winter.

These are the cycles of Nature and the holidays of the wheel. When we celebrate them, we learn the harmony written into the universe.

THE SACRAMENTS

There is another set of passages in our lives that are associated with our linear time. These are the passages that mark milestones in our life cycle: The birth and naming of a baby, the advent of puberty, dedication to the Goddess, marriage, menopause, becoming an elder, and passing over to the other side (death). As Wiccans, we don't need a lot of excuse to call a celebration, and so we celebrate all these passages as sacraments, too. They are sacred parts of our wheel of life.

We call the naming of a baby its Wiccaning. We call a marriage a handfasting. Marriage in a Wiccan church can be a legal marriage, registered with the state, or it can just be a marriage registered with the Lord and the Lady. We don't have such a thing as "living in sin," so if a couple wants to live together, we "handfast" them. The Lord and the Lady recognize it as a marriage commitment.

Making the decision to dedicate ourselves to the service of the Goddess is a big deal and requires a celebration. We do not bring children into the church, except in the company of their parents, so the dedication is an adult decision, taken of our own free will. Dedication is a personal thing, not done in a group, like initiation is. Initiation is usually when a coven takes in members. Dedication is an individual's choice to be Wiccan.

Celebrations are held for boys and girls as they reach puberty (the Wiccan equivalent of the Bar Mitzvah). They are also held for men and women as they reach menopause or "graying." A graying ceremony for a man is a celebration of his status as an elder in the church. For both men and women, the graying ceremony welcomes them to the circle of wise ones and the protection of the crone. It is a celebration of the freedom that comes from realizing you are where you were going, and you no longer have to wonder what you'll be.

The eldering ceremony is used as a type of "prefuneral," with the person still alive to enjoy it. It is taken from Native American practices, when a person might decide that they acknowledge they have led a full life, and they have reconciled with the coming of death. It should be used while a person is still healthy whenever possible, to say, "I am happy that I have had this life experience, and I am ready now for what will come." It does not mark the end of life, but rather shows gratitude for life and signals loved ones that the person is at peace.

The passing over ceremony is, of course, the funeral. This, too, is a happy time. We know our loved ones have entered a new phase, and for them this is a beginning. We wish them well on their journey.

In all things, celebration for a Wiccan is a daily experience. Solemnity is not present in our worship services or sacraments. We enjoy living and feel joy and gratitude for all it offers.

SUMMARY POINTS OF LESSON 4

- The eight Wiccan holidays are called Sabbats. They are celebrations and festivals that occur to mark the milestones of the wheel of the year.

- The holidays are: Yule, on the winter solstice, which is between December 21 and 23; Imbolc, on February 2; Ostera, on the spring equinox, which is between March 21 and 23; Beltane (pronounced Byal-tin), on May 1; Litha, on the summer solstice, which is between June 21 and 23; Lammas, on August 1; Mabon, or the fall equinox, which is between September 21 and 23; and Samhein (pronounced Sow-in), which is actually November 1, but is celebrated on the evening before, October 31. All holidays are actually celebrated from sundown the evening before to sundown of the next day. Samhein is the beginning and the end of the Wiccan year.

- The sacraments of a Wiccan life are the passages of milestones in a life: the birth of a baby, puberty, dedication to the Goddess, marriage, graying or menopause, eldering, and death.

SUMMARY POINTS

LEARNING EXERCISES FOR LESSON 4

1. Mark your calendar with the Wiccan holidays for the coming year. You will need to check an almanac to find the exact dates of the equinoxes and solstices.

2. What is the next event in your life that could be a cause for Wiccan celebration? Do you have a marriage, birth, puberty, menopause or graying, dedication, or eldering coming up? Pick a date to have a party in honor of the Goddess for your big event.

3. Plan how you will celebrate the next Sabbat. Put together a ceremony recognizing the meaning of the holiday and plan your party decorations around the theme for that Sabbat.

To join in the private online discussion forum exclusively for readers of this book, and to try the test questions for this lesson, go to:

http://www.LadyRaya.org/religion/classes/

Enter your e-mail address and the password you were given at the end of the first lesson on page 33. Then select Test 4 from the list of tests. Feedback about the test will be sent directly to your e-mail address. You can also join in on a discussion forum about each of the lesson topics.

Lesson 5
Pagan Mythology

RUN dot Child, and call your home
You were never meant to roam
Stay securely by my side.
Stem the tide.

Your Objective for Lesson 5

You will describe how pagan myths influenced
the development of mainstream religion.

In the beginning was the Word, and the Word was with God, and the Word was God . . .

Thus speaks the writer of the Gospel of John in the New Testament, sometime near 90 C.E. "I am the Word," the early Christians quote Jesus as saying, and we in the twenty-first century still wonder what words are, in terms of molecular physics. Quantum science continues to search for the unified theory that will reconcile the workings of the world to a formula that can fit across a T-shirt. Our scientists know this formula must exist, for the world we've come to understand is, in its essence, mathematically consistent. But the molecular action of thought, language, and consciousness—that illusory self-awareness that allows us to have the "Word"—has not yet been discovered.

"Is religion consistent with science?" The young atheist asks the mystic Jew. "No," the old man responds sadly. "But science is learning more each day, and we are confident it will eventually catch up."

THE SACRIFICED GOD

Ancient peoples in every civilization developed stories to explain the science of the natural world. These stories inevitably centered around a race of "gods"—superhumans who had vast and infinite knowledge and who were not limited or constrained by the laws of physics or nature. Instead, these beings had created the laws of physics and nature in order to allow the human race to exist. Because these stories attempted to explain nature, they inevitably were stories of a cycle of birth and death, seed and sacrifice. Plant the seed, sacrifice the fruit of the harvest, and eat it. Allow the death to come. Plow the dead back into the earth, for the good of the earth. See life rise again.

This cycle is the story of the wheel of the year; it is the story of the Egyptian Osiris, the Celtic Oak King, the Norse Odin, the Greek Orpheus, and many thematic myths of the ancient world. Many of the god-heroes are pierced by a spear or hung on a tree. The sacrificed god illustrates the theme of nature's bounty being provided to humanity; the god is sacrificed and eaten, then gives this sacrificed life to fertilize the earth and ensure bounty again with a resurrection the following year. Every early civilization, from the Americas to Africa, from Europe to Indochina, developed a story around this plot. It is, of course, the central theme of the story of Christ. "Take. Eat. This is my body, broken for you," says Christ. The old Scottish song "John Barleycorn" says the same thing.

There were three kings come from the East
Their fortunes for to try
And they ha' ta'en a solemn vow
John Barleycorn must die.
They took a plough and ploughed 'im down
Cast clods upon his head
And they ha' ta'en a solemn vow
John Barleycorn was dead.
But when the spring came kindly on
And show'rs began to fall
John Barleycorn got up again
And sore surprised them all.

Our human civilizations evolved in different places but drew similar conclusions about the world. Our myths and stories told the same truths; our legends painted the same pictures. Mythology is the truth our collective subconscious observes and represents concepts we are less able to express rationally. The gods and goddesses, heroes and heroines of our myths, tell us morals and ethics of the universe, to which we can ascribe with our hearts and our passions, even if we are unable to agree to them with our logic.

The Primal Creator

Pagans are said to be those who worship polytheistically, that is, worship multiple gods. Nothing could be less insightful of the pagan religion. The gods and goddesses that populate a pantheon for a particular culture are perceived to be multifaceted aspects of the One. That one is both Mother and Father, Goddess and God, Earth and Sky, yin and yang, a sacred unity and duality all the same. The primal Creator, existing before all existence, all-powerful, all-knowing, all-present, the one and only God, is the same Deity who presents to the Jews as Yahweh, the Christians as the Trinity, the Greeks as Zeus and the entire Greek pantheon, the Norse as Thor and the entire Norse pantheon, the Ephesians as Diana, the Egyptians as Ra, the Mayans as Itzam-Na, the Moslems as Allah, the Buddhists as the divine self, and the Native Americans as Grandfather. God is both male and female and neither male nor female. God is the Goddess. The Goddess is God.

When we use archetypal images of a god or goddess in human form, we are attempting to symbolize the concept of Deity in a way that we, in our limited human capacity, can feel passion for. We know, however, that the Lord is not a man and the Lady is not a woman, for to call them that would be to limit them. They are the primal Creator, the masculine and feminine principles from which creation is emitted. We are truly unable to describe the Creator, for any description would imply a limit, and the Creator is limitless. We have no ability to perceive the vastness of this Creator. And so we, as pagans, resort to myths and stories of the gods and the goddesses, attempting in some human way to envision a Creator that our minds can understand.

The Reality of Symbolism

Having envisioned our gods through mythologies, does that mean these gods do or do not exist? A way to look at it is to think of the concept of money. Money is not real value. It is an agreed-upon and arbitrary assignment of value, which has reality only as long as the society continues to agree to its value. The value of the money changes as the societal circumstance of supply and demand changes. Is the money real? No, it is symbolic. Is the value of the money real? Absolutely. The value of the money is a relative reality to the person who perceives its value. The buyer and seller must come to an agreement on that reality before the money has any value. When an agreement is reached, the money is used as a symbol of the reality of the value that has been agreed upon. If the society in general chooses to assign an absolute value to that money, then the money itself approaches a reality similar to the reality of its value.

So also with the archetypal gods and goddesses. One particular pantheon, or set of gods and goddesses, will be more useful to one pagan than to another pagan. One set of gods and goddesses will take on a reality for one pagan, making possible the achievement of magickal ends. The value of that pantheon for that pagan is reality, although the archetypal gods and goddesses are simply the symbols of that magickal value, like the money is the symbol of a value for barter. The pagan then invokes, or calls upon, the gods and goddesses of the chosen pantheon in order to achieve magickal ends. The gods are real, just as the value of the money is real, but the archetypes through which a pagan chooses to experience the gods are symbolic.

Prayer versus Magick

When Christians invoke their archetype of God, they call it praying. Few pagans like the idea of prayer, however, because the gods of many pagan pantheons are annoyed by it. Praying, as it is practiced by many today, is a form of asking God to do something for you. In praying, we tend to adopt a subservient body language and attitude and request a favor. While some god-archetypes may find this acceptable, most images in the pagan pantheons do not.

Praying is like asking your father for an allowance while magick is like going out and getting a job. Magick is a form of offering your energy to the divine in order to effect a magickal change that is in concert with God's Will. In magick, God takes your energy and uses it to enact a magickal change that will perform God's Will. You, as the practicing magician, find yourself depleted of energy for some time period thereafter. Magicians believe that the True Will in our hearts is the Will of God. That is why we say, "An it harm none, do as Thy Will," for we believe the Will is placed in our hearts by the Goddess. When you offer your personal energy to the Divine in order to change the universe in a magical way, you are sacrificing your energy in order to show your devotion to the Deity. No magick will ever be done that is not the will of Deity, for magick is a reserved province of the Goddess and the God. They decide how to implement and manifest the universe, as They are the Creators of the universe. We give our energy to Them to do magickal acts in concert with the will in our hearts, which we know is placed there by the gods themselves.

While the archetypal image we choose to help us experience God may be only symbolic, the experience itself is real. The gods, to a practicing magician, are tangible, concrete, and dramatically physical. They have egos, desires, preferences, and self. We meet them, learn from them, and know them as Father and Mother.

Invocation and Ritual

The gods—although not in reality living within our three dimensions in human form as we know it—communicate to us through meditation, channeling, insight, coincidence, circumstance, and revelation. Most pagans would agree that the communication received from the gods tells us to perform magickal acts and ritual rather than prayer. These magickal acts operate on our own inner child—our id—and also the id of the subconscious universe to interact with the universe and make us truly alive. The reality of the gods with whom we interact becomes then abundantly clear, as the currency of our beliefs and rituals proves itself to manifest when we perform magickal acts. Our gods show themselves to be real as we see their response to our reverent invocations and magickal ritual. As money shows its reality when it is empowered to buy goods and services, so also our gods display themselves in the response of the universe to our magickal intent.

Do these archetypal and symbolic gods also have an objective reality and an absolute temperament and preference? Are they likely to burn the Ten Commandments into a stone tablet? Do they have a self-image, a set of goals, a plan for the universe? Do they make rules, judge behavior, assign duties, and mete out rewards and punishments? Do they preside over courts? Do they pick presidents and emperors? Do they throw thunderbolts and erupt volcanoes? Is there a standard to which they hold humanity? Is there an expectation and a plan for each person's unique life and path? How do the gods perceive humanity, and what is their reason for creating human life?

While humanity indeed envisions the symbolism by which we each relate to and invoke passion for our gods, the gods themselves created humanity so that through this invocation the gods might in reality exist. They are both existent and nonexistent, real and imaginary, concrete and conceptual, and through interaction with the creation, the Creator is displayed.

The Dilemma of Survival of the Fittest

In the earliest civilizations, the Deity was perceived as female, and the Great Mother Goddess was the primary form of pagan worship in all early societies. She was Anu to the Babylonians, Isis to the Egyptians, Inanna to the Sumerians, Ishtar to the Canaanites, Asherah to the Jews. Over time, She became Mira (mirror, the image), Miriam, and finally . . . Mary. As civilizations and cultures changed, so the Great Mother changed in Her archetypal and symbolic form. Always, She was the nurturer, the Mother whose apron shielded us from harm. In Her form as Mother Earth and Mother Nature, She taught us Her rules.

Nature's rules could be harsh. We learned She wanted attentiveness to Her cycles and harmony with Her ways. We learned She demanded balance and moderation, and She exacted Her due. We learned that we reaped what we sowed, and that we lay in the beds we made. We learned that we depended on one another, and conflict among us would be deadly. We learned that the strong could overpower the weak, but that we as a society must band together to prevent this if we are to satisfy our needs for compassion and prevent grief. We learned that grief, sadness, and despair were the precursors to illness and death.

We learned that boys will be attracted to girls, and girls will want babies. We learned that Nature would allow the boys to "love 'em and leave 'em" and that we would have to construct societal sanctions if we were to convince men to care for their women so the women could care for the children. When we learned that there must be societal sanctions and village rules, we introduced the concept of the Dark Lord. The backbone who would teach us to live in structured society, convince our young men to do their duty by their women, and enforce rules beyond Nature became our patriarchal God. Who was He? We wondered. What would help us overcome the winter, give us the will to fight and survive, and spur us on to achievement and accomplishment? Where would humanity learn its discipline and who would enforce its societal rules?

The Patriarch Emerges

Eventually, we concluded as a society that the Great Mother had a consort, who would enforce Her societal rules and introduce testosterone to spirituality. At first, we called him Her son, the Lord of Light. In the cradle of civilization—the Mesopotamian and Sumerian lands and Canaan—the word Baal meant Lord. We worshipped Baal, the young Lord. He was in sharp contrast to the Dark Lord, the Great Mother's husband. We called Him El. Our words "Israel," "Michael," "Gabriel," were ways to say these were things "of El." El we saw as a terrible Lord, one who enforced the laws of our Mother and behaved as the dominant male of our group.

We were an evolved monkey society. The dominant male was a concept we understood. The dominant male in an ape group is the one to whom all the other males bow down. They avert their eyes, lower their heads, bend their knees. Look at the anthropology of an ape society. See how the apes will bow their heads to the dominant male. Watch how they will prostrate themselves and show signs of subservience and shame in the presence of the great one who is their lord and king. "Don't worship Baal," the Dark Lord said, "for I must be the dominant male of this group." Few pagans today bow their head in prayer, preferring instead to stand by our Mother, and lift our hearts and voices in Her honor. The Dark Lord of today's archetypal vision has evolved to be the master of our drive and ambition and the taskmaster of our achievement.

In the early days of humanity, society saw El, the Dark Lord, as the patriarch and tyrant. He had the power to destroy our crops with the weather, send hurricanes and floods, erupt volcanoes, thrust thunderbolts. He and He alone could interfere with the nurturing arms of our Mother and destroy us. He and He alone could take Her away from us and prevent us from feeling Her love. He, the Father, was the only obstacle between us, the child, and the heavenly warmth we felt from Her, our Mother. We related to Baal as our savior, our brother, the one who would save us from the Dark Lord.

In the psychology of our evolving early humanity, the conflict between El, the Father, and Baal, the Son, was as sharp and clear as it is today when a young man reaches puberty and strikes out on his own, conflicting with the father in our households. "Don't worship Baal, the Son," the great, dark El taught us, "for I am the great father and patriarch, and I will have no other take my place." This is the behavior of the patriarch and dominant male in all ape societies, and to the early humans, the behavior of El was no different. The tribe of Israel, fearful of El to the point that they refused to say His name, began to record our history in Hebrew writing.

THE BEGINNING OF RECORDED HISTORY

They wrote down our long-standing stories and legends. They wrote of a paradise called Dilmun, where El first created man out of clay. They wrote of the goddess Ninti ("lady of the rib"), who stood by Enki, the first godman, when he was cursed by Ninhursag, the Great Mother, for eating the sacred plants of Dilmun. They wrote of the serpent in the tree, who appeared in the Babylonian epic of Gilgamesh, the oldest book in the world. They wrote of the brothers Emesh and Enten, who came into conflict because the god Enlil preferred the work of one over the other. They wrote of the sea-dragon Kur who was killed by first-man Enki. All of these pagan legends transformed in the telling until they were the stories of Adam and Eve, and Cain and Abel.

The Hebrews wrote of the pious man Ziusura, whom they called Noah. Ziusura was the only one saved out of all humanity when the gods sent a flood to destroy the Earth. Ziusura was instructed by Enki to build a great boat to save his family and some animals. He releases a dove from his boat to see if land is near. When the waters recede, he reestablishes humanity on

Earth and is rewarded with eternal life. These stories became the basis of Genesis in the books of Moses, legends told and retold among the peoples of many lands, pagan history and mythology based on beliefs that carried the ring of truth to the ears of early humankind.

The wife of El, called Asherah by the Jews, was worshipped by the tribes of Israel for six hundred years, even in the temple of Jerusalem, where Solomon the King erected a statue for Her. Her tree symbol eventually became the menorah of today. Solomon, the greatest king of Israel, also became the greatest contributor to magickal thought and practices of ancient times.

The Chosen People and the Mother and Child of Egypt

While these legends were becoming accepted as history in the Mesopotamian lands of evolving civilization, the Egyptian peoples living along the river Nile also developed a form of writing and began to record their understandings of the universe. The most ferociously religious of peoples, the Egyptians, enjoyed fertile land and moderate weather, along with an isolation by the surrounding deserts that protected them from constant invasion by other tribes. This relative safety allowed them to focus attention on the arts and advancement of literature from 3000 B.C.E. until they were conquered by the Greeks under Alexander in 332 B.C.E.

In ancient days, every small tribe would have its own stories of the behavior of God, and its own naming conventions for the various gods its members knew. Each tribe felt like the "chosen people" of their own God. When tribes met each other and told their stories, the stories would be adjusted to incorporate the names and stories of each tribe. This is how the great Sun God of Egypt, Ra, became known as Amun-Ra. He was Amun to one people, Ra to another, and so they hyphenated His name to acknowledge the stories of both tribes. The Egyptians—under the guidance of Amun-Ra—made great achievements in irrigation technology, medicine, astronomy, and literature, as well as the still fantastic and astonishing feat of building the pyramids.

Pyramid building, which was also going on in the Mayan civilization half a world away, seemed to be an accomplishment that was intimately related to calendar building, and the Egyptians had a 365-day year figured out—based on a vast knowledge of astronomy. The Egyptians invoked their gods constantly to assist them in acquiring this knowledge and making these achievements, and their gods answered with superhuman force. Magick—which is another word for a technology that is sufficiently advanced—was their primary means of learning and acquiring this knowledge, and the Egyptians can be said to be the foundation civilization for the establishment of magickal practices. Mummification and the technologies of embalming came about as a result of the Egyptian understanding that the soul was eternal and their desire to provide an intact body for the soul to take on its eternal journey.

Although nearly every ancient civilization told a story of a god's death and resurrection, based on the theme of the seasons and resurrection of the Earth at springtime, the Egyptians took this theme to a new level of intellectual advancement with the story of Isis and Horus. Isis, who at this time was the name for the Great Mother, was married to Osiris, who now had taken the place of Amen-Ra, formerly Amun-Ra ("Amen," meaning "so be it").

The great God, Osiris, was murdered by his brother, Set, and his pieces were scattered throughout the universe. Now Osiris could no longer be seen in a human form, because He was everywhere and in everything. However, the Great Mother, Isis, who had consented to stay on Earth and live with Her human children, was bereft over the loss of Her husband, and She determined to find all the pieces and put Osiris back together again. Isis found all the pieces except for His phallus, so like Humpty Dumpty, Osiris could never be fully reassembled. For a great goddess, this minor detail was not an insurmountable obstacle, and Isis used what She had left of Osiris for long enough to make herself pregnant, resulting in a virgin birth. She then allowed the pieces of Osiris to be blown to the winds and distributed throughout the universe, so that God would be everywhere and in everything, but the Great Mother would remain on Earth.

When Isis's son was born of this union, he was the god Horus. His Father, Osiris, although physically not present on Earth, ruled the underworld as the judge of dead souls. After death, each human being came before Osiris and was judged as to whether or not his life was worthy of a happy afterlife. Horus grew up talking to his Father but not having his physical presence with him. At the point of manhood, Horus set out to fight the evil Set, who had killed his Father, and a battle of good versus evil ensued in the heavens forever after.

It doesn't take a rocket scientist to see the similarities between this widely held belief of the advanced civilization of Egypt and the follow-up story of Mary, Jesus, and Satan that came after the Greeks conquered Egypt. Nor does it take much extrapolation to imagine the interplay of cultures when the Israelites brought the Mesopotamian legends of El and Asherah to the land of the Nile. Moses was raised as an Egyptian, we learn, and when he throws his staff at the feet of the Pharaoh, it turns into a snake. So, also, the Old Testament tells us, do the staffs of the Pharaoh's magicians. From the New Testament, we learn that Joseph takes Mary and the baby Jesus to Egypt to hide them from the evil King Herod. The young Jesus spends his early years in Egypt, learning with the other boys, one can only suppose, the techniques of the magickal trade.

But rocket science would be perceived as magick by any early society, and much of what today's quantum physicists reveal sheds light on how magick may be performed.

THE MAGICK OF THE SPOKEN WORD

Human beings differ from animals most markedly by their ability to speak and create complex language. This language is even more advanced when it can be written and read. While some other species of animal on Earth may have developed simple language, no other animal has ever developed the written word. Writing and reading are the most marvelous advancements of humanity, pulling humanity out of the animal world and into a world of power over all the other species on Earth. This ability to make symbolic forms communicate messages to others was so astonishing and miraculous to early peoples that they began to believe that a magickal power existed in the written words and letters themselves and that the letters and symbols of the written alphabet contained a godlike power with magickal ability. To the early pagans—especially the tribe of Israel and the Egyptians of the Nile—the magick of runic symbols first appeared.

The early Israelites developed a system of twenty-two letters of the alphabet, and to each of these symbols they attributed powers and characteristics. Likewise, the early Chinese, in a more symbolic manner, noticed the patterns on the back of a tortoise and developed a system of symbols they called the I Ching. Symbols and the ability to read and interpret them became an obvious way to receive communication from the gods. Because reading and interpreting are actions that are taken at the level of our subconscious mind, not our conscious mind, people learned that they could more easily hear the gods speak if they could assimilate the ability to read and interpret signs. This complex task would turn off their conscious minds and allow their subconscious, where the id resides, to communicate. In pagan terms, it is a way of thinking that is more like the following example.

Suppose you walk into a room, and you see a kettle of water on the stove. The water is boiling. You say to yourself, "Why is this water boiling?"

There are two correct answers to that question. The first correct answer is the answer of the "literal," or rational mind. It is: "The water is boiling because the heat from the fire on the stove has caused the molecules to collide with one another, and in their collisions, they are releasing the tension from the exploding air, causing bubbles to be formed and disintegrate." If you think with your rational mind, you may believe that the way to stop the water from boiling is to remove the pot from the heat.

But there is a second correct answer to that question. It is: "The water is boiling because Grandma wants a cup of tea." In this second approach, you have interpreted the sign of the boiling water and looked further to find out how it came about to be boiling, rather than just looking literally at what is currently happening. You have used your "interpretive" mind, which is part of your subconscious id, to analyze and extrapolate from this symbol to the originating cause of the action. If you think with this interpretive mind, you will realize that removing the pot from the water will only stop it from boiling temporarily because as soon as Grandma sees what you've done, she'll just put the pot back on the heat again. You will see that your only chance to stop the water from boiling will be to appeal to Grandma and hope she will agree to drink orange juice instead.

The Symbolic Qabalah

It is this interpretive mind, part of the subconscious id, which allows us to read signs and interpret symbols. It is the mind that follows clues to deduce the cause of things, even when those clues cannot be conclusively proven. It is the part of the mind that stores the system of beliefs and premises of faith. It can be called the "irrational mind," although its reasoning is not illogical but intuitive, based on leaps of faith.

Among the early mystics of pagan days, most particularly in the sects of Judaism but joined also by the mystics of Gnostic Christianity and Islamic Sufism, an intuitive analysis developed from the irrational mind that came to be known as Qabalah. Uniquely combining the symbolism of numbers and letters, Qabalah alleges to define the existent and nonexistent cosmic universe. This system says that the letters themselves created the universe. That is, the universe was illusory, and except for consciousness and awareness, there was no objective reality. Consciousness and awareness came about through a knowledge of history and time, as a function of association and symbolism found in written record and oral tradition.

The Qabalistic system set about describing a "Tree of Life" and a progression through four worlds. From the first world comes emanation, the Qabalah said. From the second world comes conceptualization. From the third world comes formation. From the fourth world comes manifestation. Moving among these worlds creates what will be. If we think of something, it will come to pass, because it will be created at some level and move through the worlds until we meet it one day on the road. We all know this to be true from common experience. This is why we must think good thoughts.

THE ILLUSION OF BEING

In the Eastern cultures, the concepts of an illusory world took great hold, and the theologies of Buddha, Krishna, the Vedas, and the Tao expanded on the theme. The Qabalistic concept became more and more detailed and concrete. The Tree of Life developed ten branches. There were four worlds, and each of them contained ten dimensions, the mystics said. The letters of words, when associated with numbers and added symbolically, would describe the universe. "Don't ask us how we know," they told the uninitiated. "It is knowledge contained in the aether."

Today as we begin the twenty-first century, our physicists tell us they believe they are learning the structure of the cosmic and microcosmic universe. Einstein's theory of relativity joins with the theories of quantum gravity at the point of superstrings. Superstrings, pagans say, join with consciousness at the point of Qabalah.

Physicists say that the cosmic universe has ten dimensions, and it is probabilistic rather than certain. The ten dimensions live in Quaternion Hyperspace, which contains the Real, the Imaginary, and the J and K worlds. It is from a folding hyperspace that wormholes connect us to other times and other universes. We are unable to say where a particular electron may be at any one time. It is illusory in its position. Our DNA is made of four elements, and these elements combine in exactly the number of combinations as the I Ching.

Today's pagans say the propelling factor in guiding the electrons is Will, the Will of the mind, which is the Will of God, and the technology that derives it is magick. Yesterday's pagans—Aristotle, Plato, Euclid, Pythagoras, Hippocrates, Philo, Paracelsus—would have surely agreed.

THE FIFTH FORCE OF NATURE

When we draw the pentagram, we recognize intuitively that the forces of Nature are five. They are Air, Fire, Water, Earth, and Spirit. Science has learned that the force of Air is electromagnetism; the force of Fire is the strong nuclear force; the force of Water is the weak nuclear force; the force of Earth is gravity. Soon, science will announce a fifth force, the force of sono-luminescence. Pagans will know this is the force of Spirit, which is the breath of God. We call upon that spirit when we light a candle, invoke the gods, block out our consciousness, and allow our intuitive minds to do the following.
(Read this *out loud* or play track four on your *RUN dot Child* CD.)

THE ROSWELL EXPLANATION

Goodness, Gracious, what's IT mean?
How'd the X-files make the scene?
Lords have Ladies, don't they? Well,
Shouldn't Ours be married? Spell
Out the lesson told by John.
Sure enough, you'll find the Con
Hidden in the Holy Word.
Hang on, Pete. The Rooster's Heard.
But that Bird's no Raven, Poe.
Read aloud and say it slow.
Fifty One in Roswell says
Monica takes down the Prez
Then you look the other way
While the Year Two Thousand Day
Builds to its expected SMACK
And the Lord turns History Back
To the TIME when Men were Men
And the Ladies birthed again
And again as Nature called.
Shave that Eagle! Name it BALD.
Mother, Daughter, Sister, Wife. Giver, Nurturer of Life, Bringing forth the Shining Sun,
King and Lord. And if He won Hearts, then She would step aside,
wouldn't She?
Maiden, Virgin, Mother, Crone, Made the Universe Alone
But for Him, Her Other Side. She could be His Earthly Bride,
couldn't She?
Then when Evolution crowed She could set the markers. Road
To the Karmic circumstance Could be Guidance, not be Chance.
Shouldn't She?
Woulda', Shoulda', Coulda', Will, Wrapped inside a Karmic bill.
Walk the Way and pay the Price. Mother's Hand can guide the Dice.
Will She?
Now I learn My A-B-C's. Is the Moon still made of Qi's?
Mother takes me by My Hand. Firmly I learn I can Stand
On my own and face my fear while My Mother's standing near
So I listen for Her voice and I know that my own choice
Is Her Will.

For I'm Hers and She is Mine.
I'm the Sun. I'll always Shine
In Her Eyes and be Her Star.
Twinkle, twinkle. What we are
Is what She wants us to be.

And when I saw Her, Mother
Was flecked with gold. Arrayed
In flowers, birds, and honey,
Her splendored bounty paid
The ransom. On my heartache
She seared the memory
Of Who, and Why, and Wherefore,
Evolved the Part called "Me."
So I returned to Mama
And She reclaimed my soul
Within Her warming bosom
I found the Human. Whole
Again inside Her family
I followed in Her path
And She drew lines around me.
Now, if you knew, the Math.
And Engineering drawings
Reveal the Reason. There,
But SHE has hidden meaning
In each electron. Pair
Or Apple, Peach, or Orange,
The Fruits of Passion bloom
And pollinate seduction
Of depths beyond the tomb.
And with my new found freedom, I learned the Ups and Downs
Of Rocks who wore their Hard Hats
And Holes who wore their Crowns
And there I learned that Rhythm
Can change in just a Flash
Like Floods of Credit Offers . . .

Tick Tick Tick Tick . . .
Ta da Bonk ta da da Bonkers
Ta da Bam ta da da Boom
Every vice has been a Virtue;
Every good was once a Crime.
All in context, as its Nature,

Thus the essence of Sublime
TRUTH and BEAUTY. Is Illusion
Setting up or Plowing down?
Reach inside you for the meaning.
Be a FOOL, thou Sacred Clown.

Make a mending stitch in FaceTime;
Sew a pocket on a patch.
Be a Living Child. The Mother
Mixed the cookies from a batch
All in order where she found it—
Lyrics by His salty "C".
There I followed to receive Him
And He opened arms to Me.
Man or Woman, I'm His lover.
Quantum forces pull my strings.
Hear the music from my subtle
Heart vibrations.

I have Wings!

So, GO, my ancient pilot
And fly the storming C
As Pirate, Friend, and Lover
Who answered calls from Me.
And let this be the MANTRA:
I came, I lived, I saw
And ACT not on temptation
But hear Hecate's Caw

Right then I lived the Rapture.
My Lord relieved the pain.
He carried me to freedom.
She cleaned away my stain.
So I was a new person.
I died, and lived anew.
The guilt of many ages
Dissolved in Witches' Brew.
And I stood tall beside Her,
My Mother's child at last.
Oh, Mary, Queen of Heaven,
The Isis of our past,
The Guide to all our Musick,
The Hand our cradles rock,

The Key to sweet Nirvana —
Our Mother.
                    ZIP.

                                        Unlock.

Sow this, My Seed of Glory,
        And Reap the Mystic Light.
                        When ONE embraces Mother
                        The TWO entwines His Might.
                And This is how the Mystic
                        Recovers from the "C"
                                That washes Inner Vision
                                        And Carries Clarity.
                        For Once Upon a Cupcake
                        I came, I saw, I fought.
                        But Cinderella's pumpkin
                        Transformed and I was caught
                                Unslippered. Unzippered. And Free.
(Who has Eyes and Ears can sense:
        This is "Food" in Present Tense.)
                "I" calls this the Reconciled
                        Version of the Holy Child
                                Who has always been THE WORD.
                                    Hang on, Pan! The Pot's been STIRRED.
                        From the Frying Pan we got
                                Time and Spaces. Tie the Knot.
                Well, TIME has told that Cat's Alive
                        Or Dead cannot be sure.
                And in the Quantum World of Men
                        The Skeptic must endure.
        So that's BECAUSE. Now what's the OUT?
                It's WILL. For if you're Free
        Then you must not be Scheduled. Take
                A Break to pass the Brie.
        With Crackers comes the Qi's of Life
                And Nuts too tough to Shell
        Their Skins. What Snake could lure the Wife
                Of Adam? Straight to Hell
                I'd go if it would clue me in
                On what This Living's FOUR
        And Two are Sicks, They pick up Styx
                And carry Tunes. Folklore
                And Fantasy may tell the truth

More frequently than News.
So here's my Take, I'd rather Brake
A Tale than Sing the Blues.
Sew right me up and dress me down,
I'll stand for my "Eye" Deal.
And fork the path with Spiral's Math
The Turning of the Wheel.

Now you count what "I" has writ.
And you'll learn that bit by bit
Byte by byte and Pack by Pack
Lord is SERVER.

You ACK-ACK

Source above and Source below
Flow through me and make it so.
Cause no harm, and bind by three,
Live by love, the law for me.

In the beginning was the Word, and The Word was with God, and the Word was God.
Blessed be.

SUMMARY POINTS FOR LESSON 5

- The sacrificed and eaten god is a common theme in pagan mythology. It arises from the observation of crop growth.

- The all-knowing and ever-present god is represented by archetypal imagery in the many gods and goddesses of paganism. Regardless of their names, they are all facets of the One.

- The symbolism of various gods in a pantheon is useful for a magician's mental focus and direction of energy.

- Magick is a form of offering personal energy to be used by Divinity for Divinity's own ends.

- The gods show themselves through circumstance. Magick manifests through apparent coincidence.

- The patriarchal god arose in response to humanity's need for structure and law.

- Pagan myths of Dilmun, Ninti, Enki, Emesh, and Enker became the creation myths of the Hebrew Bible.

- Pagan legends told of the virgin birth, the hero-king son, a heavenly battle between good and evil, and the sacrificed lord.

- Greek pagans made great discoveries in science and mathematics. At the time, religion, philosophy, and science were all the same concept.

LEARNING EXERCISES FOR LESSON 5

1. Read one book on Qabalistic theory and one on quantum physics and superstrings.

2. Research some of the various cultural mythologies. Learn the stories and legends of a particular pantheon of gods that interests you. Try to contact those gods in your meditation.

To join in the private online discussion forum exclusively for readers of this book, and to try the test questions for this lesson, go to:

http://www.LadyRaya.org/religion/classes/

Enter your e-mail address and the password you were given after the first lesson. Then select Test 5 from the list of tests. Feedback will be sent directly to your e-mail address. Feel free to join in on the discussion forum about each of the lesson topics!

LESSON 6
THE HISTORY OF WITCHCRAFT

RUN dot Child, but let it be.
Vengeance never sets you free.
Let the winds resolve your plight.
Be the light.

YOUR OBJECTIVE FOR LESSON 6

You will define witchcraft as it is practiced now
and as it was practiced throughout history.

THE DEFINITION OF WITCHCRAFT

"You what?" her mother's voice screeched across the dining room table. "How dare you ruin the good name of this family with such shame?" The child cringed at the outburst. The fire in the hearth crackled a spell of doom and eternal damnation. Inside herself, the young girl curled back to her infant state. Her eyes begged for a sign of mercy from the father she adored. But there was no mercy to be found in her father. "I will not have my daughter behaving like a trollop!" he shouted, storming out of the room. The child, feeling palpably the hatred and disdain of the rest of her family, suddenly could not catch her breath. She felt weak.

"Now you see what you've done to this family . . . " her mother started to say, but noticing her daughter's sudden illness, she changed to, "Oh, here we go again. Another dizzy spell. Well, you're certainly famous for that." The child stumbled out of her chair and crawled to her bedroom. The shortness of breath and heart palpitation continued. Doctors were called. Prescriptions were written. Diagnoses were presented.

But when the war came, Florence Nightingale managed to find it in herself to overcome her fear of the hostility of her wealthy family. She finally began to practice the nursing profession she loved, against her father's will. Her weakness and palpitations ceased immediately. She became a symbol of courage, bringing the nursing profession an international prestige. But Florence only served the British Crown as a nurse for two years. When the war was over, and she returned to her family, her symptoms returned. She immediately became bedridden.

And she remained that way until her death, over fifty years later.

Witchcraft is the act of imposing change on the world using our will. When we use our power and influence to manipulate another's feelings, when we cause others to cringe and feel small, when we label and stereotype people, when we assess moral judgments based on how others look, or dress, or behave, we impact those people, and we change their world. Throughout history, human culture has recognized that the words and the acts of one person can impact the life of another person. "You hexed me," humans have accused throughout history, and as we see in this story of Florence Nightingale, it has often been entirely true.

But the parents in this story had no idea they were issuing a curse. The doctors had no concept of the energies and the powers of The Word. Parents and teachers working with children every day are usually unaware of their ability and opportunity to hex the minds and bodies of their young charges, and so they accidentally issue damning curses and crippling sorcery on children regularly. "You idiot!" a dysfunctional father screams across the dinner table when a child spills his milk. And when the child's mind shuts down to live up to its label, our doctors wonder why.

THE POWER OF THE WORD

Archaeologists can exhibit ancient notes and hieroglyphics hexing friends, family, and neighbors. "My neighbor killed my cow," one ancient note excavated from the ruins of a Hebrew tribe reads, "and so I ask God to cut off his ears and slit his throat." People, since the beginning of time, have filled with anger and lashed out. Invoking the God to assist in revenge has been a reaction from the beginning of human time. "In the beginning was the Word," says the writer of the Gospel of John, "and the Word was with God and the Word was God." Using words to hurt others, cripple their self-image, and "mess with" their minds is an invocation of that God who is the Word. The power of the Word is undeniable. "I am the Word," Jesus Christ is attributed as saying, and when we take that statement literally, we can see what power the Word contains.

THE ORIGIN OF WITCH HUNTS

Because people knew from observation the power the spoken word exerts, humanity began to speculate what power could be exerted if this word were spoken in secret. Perhaps since we know a particular person has power over us when present—by speaking clearly and honestly or by aggressive and dominant behavior—maybe that person is able to have even more power when absent.

Maybe that person can speak privately to the Creator and make a deal. Maybe the words that are so powerful when we hear them are even more powerful when spoken in ritual. After all, we know how moved we are emotionally when we hear a song. Songs are poems and chants, are they not? What if a private song to a powerful god can be used to hex and curse someone when they are not in the room to hear it? Could someone be doing that? Just as we know in our hearts that our illnesses and pain and emotional trauma can be caused by the words someone once said to us long ago, is it possible that *all* our illness is caused by someone sitting privately in a room and chanting curses to the Deity? After all, humanity reasoned, if this illness has stricken me so severely, God must be punishing me. Why would God punish me, such a good person, unless someone else prevailed on God to do so?

In the story of Job, Satan prevailed on God to allow him to send tribulation to Job, a good man. "I'm good," the person rationalizes, "so someone must have prayed to Satan to cause this trial and heartache to strike me." It is easy to envision a thought process like this resulting in a public outcry: "Find the witch!"

CHEMICAL EMOTION

This set of premises results from a belief system humanity developed over thousands of years of observation of the action of the world. Words count. Words repeated in a rhythmic manner invoke emotion. Emotion is chemical. Chemical responses change the body. The body is physical matter. Words cause physical reactions. Ergo, magick happens. Witches are people who consciously and with intention use this ability to make words cause physical responses in the universe. We can see the truth in this by watching how Madison Avenue uses TV commercials to make people buy Froot Loops.

Every politician, every corporate leader, every charismatic evangelist, every inspirational writer performs witchcraft in the course of their mission daily. The world, without the action spurred by the words of these witches, would be a different place. Their words caused a change, and this change was magic. Now the question arises, how controllable is this change, and did the witch know what action would result from the witchcraft? More importantly, knowing that our words mean something to somebody, can we learn to perform this witchcraft intentionally and with positive purpose, ending our human tendency to do it accidentally and without control? Throughout the history of human civilization, the quest to perform witchcraft ourselves and prevent others from performing witchcraft on us has been part of our societal goal.

The Technology of Magick

Of course, every sufficiently advanced technology is indistinguishable from witchcraft. Perhaps, performed correctly, witchcraft itself is a technology. Perhaps it has rules for performance. Perhaps if we follow those rules of performing witchcraft, we can make it behave in a predictable manner, the way electrons behave as they rush through wires to tame the force of electricity in our homes. Whatever the rules of performance of witchcraft are, we know one thing is certain: If we cannot be witches ourselves, we cannot afford to allow witches among us. "Die, witches, die!" the fearful, petty, and jealous chorus, and so the truly magickal follow the law of silence.

To be silent about your powers in witchcraft is a primary rule to making them work. Magic performed for an audience is the trickery of a magician's parlor show. Magick performed in earnest is the social change invoked from behind the veil. Your magick will work if you do it privately and silently, never for an audience, and never as a show. The history of witchcraft in world religion is the story of humanity's search for the power and worry about taming it. When we open the mind, we run the risk that our brains will fall out. Too many people, searching for the power throughout history, came down on the wrong side of that risk profile. When we raise our hands and say, "I want to be a witch," we must acknowledge that an open mind is the antithesis of an empty head. We keep our wits about us by learning to use our rational abilities as well as our intuitive ones. It is rational to keep silent about the practice of witchcraft when in the presence of those who are oblivious to its nature. There is no positive outcome to be had by awakening ancient and primordial fears in those who have not been called to the craft.

Aboriginal societies feared the witch, believing witches had power to become invisible, to change into animals or birds, to foretell the future, and to reveal the past. Any schoolchild of high intelligence has known the disdain of classmates aroused by envy.

If a Native American warrior knew a secret passageway through a canyon and used that passage to appear on the top of a ridge when no one saw him climbing it, his tribal brothers would say he flew up there. If the man wished to exert influence over his brothers, perhaps he would let them continue to think that. People throughout history have attributed magickal power and witchcraft to those who knew hidden secrets and held creative talents. Myths and legends were built around the misunderstood, but the venom exhibited toward the "witch" by those who feared the witch's special abilities has a unique place in world religion.

The translators of the King James Version of the Bible institutionalized this poisonous hatred in dozens of places in both the Old and the New Testament. "Thou shalt not suffer a witch to live," thunders Jehovah in Exodus, chapter 22, verse 18. Even today, many otherwise good people feel obligated to carry out this (mistranslated) commandment.

The Witch in World History

Among ancient peoples, one in each group would emerge as the tribal "witch doctor." The medicine man or wise woman learned the properties of indigenous plants to cause vomiting, reduce fever, heal wounds, and ease discomforts. Herbalist, psychotherapist, hypnotist, and dramatic artist, the witch doctor was a healer in every sense of the word. Awareness of disorder in both the psyche and the soma, the witch doctor developed a following and became a leader of his or her village or tribal group. In every society, the ability to heal became associated with the ability to attain favor from the gods.

As the evolving human species built its societal structures, leadership of the group became a struggle between those who provided military protection—the warriors—and those who intervened with the gods—the healers. Who would lead the village was a dependency of which threat—military invasion or disease—was felt most strongly by the villagers. Just as everyone is not called to military heroism, so also everyone is not called to the magical sciences.

The religion of just about every human culture in the days before the introduction of Buddhism was fairly consistent across the world. Everyone believed there were gods who created the world. These gods could be an impersonal energy force, such as the Tao, or they could be the capricious, superhuman characters of Teutonic and Celtic legend. Stories were told and passed on from generation to generation about these characters. Learning the stories and telling them correctly was a job for the shaman and medicine woman. The stories held the wisdom developed over generations. They were a way to teach lessons learned by one generation to the next generations, so that evolution would allow us to learn beyond the timeframes of our short life spans. In every culture, the stories and lessons of our gods described truisms of how we observed nature to respond, whether the tale illustrated the nature of humanity or the nature of the physical world.

There are five forces of nature, according to the European pagan religions. Four of them are air, water, earth, and fire. With a few minor variations in the element names, Native American, Mayan, Egyptian, Chinese, and Hindu cultures independently reached the same conclusions that correspond to each other.

THE INTRODUCTION OF BUDDHISM

Around 600 B.C.E., a movement took place in China to introduce a religious philosophy we today call Buddhism. The Buddhist thought transcended pagan religious thinking of the time to point out that all was illusion. It is not God who is imaginary, the Buddhist said, but we who are imaginary. God is the only reality. We are but a product of God's dreaming brain. As a result, the Buddhist thought proposed, we should spend less time in the anthropological pursuit of monkey business, and end our animal instincts that pull us to war and drive us to aggression. We should remain at peace, both within and without, and this will awaken us from our sleep of unconscious behaviors. Through the focus of our mind's energy, Buddhism taught, we can conquer our animal nature and reach the higher goal of nirvana toward which our soul is destined to evolve. Buddhist thought met Jewish mysticism in around the sixth century B.C.E. and inspired Zarathustra and Zoroastrianism.

THUS SPAKE ZARATHUSTRA

Zoroastrianism was a blend of mysticism and science. It taught that there was a dualism between good and evil. All good came from God, and all evil came from a fiendish supernatural spirit and his assistants. The God of Light was called Mithra. At first, Mithra was a Persian god, but he traveled to Rome about 68 B.C.E. and became a popular god among the Romans. Good was associated with truth, while the evil spirit was a liar. After people died, they would be judged to decide if they would go to heaven or hell. Mithra was a bachelor god, without an associated goddess; he was a shepherd of his sheep and a leader of his soldiers. The similarities between Mithraism and Christianity result from the influence Mithraism exerted in Rome at the time of Christ.

DO NOTHING: THE WORLD WILL ORDER ITSELF

While Buddhism remained a movement that attracted followers from the ancestral paganism in some places in China, most of the Chinese people continued their village religious practices, which were very similar to the beliefs and practices of indigenous peoples in Australia, Africa, and the Americas.

Another movement in China, which relied considerably on ritualistic magick, was Taoism. The Tao is the great energy force, all being and wise. If we consciously focus on being in harmony with the Tao, the Tao will order all things. Religious Taoists filled the void for healers and medicine men among Chinese villages, offering magickal ritual to solve problems of daily life.

As we know from our double-blind clinical drug tests, a good percentage of people will be cured by a placebo. If a drug being tested cures any more than a placebo, it is considered a successful medicinal remedy. Yet millions of people are cured by their faith in the placebo. So, also, the healing rituals of magick cure. If one believes the ritual will heal, then indeed the ritual will heal.

The Oldest Scripture on the Planet

India, however, while adopting Buddhism in some places, for the most part continued to be Hindu. Hindu is a form of pagan religion, one which believes in reincarnation and recognizes multiple gods. While the gods may have different behaviors depending on the village telling the tale, Hinduism shares many characteristics with the village religions of the indigenous peoples from every continent.

Unlike the spontaneously developed, oral-tradition, indigenous religions, however, Hinduism boasts a long and sophisticated literary heritage from the Vedic writings, and more than five thousand years of recorded literary history. If other societies could be considered primitive in their theology because of a lack of written scriptures, the Vedas proved that pagan thought was deep and insightful. Written thousands of years ago, their complex revelation has led some to suggest that human history may have had civilizations more advanced in the past than it does today. The Vedas described a God that was threefold, both male and female, seven worlds plus a triple-godhead world. Poetically beautiful in their language, Vedic writings hold truths we have yet to learn. They are acknowledged to be the oldest writings on Earth, possibly from about 3000 B.C.E. There are four Vedas. One of them, the Atharta Veda, is devoted entirely to the record of ritual magic.

While every village had its own name for the gods and goddesses of the world, five civilizations stood out as having great influence on the evolving Western world. These five civilizations provided much of our religious practices and cultures in the West: the Egyptians, the Babylonians, the Greeks, the Romans, and the Jews.

The Witch in Egyptian Religion

Magickal practices were essentially defined by the Egyptians. The priests of Egyptian religion were magicians and practitioners of healing arts. When Moses threw his staff down in front of the Pharaoh and turned it into a serpent, the Pharaoh's priests were able to match him in his magickal displays. When one considers that Moses grew up in the Pharaoh's palace and would have known the same religious teaching as the Pharaoh's priests, perhaps this is quite understandable. Egyptian religion tied astronomy, numerology, and magic words to the practice of theology. The witch was a respected and honored priest of the gods.

The Witch in Babylon

The civilization in Babylon, however, was considerably more freeform and diverse than the structured Egyptians. Trancing, fortune-telling, consulting oracles, predicting the future through the stars, and speaking to those who had passed on became a common practice among what we might describe as Babylonian "New Agers." Breaking with the Egyptian tradition of magick as a theological science, the Babylonians lost touch with the basis of divinity in magick and allowed witchcraft to become another word for "loose women." It was in Babylon, home to an abundant society, that the word "witch" first got a bad name. One could purchase the services of a witch to hex or curse another, and the concept of divine intervention lost its connection with magick.

The Witch among the Jews

Among the patriarchal society of the tribes of Judaism, the Babylonian style "witch" was the equivalent of a hooker. Even so, it was not unheard of for a staid and married Jewish man to spend some time with one. The society needed to keep its women close to home, however, for if a Jewish woman were to marry outside the tribes of Judah, her lands and fortune might leave the family. Jewish men, however, seemed to make it a habit of marrying the women of Canaan and other tribes, constantly bringing pagan thought and worship practices into Jewish circles. The great King Solomon, writer of the Biblical books of Ecclesiastes and Song of Solomon, hero of the Jewish nation, and builder of the great temple of Jerusalem, was one of the greatest witches of all time. In addition to defining the lesser keys of the Goetia, Solomon ensured that the temple in Jerusalem was also the site of worship for the Goddesses Asherah and Aneth, considered to be wives of Jehovah.

Solomon himself had hundreds of wives, many of whom introduced him to Goddess worship.

The Jewish people did not always have such a beautiful temple, and many of them were unable to travel to Jerusalem to worship in it. Their standard for worship was defined in the Torah. The Torah told them to appoint a member of the tribe of Levi to be their priest, and the Levites were given specific direction on constructing a worship space and altar inside a tent. The Levites discerned the word of God by divination with a Urim and Thummim.

The word in the Torah translated as "witch" is more correctly translated as "poisoner." "Thou shalt not suffer a poisoner to live," says Jehovah. A society living in the desert, where a poisoned well meant death to the tribe, could need this rule.

The Witch in Ancient Greece

The heyday of Greek civilization, which produced such advanced pagan thinkers as Aristotle, Plato, Hippocrates, Euclid, and Pythagoras, was shortly before the time of Christ. Greek civilization had spread throughout the lands known as Palestine, and the Aramaic lands in which Christ is said to have lived were heavily infused with Greek philosophy and thought. Although the Romans conquered Greece before 1 C.E., Roman and Greek religion were closely allied. Both civilizations were greatly influenced by Egyptian religious thought. Both the witch-as-priest and the witch-as-hooker flourished in Greek society. Philosophy, religion, science, astronomy, and mathematics were seen to be integrally tied. Greeks believed humans had a threefold character: psyche, or the mind; soma, or the body; and nous, or the soul. The psyche-soma-nous could be influenced by forces that came from the stars.

The witch in ancient Greece was everyman. Learning was valued. Achievement was honored. Astronomy and mathematics were parts of the soul. Pagan religion was the core of Greek society, and the practice of magick was also the practice of science. Who could tell which was which? The great thinkers of Greek society were considered by the people to be sons of god.

The Witch in the Roman Empire

While the Greeks made great strides in scientific studies and athletics, the Romans were focused on military structure and law. Great court systems, rules and disciplines for Roman citizens, calendars and schedules, the rights of a Roman to due process—these were all focuses and features of Roman thought. Caesar Augustus, self-declared to be "Son of God," ruled the empire during the time Rome had conquered Jerusalem and Palestine. These same lands had previously been conquered by the Greeks.

Religious thought was diverse, and temples to many gods and goddesses coexisted. One primary god of Rome, however, was the Persian god, Mithra. Mithra, like the Romans, was a warrior-god. He, nearly alone among gods, had no goddess consort. He was a soldier. His followers believed He was born in a cave to a virgin. They thought if they ate His body, they would be taking His strength into themselves, and so they devised a ceremony whereby they ate something that was "transubstantiated" to be the God Himself and took His essence into themselves to make them strong in battle.

As the Roman Empire expanded, each village it conquered had a name for god. Knowing that one cannot conquer a people if they believe you are attacking their god, the Romans added each village's god to their list of gods. The various names and stories about the gods and goddesses grew longer and became intertwined. As people traveled, they brought more stories of gods with them, and, since there was no TV, storytelling was a prime source of entertainment. The gods of many lands became fused, and their tales and paths crossed.

Both Roman and Greek religions had sects of mystery cults. These cults practiced their religion secretly and required initiation and membership before being allowed to worship. The practices of these mysteries included the carrying out of plays or scripts to depict events in the lives of the gods. The four gospels of the New Testament, three written in Greek and one in Aramaic, were written in the dialogue style of mystery plays. The practices of magick, much carried over from Egyptian sources, were part of the mystery religions. "Out of Egypt I have called my son," the writer of the Old Testament Book of Hosea tells us.

THE CELTIC, TEUTONIC, AND COUNTRY-PEASANT WITCH

While the conquering Roman and Greek civilizations can be called pagan, the religion we know today as Wicca was a brand of paganism practiced in the outbacks of civilization—the Norse, Slavic, Welsh, Gaelic, Irish, and peasantry of European life. Far simpler in theology than the complex legends of the god-residents of Mount Olympus, practitioners of the country religions built localized tales of gods and god-men to describe their concepts of the meaning of life. These gods drank at local watering holes and bedded local women. They lived on local mountains and swam in local lakes. They were present in daily life and cared about local issues. They voted in local elections and looked after local fields and crops. They presided over the peasant festivals that signaled the planting schedule for agrarian society. The witch was the village herbalist and medicine woman—powerful in her tribal group, respected in her knowledge.

The Witch of Christianity

Now as the peak of Greek civilization passed and the Roman Empire expanded, a movement began to identify another son of God, a man who lived in the Aramaic lands of Palestine. At the time of the beginning of the movement, it was one more variation in the diverse richness of pagan worship. This movement identified a man named Jesus as the current son of God and was initially confined to the Jewish tribes. However, internal conflict between followers who had known the man Jesus personally and a latecomer named Saul of Tarsus—converted by a vision of a ghost after Jesus's death—caused the movement to break into two parts: the Petrine church, followers of the disciple Peter, and the Pauline church, followers of Saul of Tarsus. Saul, renamed Paul, worked to convert the gentiles; Peter worked exclusively among the Jews. The gentiles, of course, were pagan, and knew the intricacies of pagan mysteries. Particularly, Paul worked in Ephesus, home of the great statue of Diana that had fallen from the skies, and residence of great mystery cults.

Paul preached the gospel of Jesus to pagan worshipers, people who knew the basics of how to call the quarters and invoke the gods. Given the background of early Christians, it was understandable that in the early church, there was much discussion over which god Jesus was the son of. Reincarnation—a standard belief among aboriginal peoples from every culture (after all, the crops return every year; why wouldn't we?)—was also a standard belief among early Christians. "Who do they say I am?" asks Jesus, and his disciples tell him that some believe he is the reincarnation of John the Baptist. Ideas of the judgment, Satan, the break between the all-good God and the devil, the shepherd-god, the soldier-god, and the fiery apocalypse all came from existent philosophies of Zoroastrianism and the Mithra cults. These concepts, discussed in pagan forums by other commonly considered "sons of god"—Plato, Philo, and Aristotle—were philosophies of the Greek and Roman culture, imported from Persia. The gospels were written in the pagan style of mystery plays. There is no objective evidence that the miracles of Jesus, or even the physical and historical life of Jesus, ever existed in fact. The man Jesus left no writings. The Roman court documents record no trial.

Stay away from "pharmakomen," the New Testament tells us Jesus said. But the New Testament was written almost entirely in Greek, a language the historical Jesus never spoke. It was also written between thirty and ninety years after the events were said to have happened, in a land where legends and tales of gods and sons of gods were the equivalent of today's prime time TV. "Pharmakomen?" Does that translate to "witch"? Or in today's society might that not be the word for pharmacist, drug dealer, or even HMO and health insurance company?

"In the name of Jesus, take up your bed and walk," Peter tells Annaeus in the Book of Acts. The crippled man rising is not a miracle performed by God, for if it were a miracle, God would have needed no intervention by Peter. This is magick, with all its precepts. The magician, Peter, invokes the patron god (Jesus, in this case), and commands the action. The crippled man, by his belief in the magick, is healed. Magick requires belief, above all else, and with that belief, the mountains can move.

The Roman Catholic altar, like the pagan altars of the time of Christ, is the central place to keep flowers, to represent the Mother; a crucifix, to represent the Father; candles for the element of Fire; incense for the element of Air; salt (used to make holy water) for the element of Earth; and water for the element of Water. This is quite understandable because the original Christian churches were converted temples of Mithra. The eucharist given to Catholics in Mass is "transubstantiated," or transformed by an act of magick, into the actual, physical body of Christ. Believers eat the body of Christ for strength, just as they ate the body of Mithra. The Catholic saints are the historic relics of the pagan village gods. St. Brigette, for example, is in fact the Celtic goddess Brigid, rather than a real person. Veneration of the Mother, a key and important element in Roman Catholicism, is history's transformation of the Great Mother goddess.

The Islamic Witch

A few hundred years after Christ, the prophet Mohammed founded the religion of Islam. Islamic people share the heritage of Christians and Jews. They are descended from Ishmael, Abraham's son by his handmaiden, Hagar. According to Jewish scripture, God told Abraham both his sons would be the ancestors of great nations. Abraham's son by Sarah, who was Isaac, became the patriarch of the tribes of Israel; his son, Ishmael, born to him through Hagar, was the patriarch of the Moslems.

Islamic law, as presented in the Qur'an, is specific in many areas of life. While most Westerners think of Islam as suppressing women, it is not the Islamic religion that teaches an unequal status of any peoples. In fact, the Islamic religion is said to have been largely responsible for improvements in the status of women and equality of all peoples. Like Buddhism and Christianity, Islam's theology teaches harmony, equality, and peace among all. Followers of Islam, called Moslems, say, "There is no God but Allah," meaning of course, that Allah is all-great, all-knowing, all-powerful, and beyond comprehension by the limitations of the human mind. Allah is the same as the Jewish Yahweh and is perceived as being the god of Abraham. Moslems, like Jews, reject the premise that Jesus was God incarnate and see Jesus as a prophet, rather than as a god. A mystical sect originating from Islam is known as Sufism. Sufis practice mystically and achieve ecstatic states of mind to perform powerful magickal acts.

THE BURNING TIMES

After Emperor Constantine mandated Christianity as the official religion of all peoples of the Roman Empire, peasant religions and country-village festival practices were either changed to reflect a Christian theme or vilified as a means of convincing the people to switch their allegiance to the new god. The switching of allegiance was hard to pull off. It became necessary to make fun of the tall pointed hats worn by country peasant women and to characterize the village grandmothers who dispensed needed herbs and wisdom as warty old demons. The Old English word *wicce*, used to describe the nature religions of the countryside, became an epithet: "witch," commonly depicted as a woman with green skin, a wart on her nose, and a pointy black hat. She flew on a broom, stole children, and cooked up potions of lizard's breath and bat's eyes. In fact, many of the plants and herbals used by the village herbalist were colloquially named lizard's breath and bat's eyes because that's how local botany developed. It isn't likely, however, that Granny used animal parts in her herbal medicines.

Beginning around the twelfth century, however, the church, which was wedded to the state, realized it would need to take drastic measures to ensure its political power over the vast empire and root out any possible pockets of informal, local power. A hunt ensued in Christian Europe for those who were not committed to Jesus Christ. Using the Biblical passages that were now interpreted as prohibiting "witchcraft," the church/state decided it would be necessary and divinely desirable to eliminate all those people who were "witches." By the fourteenth century, the *Malleus Maleficorum* pronounced a death sentence on anyone who appeared to exhibit the power. For hundreds of years, even extending into the New World, witches—or, rather, those appearing to practice witchcraft—were sought out and persecuted.

Fortunately for the religion of wicce, the public persecution focused on those who were suspected of being witches rather than those who actually were. Practitioners of the craft took their visible symbols off the walls and hid their magickal tools in plain sight with the kitchen utensils. Never needing a group to practice the craft, witches took to solitary and private worship, away from prying eyes. Noticing behavior with the eye of an astute observer, they wisely hung the crucifixes on their walls and the rosaries around their necks. They watched their children to see who was called to the craft and passed on their private wisdom only to the children who could keep the secret. Witchcraft is a relationship with divinity that requires no communal forum. Most of the millions of people executed for witchcraft were not witches. They were simply people who got on the wrong side of their neighbors.

It was not until 1952 that laws prohibiting witchcraft were taken off the books in England. In 1954, Gerald Gardner published *Witchcraft Today*, describing the practices of "wicce" as still alive despite hundreds of years of persecution. As we enter the twenty-first century, Wicca is the fastest-growing religion in America.

Tʜᴇ Пᴇᴏᴘᴀɢᴀɴ Wɪᴛᴄʜ ᴏꜰ ᴛʜᴇ Tᴡᴇɴᴛʏ-Fɪʀsᴛ Cᴇɴᴛᴜʀʏ

One does not have to ascribe to the religion of Wicca in order to practice witchcraft, as the Florence Nightingale accidental hex example at the beginning of this lesson revealed. But Wiccan theology teaches ways to prevent the unintended witchcraft we might all stumble into every day. Our daily lives provide constant opportunity to hex or hope a situation. The neopagan witch of the twenty-first century studies the techniques to perform magick intentionally and in tune with the universe, working in concert with the Will of the Divine.

Magick spells are about mastery within. You cast a spell on yourself to learn to control your subconscious behaviors and manage your mental precepts. These deeply hidden precepts control your subliminal behavior and your subconscious actions. They control your body language, your facial expressions, your emotions, your priorities, your language, your responsive behavior, your blood pressure, your cholesterol level, your amino acid production, and your overall physical and mental health. You can cast spells to heal yourself. You can cast spells to get your paper accepted at a world conference. You can cast spells to get a new job. You can even cast spells to fix your car. You cast spells to get rid of bad habits. You cast spells to be a better you. Your first duty in this life school is to become what the Goddess wants you to be. Mastery within is your goal in magick.

Here is an example of a twenty-first century magickal working.

The First Magick Spell

To begin, make a very specific, results-oriented list of all the things about yourself that could use some self-examination and primal rework. This is what you're going to be writing spells to work on. To get you started, here's the first spell I ever cast:

I need to improve my family life. My kids are behaving disrespectfully. My husband and I seem to have nothing in common. Our home has no warmth and welcoming feel to it any more. I'm developing a cough. I think I'm allergic to something in the heating ducts. I'm unloved.

Our family budget isn't working. We can't seem to make ends meet. The creditors are closing in, and there seems to be no way out. I'm stressed. I don't know that I've really found the job that fulfills my potential and actualizes the real me. I need a new job. I need guidance to find what it should be. I'm unfulfilled. I've gotten myself into some trouble by being less than honest with another person. There could be legal repercussions. I'm scared. I'm having a recurring nightmare. It frightens me. I'm starting to have panic attacks. I feel anxiety, and sometimes it makes me lash out at the people I love. I'm worried. I get feelings of being out of control.

Sometimes I wonder if there really is a God. The world seems so crazy and senseless. I feel violated when I realize I can't walk down a city street without worrying about a drive-by shooting. I have to go back twice and check the front door to make sure it's really locked. I don't know why God would let the world be like this. I don't know how God could allow the atrocities I see on the TV news each night. I'm insecure. I'm disconnected from divinity.

I'm unloved. I'm unworthy. I'm stressed. I'm unfulfilled. I'm scared. I'm worried. I'm insecure and disconnected.

Seven problems. Seven spells.

And then *POOF!*

Magick happens.

You've made your list and realized it looks overwhelming. Could the Goddess really solve your problem about dishonesty without impacting those nightmares? Would a more appropriate job, possibly at a lesser income, be separable from the problem with the creditors? Would you be healthier if you felt you were loved? If you felt you were loved, would the world look less threatening and godless? Are there seven problems here? Or are there seven aspects of one problem? Is anything on that list any more than a manifestation of an imbalance in the field of the energies surrounding me? Have I not described a disruption in the ever-flowing Tao? And the big, big, big question:

If I could learn to control my personal energy field,
Would my children behave differently?
Would my allergies go away?
Would my body change shape?
Would my finances work out their own solution?
Would I feel satisfaction in my work?
Would my neighbor resolve his differences with me?
Would I sleep better and dream peacefully?
And most importantly.
Would the world change?
Now deep in your subconscious there is a Little Voice. And as you read that question, that Little Voice said to each of you:

YES.

Yes, if I change My Self, i will change the World.
Yes, if I give out Love, i will receive Love.
Yes, if I think good thoughts, i will perceive good responses.
Yes, if i learn to forgive, my body will respond to my forgiveness.
Yes, if i understand honesty, i will be treated with sincerity.
Yes, if i embrace humility, my needs will be provided for.
Yes, if i release my ego to God, i will achieve fulfillment and inner peace.

Words, words, words.

How, in the name of the Goddess,
Might I learn to put them into *action*?

The first rule of casting magick spells is:
Paint the picture of your dream.
And send it out into the world with a sense of timing.

The universe has been implemented in a quantum manner. There are many possibilities, many influences, but all is connected. This universe is not *just* created. It is also *crafted*. To design your spell, you need:

A purpose statement described in a visual manner. You must *see* the end result in your mind. I *see* myself healthy. I *see* myself coming home to a loving family. I *see* myself working in a job I love. I *see* myself making amends to my neighbor. I *see* myself feeling at peace and enjoying a spring day. I *see* myself happy and healthy. I *see* myself living in the Garden of Eden with God.

You must have the best possible vision of this end result. Spend a good deal of time imagining and envisioning what that end result would be like.

In your mind, paint a picture of yourself doing those things. What clothes would you wear? How would you move your arms and body? What would you feel inside? What would your typical day be like? What feelings would you *stop* having? What actions would you take differently from actions you take today? What *exactly* would change in the minor and trivial details of your day? What are the tactical and small details that would be different?

Get out a piece of paper and handwrite the best possible, most detailed description of exactly how you would behave differently if you lived in the world described in your dream. Don't bother writing out how other people would behave differently. Only write how you would behave differently. You don't need seven spells. There's only one problem here.

Look in the mirror.

You just saw it.

Once you've envisioned the solution to your problem and seen how your behavior would change if the problem didn't exist, you need to contact your subconscious and convince yourself to act differently. At first you think that's ridiculous, but think again. We are all connected. Right now, this problem is changing your behavior at a subconscious, subliminal level. If it wasn't, you wouldn't have been able to envision yourself acting differently, and then there would not actually *be* a problem. If you consciously, and with an act of Will, change your own behavior to deny and negate the problem, *the problem will have to change in response to your denial and negation of it!*

Your primordial id is very strong, and it can be very stubborn. The energies that are causing your body language and subliminal behaviors to be as they are still exist, and they constantly pull at you to respond to them. To push back and change those energies, you must exert Will, and this Will is at a deep, subconscious and primordial level. To reach it, to talk to it, to reprogram its conditioning, you must get to it at its own level. Its level is the level you attain in sleep. It is primordial. It is primal. It is at times, very sexual. It is where Fear lives. It is where Horror lives. And it is where you must go to perform magick . If you are of little faith, you cannot do it. If you believe at the core of your being, you have the power to make the world change.

So you've got your solution defined, on a piece of paper, in your own handwriting. You didn't type it on the computer, because at this level of training, handwriting is a big part of the process. To do a spell, you must first *hex* the problem, and then *hope* the solution. For your initial steps toward self-mastery, you'll need to do this in steps. You hex during a waning Moon, that is, between the Full Moon and the New Moon. You hope during a waxing Moon, that is, between the New Moon and the Full Moon. This is what makes the dark Moon so wonderful. You can *hex* a problem before the moment of the dark Moon, while the Moon is waning, and then turn around and *hope* it just a few minutes later, when it starts to wax again.

The hex part of the spell requires that we identify what we're getting rid of. As I look through my list of problems, I see I need to get rid of the following.

A green flavor in my house. This comes from all the people in my family thinking too much about money.

A gray cloud over my forehead. This was generated by the conflict with my neighbor.

A purple wound in my heart. This was put there as a scar from childhood, and I haven't been able to shake it.

A red flag on my future. This is the inevitable outcome of working in a job I don't like.

Go through your list of problems. Express them as colored objects to be eliminated. Use as many language idioms as possible. That's why your subconscious is called "the id." It speaks in idioms.

For the hex, I gathered together objects to represent each of the things I was going to eliminate. I needed a green flavor, a gray cloud, a purple wound, and a red flag. For the green flavor, I picked a lime Popsicle. For the gray cloud, I chose a handful of cotton balls and spread ashes on them. For the purple wound, I had some trouble. This was a deep, long-lasting problem I'd lived with for years. I needed something very seriously significant, that would truly reach my primordial id. After some extremely deep soul-searching, I chose my dead father's army dog tags. I went to the drug store and bought purple nail polish and I painted them purple.

Like I said, if you're going to be a witch, you're going to have to go places that might get pretty raw and upsetting. You have to have the courage to really see your own psyche and what has occurred to it over the years.

For the red flag, I chose a red flag.

Then I took my objects—elementals, we will soon be calling them—and I chose a cardboard shoebox to be their coffin. Soon, they would be resting in peace.

Do you understand why you have to design your own spell? You must make contact with your primordial id. It speaks in dream language. It speaks uniquely to you, about experiences known only to you and God. To reach it, you must choose representative activities and items that feel right for you. The significance of anything you do as a witch is a unique significance—a secret between you and God. In your subconscious, you know what your problems are. In your dreaming state, your subconscious tries to tell you what your problems are. You must speak back to your subconscious, using its idiomatic terms: red flag, gray cloud, purple wound, and green flavor.

If you dream that you turned into a turtle, it's because you wanted to have a hard shell. You needed protection. Your id speaks in these terms. To cast spells, you must speak in those terms, too—archetypes, C.G. Jung called them—the wisdom of the ancients.

To begin my spell, I waited for the dark Moon, and I carefully built my sacred circle and constructed my temple. I picked up each object, and I declared it to be an elemental. I named each one: Green Flavor, Gray Cloud, Purple Wound, Red Flag. I told each of them they would be tasked to bear the burden of the problem I had identified them with. I told them this problem would live in them. They would *be* the problem. Their purpose in the karmic universe was to *be* the problem. I told them to breathe. I said that they were animated life forms and that they were alive for the purpose of being that specific problem.

I envisioned the vital force of that problem going into them, leaving me and spiraling into their twisted little bodies. I gave them a few minutes to enjoy their new life. I verified that they had left me, and were living in their new vessels, by asking them to tell me how they felt. "Slimy," said Green Flavor. "Artificial and slick. I'm full of superficiality because I pretend all day." "Heavy," said Gray Cloud. "Full of expectations not met and greed not satisfied." "Ill," said Purple Wound. "Confused, shaken, betrayed, and patronized. I'm the embodiment of unmitigated selfishness." "Dead," said Red Flag. "I am anathema. I live to strangle life."

"Yes," I told them. "I thank you for taking the burdens, and bearing them for me." Then I put my elementals into their tissue-lined coffin where they could be surrounded by my tears, and I sent them to their grave. Here is a guide for you to try for yourself.

The Hex of the Elementals

(Say this out loud, strongly, and loudly. Put the elementals on the floor to do it, not on the altar. Use black candles during the hex ritual.)

Beasts and Ghoulies, pains and strife,
I will end your sordid life.
You will carry power no more.
I will ground you through the floor.
Never shall you visit me.
I have closed the door to thee.
Popsicle, your time has come.
Cotton ball, I cast you from

> Life. And Dog Tags, you will go
> To the earth where you will know
> Pain that I could never bear.
> Flag it, Future. I *WILL* care.

Needless to say, the Popsicle melted really fast. But I knew it would, so I had a black garbage bag ready to wrap the little cardboard coffin in.

You have to build yourself a little psychodrama to get rid of the problems before you can start anew on the rebuilding. This is something you must do for yourself. By meditating and doing the pathwork and reading the scriptures, divinity will come to help you. *Any help from another person only impedes the action of divinity.* You must turn to God and ask God's help. Your relationship with God is between you and God. When I say God, I mean the Goddess sometimes, and I mean the God other times. It doesn't matter what I mean. Deity is not human, neither male nor female.

Since you wisely chose the dark Moon for your ceremony, you now have some time to be comforted in your circle by the faeries. You have to wait for the Moon to pass to the waxing phase so you can continue with your hope ceremony. This is a time to be still and listen for guidance from the ancients. The passing of the dark Moon is the time when they are most able to speak to you. Don't be afraid now. You have opened the door, opened it with strength and presence. You have declared yourself to be a witch. Demons are cowards. They will run.

As the Moon begins waxing, you will feel your power building. You were drained of power from the hexing. You felt the drain. Now you feel the replenishment. More importantly, Mother is pleased by what you've done. You took the first step. You announced your intention to be master of your self. You uninvited the unwelcome guests who were diverting you from finding your path. Now you are a new person. You no longer need to carry the hurts and burdens that were bothering you and causing you to respond with rage and anger. The green flavor has melted. The gray cloud is dissipated. The purple wound is bandaged, ready to begin its healing process, and the red flag is lifted—gone, all of them—gone. Nothing prevents you from behaving in the manner of your vision now. You are ready to build the hope.

> *I come to the Garden alone*
> *While the Dew is still on the Roses*
> *And the voice I hear*
> *Singing in my ear*
> *Must be the God.*

Because I Will it.

Read the following *out loud*.

THE HOPE ROPE

Two Cubed, Three Squared.
      That's the Key. Where'd
         X go? Why'd She
            send THAT to Me?
     D-Ride, D- Rail,
        IT's ALL e-Male.
           And THIS old Goat
           Don't need no Coat
               Of Arms to be
           The King of Three.

So HEAR's the Rule.
     "U" SEIZE the Tool
            And Pull.

Don't Push. Don't Pant.
     Don't Strain. Just Chant.
        And Let the Chips
          Fall. If they slant
            Then turn aside
              And make a Why'd
                He do Dat?

And If the Lesson isn't clear
Then sit upon a Tuffet, Dear,
Until you know the Tao's the Way
Don't move. Don't rock. Just let it stay
              Unanswered.

For Order is as Mother does
     And chaos never will or was
        So set aside your works of clay
           And let the True Creator Say
              "The Word."

For Words get to Mapping
And Mirrors get Fogged
And when we hear Music

The System's been logged
And that be the Reason
Now here be the Rhyme
It's chanting that makes Will
Be scored in Our Time.

A map or a mirror, it's one and the same.
Without a reflection, there's only the Game.
For what you see always decides what you get,
And when you see Mother inside you have met
                    Your Maker.

So run to the Goddess and let Her inside.
She hides in the brambles and looks like a Bride.
But She has a husband; Her consort's The Fool
And if you can Center, She'll take you to School
                    For Witches.

And there you'll do Magick and wiggle your Knows
And conquer the demons who live in your clothes
And set all the Tickers to Half Past the Ten
So Tongues that go Wagging can fuel fires again
                    Inside you.

And you'll be The Lady, and She'll be The You
And God Help the Bastard who doesn't ring True
For False sets a Timer and Wrong clicks a clock
And only within you can simmering mock
                    The Lady.

Now Stand to your Nature and Snap to your Guide;
The Person She made you is ready to Ride
The Winds to Tomorrow, the Fates to Today
And when you hear Music you'll know it says, "May

                                        I, Mother?"

And Mother is with you. Her Word is Your Law.
The words from another just stick in your craw.
For YOU hear Her voice. You need no one to say
What you do, for you know what She says. The Way

                                        is open.

So that's the directions. Now where is that map?
I know I once had it — but what is this crap
All swirling around it? It's covered in Goop!
Oh, heck. Now it's useless. I guess I'll just Stoop

To following StarDust.

And where the StarDust leads, the "I" will meet you.

Now by My Hand, this work will be
As blessed as She chooses. See
I cannot do, I cannot act
Without My God. That is the Pact.
And so I say,
"If She Wills," May

I, Mother?

Your song and psychodrama of hope must be built on a sound basis and a solid discipline. The God will help you with that. The Goddess will bless your effort. The magick must be all your doing, with the guidance of Divinity. The Witch of the twenty-first century is a human being who chooses to be truly alive, awake, and aware, who takes those steps that witches have taken throughout history: to live in harmony with the universe and follow the Master's plan.

Blessed be!

SUMMARY POINTS FOR LESSON 6

- Witchcraft is an expression of power that comes from the Word. God is the Word.

- The witch throughout history has been alternately a respected and powerful priest or a feared and powerful prostitute. When a priest is not focused in alignment with Deity, there is no difference between these two.

- Magick is a function of operating on the subconscious of the universe, using rhythm and rhyme. It works on the dreaming brain to create change and speaks in the idiomatic dream language.

LEARNING EXERCISES

LEARNING EXERCISES FOR LESSON 6

Review your current life situation and write a succinct, one paragraph statement about what magickal acts would benefit you. What magick are you doing accidentally that you need to reverse? Set aside meditation time to discuss this with the Goddess.

To join in the private online discussion forum exclusively for readers of this book, and to try the test questions for this lesson, go to:

http://www.LadyRaya.org/religion/classes/

Enter your e-mail address and the password you were given at the end of the first lesson (page 33). Then select Test 6 from the list of tests. Feedback will be sent directly to your e-mail address. You can also join in the discussion forum about each of the lesson topics.

Lesson 7

The Meaning of the Wiccan Rede

RUN dot Child, and try your wings
Angels breath beneath you brings
Luck and love. It is your fate.
Be Thou Great.

Your Objective for Lesson 7

You will recite the Wiccan Rede and
give specific examples to explain its meaning.

"An' It Harm None, Do As Thy Will"

While the religion of Wicca has no defined scripture, there is one and only one law that can be said to be the complete moral guidance of the religion's followers. It is "An' it harm none, do as Thy Will." Many people who do not study Wicca are confused by this. They think it says, "Act however you want to act; do whatever you want to do." Witches know this is not the meaning. In fact, this one law is so difficult to follow, it would be an unbearable burden if we had any additional laws. How do you manage your life without harming anyone, particularly when that law includes not harming yourself?

Ninety-nine percent of all harm that comes to humans is self-inflicted. How can we avoid the inevitable stresses that cause us to make ourselves ill, drive us to lash out at our families, and seduce us to engage in self-deprecating behaviors? How can we prevent the self-immolation that causes us to get involved in hopeless love affairs, demeaning relationships, and enslaving financial structures? How can we detour the crushing road-blocks that seem to appear in our lives and stop us in our tracks? How do we handle the conflicts that arise when "harming no one" seems to be an impossibility?

The law has two parts. In the first part, we look for the way to "harm no one" by our actions. In the second part, we strive to "do as Thy Will." What is our Will? How do we know what it is and what it tells us to do? Whose Will are we talking about when we say "do as Thy Will"? Discerning our own True Will is a difficult task. It means we must understand ourselves very well, and we must know the path the Goddess has chosen for us. In our every thought and act, we must strive to find the Will and the path She has set before us, and we must follow that path without harming either our-selves or others. It is a very complex task and law to follow, and we work at following it our whole lives.

When we succeed at following the Rede, we find that we are on track with God's Will, for we believe that the Will in our hearts *is* God's Will and was placed there by our Creator. Our Creator is a merciful and loving God, and She shows Her mercy by giving us the desire, the will, and the ambi-tion to follow the path She has set for us. We need only to follow our hearts and dreams, and they will be the guideposts that lead us to Her service. It is difficult to understand this concept in the abstract, so let's take a look at some specific examples.

The Story of Tamar

Long ago, there was a woman in the pagan land of Canaan who was wid-owed at a young age before she had children. It was the custom in her tribe that a widow would be wedded by her husband's brother so that the child resulting from the union could inherit the original husband's property, and that child would be legally considered to be the child of the dead husband, as far as inheritance of property was concerned. But Tamar's brother-in-law didn't like the idea that an inheritance that would otherwise be his, as a result of his brother's death, would instead go to the child of this Canaanite woman. When he went to her bed, he decided to "spill his seed on the ground," rather than give this woman a child. Shortly after the brother-in-law did this, he also died.

Now there was one more brother in the family, but this brother was too young to provide insemination service for Tamar, and so her father-in-law told her to go back home and live with her mother and father until the younger brother was of age. Tamar did this. In her society, she was no longer available for marriage. She had to wait for the third brother to grow up, or she would never have children. It was very important for Tamar to have children, for in the society in which she lived, children provided for their aging parents. She would have no one to take care of her in her old age if she were barren. She would also have no inheritance or property, as the property of her husband was destined to be given to her children and not to her.

In obedience to her father-in-law, Tamar waited at her parents' home for the third son to come to her. But time passed, and the third son was not sent. It seems that Tamar's father-in-law was worried that Tamar might be a witch. After all, both his sons died after going to bed with her. Maybe it was her fault. Now he had only one son left. Should he risk this one, too? So the father-in-law never sent his third son, and Tamar began to age.

One day Tamar heard that her father-in-law was going to pass through the land where she lived, on his way to do some business. It happened that her father-in-law's wife had recently passed away, and she knew he was grieving. As a woman of Canaan, Tamar knew that the Goddess Hecate ruled crossroads. At these crossroads, prostitutes waited under Hecate's protection for travelers to come by. Tamar consulted her Goddess and determined what she would have to do. She dressed as a prostitute, veiled her face, and stood by the crossroad as her father-in-law passed.

As expected, he stopped to sample her wares.

"What will you give me to allow you to come in to me?" The daughter-in-law disguised as a prostitute asked.

"I'll give you my best new-born goat," the father-in-law answered.

"Well your goat is not here with you," the daughter-in-law said. "Give me your signet ring, your bracelet, and your staff as a pledge so I'll know you are sending the goat. I'll give them back to you when the goat arrives."

The poor, grieving father-in-law agreed.

Now when the father-in-law returned home, he immediately sent a messenger to deliver the goat, but the messenger was unable to find the prostitute by the crossroad. No one nearby knew of a prostitute who worked in that area. The people laughed at the messenger, and said, "What are you thinking? We have no prostitute near here."

Three months later, the father-in-law received word that his daughter-in-law was pregnant. He, as judge and patriarch of the tribe, determined that she must be burned to death for behaving as a whore instead of patiently waiting for him to send his third son to her. Tamar and all her family came to the court to hear her death sentence.

Tamar sent her mother as a messenger ahead of her to see the judge privately. "Here is a package," Tamar's mother said. "The contents of this package belong to the man who fathered my daughter's child."

Inside the package, of course, was Judah's signet ring, bracelet, and staff.

Realizing, finally, that he was wrong to withhold his third son, in addition to his complicity in the whorish act, the father-in-law canceled the death sentence and never saw Tamar again. In time, she bore twin sons, Pharez and Zarah. Since her father-in-law refused to have anything to do with her, Tamar raised the boys as a single mother in the pagan land of Canaan. Her son Pharez went on to have a son Hezron, who had a son Ram, who had a son Amminadeb, who had a son Nahshon, who had a son Salmon, who had a son Boaz, who had a son Obed, who had a son Jesse, who had a son David, who slew a giant and became King of Israel.

So Tamar behaved as a prostitute in order to force her father-in-law, Judah, one of the twelve patriarchs of Israel, to do his legal duty to her. If she had not followed the law in her heart—to do her will, but harm no one—there would never have been a House of David or a Messiah descended from it.

You can read this story in the Holy Bible, Genesis, chapter 38. The genealogy tracing Tamar's son to the birth of King David is found in the Book of Ruth, chapter 4, verses 12 to 22.

THE FUNCTION OF INTENT

The story of Tamar gives an excellent example of a woman following the law of the witch. She takes responsibility for her own happiness. She needs a child. It's required of her to have a child if she is to live happily in her society. She wants to get a child safely; she doesn't want to be executed as a result of fulfilling a need that the society has forced her to have. She knows Judah is wrong by withholding his third son. By law of the tribe, any appointed family member could have serviced her in this way. Judah himself could have done it, but he shirked his responsibility to her. So she uses her brains and her ability to think of a way to protect herself and still get what she wants—a child. She plans and schemes to have Judah's signet ring—the ring he uses to seal contracts—in her possession as an insurance policy.

Tamar doesn't just do the act without planning a way to protect herself, for that would put her at great risk of being harmed, and a witch is literally commanded not to harm herself. Her plan has a happy outcome for everyone. No one is hurt by it. She gets a baby. He gets a son—two sons, in this case, because she had twins. And God? God gets the House of David. Tamar is, indeed, a powerful witch, as we see by this story. She is a witch, a single mother, and, we cannot forget, the matriarch of the lineage that led to the birth of Jesus. In fact, since Judah had no hand in bringing up his sons, it is more accurate to say that the line of Jesus springs from the Canaanite witch Tamar than it is to say it comes from the House of Judah.

THE MEANING OF THE WICCAN REDE

The Will of Tamar, in this case, was fully in concert with the Will of God. Apparently, it was God's Will for Tamar to act the whore this time. As witches, we understand by this example that it is not possible for us to say, "Prostitution is wrong," with any absoluteness. Here is a case when prostitution was right. It all depends on the intent. Tamar's intent was correct. Judah's intent was not correct. Yet, God used Judah to provide Tamar with the child who would continue the line of David, so we say God gave Judah the desire to visit with that prostitute at that time. Judah did the Will of God when he visited the prostitute because it was Judah's Will. The feelings in our heart are the Will of God. When we follow them, God makes it all work out. Judah's fear kept him from doing what was right by Tamar, but God wanted her to be the mother of the House of David. Judah's fear kept him from hearing what God wanted, so God used Judah's other desires to ensure that the outcome would still be right.

Now we've seen an example when Wicca teaches that prostitution may indeed be right, given the correct intent. What other things we think of as moral wrongs could, by the law of Wicca, sometimes be right? What about incest, for example? Could there ever be a time when incest would harm no one and be the Will of God?

THE STORY OF LOT'S DAUGHTERS

There was a city named Sodom that was filled with crime and gangs. One day two strangers came to this city, and a man called Lot offered to let them stay at his house. They said it was all right; they would just stay out in the street because there was no place else available, but Lot insisted they should stay with him, saying the streets of the city were very dangerous.

Sure enough, that night the gangs of the city came beating on Lot's door. They wanted the strangers to be sent out to them so they could "Sodomize" them. This was apparently a practice of the city. Lot, being a good host, refused to give the strangers to the crowd. Instead, he offered his two young virgin daughters to the crowd, saying it would be better for the crowd to do whatever they wanted to his daughters rather than for men to lay with men.

In this society, we see that a man's honor is preserved more by being a good host to other men than it is by being a good father to two young girls. Fortunately for Lot, the two strangers turn out to be angels in disguise. Since Lot was so honorable as to save them from the crowd, the angels stepped in and saved Lot's daughters. They took Lot, his wife, and his two daughters out of the city, just as God reached down and struck Sodom with a great fire, destroying everyone in it. Lot's wife turned around and looked at the fire, and for this disobedience God turned her into a pillar of salt. By the time Lot and his two daughters got a good distance away from the city and into the mountains, the angels have disappeared, as angels are wont to do, and the two girls believe they and their father are the only people left on Earth.

The girls, hopefully oblivious to the fact that their father offered them to the crowd to be raped and murdered, decide that with their mother gone, it is their responsibility to repopulate what they think is a devastated planet. They just happen to have brought a few bottles of wine with them as they were running out of Sodom, so they get their father drunk and take advantage of him. One daughter bears a son who will become the patriarch of the Moabites; the other daughter bears the patriarch of the Ammonite nation. And of course, as we all know, if it weren't for the Moabites and the Ammonites, the Jews wouldn't have had anybody to fight with. So God approved this incest in order to make multiple nations in the land, so they could live in constant conflict, thus fulfilling the prophecies and scriptures.

The hand of God works in strange ways.

You can read this story in the Book of Genesis, chapter 19.

Scripture as Erotic Literature

Prostitution, incest, extra-marital sex, polygamy, slavery, harems, eunuchs, homosexuality, child sacrifice, wars, executions, and erotic poetry: these are all topics of discussion in the scriptures that are the basis of the religions of Judaism, Christianity, and Islam. The Bible, as erotic literature, sustained its power to evoke human passion through thousands of years. Language tha evokes erotic emotion is the hallmark of the poetry of Rumi, founder of Sufism, and it is the basis of the Vedas. The Deity chooses to have the human species continue and not to become extinct. She uses our feelings for erotic sexuality to invoke spiritual experience. God is love, in every sense. When ancient peoples constructed their worship service around hope for fertility, they did so for reasons that were not just practical in an agrarian society—but also inspirational and divine.

As we strive to learn the meaning of our one rule, "An' it harm none, do as Thy Will," we put aside any thoughts of sexuality as a moral wrong. Sanctions against sexuality, we know, were put in place in historic societies in order to convince the men to take care of the women, so the women could take care of the children. God doesn't see sex as dirty. If any sexual acts are performed in accordance with the freely-chosen Will of both parties involved, and if they harm absolutely no one, they do not break our law.

tHE Fly in tHE OintmEnt

While we see sexuality and nudity as beautiful gifts from our Creator, we recognize that it is extremely difficult to perform sexual acts outside of marriage that hurt no one. Women have a powerful desire, placed within them by nature, to bear children. Generally, in a sexual situation, a woman's emotion will engage before a man's emotion will engage. She may be giving sex to get love while he's busy giving love to get sex.

It could be very, very hard to avoid breaking our rule in regard to sex outside the confines of a happy marriage. Might a child result from the union who would not have a stable home? Might a birth control method be used that would harm the health of the woman? Might one of the parties be confused and not know his or her own will or be coerced without clearly letting the other party know his or her feelings? Might the woman become accidentally pregnant and face a set of unacceptable alternatives? Might one of the parties have a deeply repressed guilt or trauma that could be triggered by an unloving sexual experience? Might one person be scarred by the experience?

Remember, we believe our souls live again, and all our traumas remain etched in our cells. Do we know that a soul has not been assigned to that fetus? If we abort, could we be sentencing a soul who was waiting for a new life to lose his chance for another round in our life-school called Earth? Would the soul who had this experience be harmed by it? When all the considerations are made, the Wiccan who earnestly strives to follow the Rede may find few instances in which sex outside of marriage will pass the test of our law. Yet although we may say it is unlikely that our law will allow sex outside of marriage, it is certainly possible that it will, depending on the specifics of the instance. All is in context, in our way of thinking, and one person can never know the Will of God for another person. We say:

> Every vice has been a virtue; every good was once a crime.
> All in context, as its nature; thus the essence of sublime.

In each instance, we must consider the context of the situation and our own intent. We must discern whether our action breaks our law or abides by it. We have no absolute measure of right or wrong. This is why a jaguar is not evil because it kills a zebra, but a zebra could certainly come to think of a jaguar that way. Each situation has a viewpoint, and it is hard enough for us to truly understand our own viewpoint. The witch who follows the Rede must say, "It is enough for me to know my own Will. I have no hope to understand the Will of another."

For this reason, our doctrine makes no pronouncement regarding what is good or what is bad, what is the Will of God, or what is not the Will of God. Each witch must contact Deity and receive personal direction. Those of us who are observers of another's behavior may see that one person is hurting another person or hurting him- or herself, and by that we would know that the Rede was not successfully being followed.

Like Tamar, planning her strategy to deal with Judah's refusal to provide for her, the witch who follows the Rede must contrive an outcome that harms no one. If necessary, that outcome may require her to do extraordinary things. This is what makes the law so difficult. It is a demand for personal responsibility for our actions and our outcomes. The witch can't say, "Oh, poor me, my life is a mess because of this problem and that problem, and that reason and this reason." As witches, we have no devil to blame for our temptations, no Satan to seduce us to go astray. We recognize that our predicaments and dilemmas are problems between ourselves and our Creator, difficulties to be resolved by getting straight with our God, challenges placed before us by a loving, relevant, and present teacher. The witch must say, "What can I do to fulfill the Goddess's command to be all I can be, use all my talents, and follow the path She set before me? How can I change my life and my self so that I harm none, but I become all She intended me to be?"

The personal responsibility inherent in that one sentence, "An' it harm none, do as Thy Will," is a demand greater than a library full of specific commandments.

The Question of Charity

The question arises: Would a Wiccan intervene if he or she saw someone hurting another? Do Wiccans help people? Are they charitable? Again, the answer is contextual. For the most part, we believe the Goddess is the Mother of all people, and She is present in everyone's life. We believe there are no accidents or random coincidence; all is in concert with Her plan. In general, we do not intervene in another person's life, and we make every attempt to avoid interfering with another person's deal with the Lord and journey to the Lady. We basically assume that God is handling it. We know that, in most cases, "help" from another person only impedes the action of divinity in that person's life.

We each know that we have a full plate, and we try to eat what we've been served without dipping into someone else's soup. For this reason, we generally do not actively run charity operations or participate in public demonstrations to save the rainforest. Of course, there are no absolutes in

Wiccan theology, so maybe we don't and maybe we do. It depends. It all depends.

If another person's drama unfolds in front of us, however, we have to assume the Lady is putting it on our plate. While we do not go looking for trouble, if trouble knocks on our door, we are obligated to respond. If our sister's husband abuses her, or our neighbor's children show up in the yard with bruises, we will expect that the Goddess wishes us to give up our energy for Her action. Spell craft and magick, while most often used to help ourselves self-actualize, are also used by the Goddess's command to pay our karmic debt in helping others. We know that the Lord and the Lady are energy forces, and in Her service we may be required to offer our energy to do Her will.

"An' it harm none, do as Thy Will," is our law. If She wants something, we can count on it to become our desire. By learning to feel the desire in our heart, and using our minds to fulfill our desires in ways that harm no one, we obey Her command.

SUMMARY POINTS FOR LESSON 7

- The Wiccan Rede, "An' it harm none, do as Thy Will," is the only divine law for practicing Wiccans. This law is difficult enough to follow in itself; additional laws are unnecessary and excessively burdensome.

- The Rede is particularly hard to follow because it includes not harming ourselves. Almost all human harm is self-inflicted.

- Wiccans believe the will of God is written into our hearts. When we learn to discern the True Will of our hearts, we are following the path God intended.

LEARNING EXERCISES FOR LESSON 7

1. Witches also say that anything we do will come back and hit us three times harder. This is sometimes called the "Threefold Law." There are no accidents in our world, and coincidence is the tool of the Goddess. If, on your way out to work this morning, you see that your car has a flat tire, what will you review about your

LEARNING EXERCISES

thoughts, actions, and energies in the last few days in order to ensure this problem indicator does not expand into an all out "when it rains, it pours" emergency?

2. Nudity, or being "skyclad," is sometimes part of Wiccan ritual. When used as a means of freeing ourselves from the bondage of societal sanction, nudity helps us draw closer to the Goddess and become more accepting of ourselves. People who are not close friends are unlikely to be capable of the purity of thought that nudity requires. Practice your own rituals skyclad, privately or with loved ones*. Record in your Book of Shadows (such as *The Book of Dreams and Shadows*) what nudity does to your experience. Recognize that nudity is natural, and the human body is a wonderful gift from our Mother. Sentient experience is part of our training in our life-school called Earth. If the experience is uncomfortable for you, try to find the beliefs and premises that are causing your discomfort. These beliefs could be branching out and causing other problems in your life. Check on them.

*Note: Skyclad ritual is for close friends, not acquaintances or strangers. Our society is not evolved enough to assume that people you do not know are able to approach the ritual honestly.

3. The Will comes from four sources: The Will of the head, the Will of the loins, the Will of the ego, and the Will of the heart. When we speak of doing our Will, we mean the True Will, which is the Will of the heart. It is difficult to discern whether our Will is from the heart unless we practice unconditional love. Unconditional love is accepting of each other and of ourselves with all our faults. We release the concept of needing someone to love because love that is accepting and unconditional is not needy.

In our society, we often partner with someone out of needy love, rather than unconditional love. This is the Will of the loins or the head, not of the heart. Sometimes we choose a mate based on financial distress, or simply because we want someone to be an escort at social functions, or because we feel unfulfilled and incomplete without a mate. Sometimes we marry in order to have children or provide for children. The True Will that leads us to our heart's desire has no needs. If we love in the manner of our heart, our concern is for the other person's happiness. With this inner love, we no longer need anything external to make us happy because we are in a state of being happy at all times.

When we love in this way, we feel no jealousy, no need to control or manipulate, and no desire for revenge. Our True Will will never manifest as a need for vengeance.

"Vengeance is mine," said the Lord. That means it's not yours.

The Dark Lord—who is the guy who said "Vengeance is mine"—has his own will. The witch concentrates and focuses on discerning the desire in his or her heart, which is placed there by unconditional love and absolute acceptance of both others and ourselves. Remaining in that state of being is the best way to act in accordance with our own True Will and stay out of the Dark Lord's way. In this manner, we believe we are able to follow our own paths in life, and karma is not required to guide us back in line by giving us flat tires, causing accidents, and otherwise wreaking havoc.

For the next few weeks, focus your meditations on discernment about your own True Will. When you feel a desire or an emotion rising, stop and meditate. Try to feel the location of that desire. Is it in your head? Is it in your loins? Is it in your ego? Or is it in your heart? Only the desire of your heart will keep you out of trouble with karma.

4. Wiccans do not believe in original sin. In our theology, we are all born blameless, as children of Deity. A child who is allowed to blossom, and not taught to feel shame or guilt about the self in any way, is enabled to find the path to the Goddess more easily. How would you explain to a child the difference between the Will in your heart that is put there by the Goddess and the ego-based desire to take someone else's toy? How would you explain to your best friend what causes you to know something is in your heart rather than in your ego?

5. The ego has been likened in magical thought to the lingam, which can be described in analogy like a karmic penis. It is necessary to have one for survival purposes. Our survival instinct requires the ego in order to operate, but when survival is not threatened, a ready lingam, like a blown-up ego, gets in the way. This is why we use the expression "to deflate the ego." Practice in your meditation looking for parts of your life that are ego-driven. Invoke your patron god (not goddess—this is a testosterone thing). Ask Him to assist you in keeping your ego in a

proper state. The ego should be neither inflated nor inverted. It is not good to have a low self-image, nor is it good to have an inflated self-image. If you invoke the God successfully, be prepared for some ego-deflating, or ego-supportive, experience to arise shortly.

When it does, learn from its lessons, and thank the Goddess and the God for their assistance. Gratitude is healthy.

6. Go to page 227 and read "Catechism of the Tradition of Elijan Wicca." What part of the catechism do you find difficult to understand? Prepare your question list and post it to the Website discussion board.

To join in the private online discussion forum exclusively for readers of this book, and to try the test questions for this lesson, go to:

http://www.LadyRaya.org/religion/classes/

At this URL, you will find an online test for each lesson—feedback for which is sent directly to your e-mail address—and a discussion forum about each of the lesson topics. Enter your e-mail address and your password found on page 33 of the first lesson. Select Test 7 from the list of tests.

LESSON 8
SPELLING AND CONJURING

RUN dot Child, and see the truth.
Faeries seal your precious youth.
You'll be young forevermore.
At your core.

YOUR OBJECTIVE FOR LESSON 8

You will list various methods for spell casting and describe the basic rules of spelling and conjuring.

WHAT DO MAGICK SPELLS DO?

Primarily, we cast spells on ourselves to convince our subconscious, primordial inner mind to change the music. These spells are extremely effective when done properly, in accordance with the rules of magickal workings. By changing our minds, we change our associations and thought processes. By changing our thoughts, we change our world. Our associations and behaviors build the worlds we live in. Magickal workings operate on the structures of our world and create tangible change. When we practice magick in a regular way, the coincidence and circumstance that surround us respond to our intent. The magick does, in fact, make things happen in a real and tangible manner, in accordance with the laws of the physical universe.

There is nothing supernatural about magick. It is physics. Science will learn this, eventually, but for now, it's a matter of religious practice. Witches believe the circumstance and coincidence in our world is intentional, part of a karmic purpose; by understanding and harmonizing with that karmic design, we can influence the real world. Karma uses accidents and tragedies and inexplicable opportunity to keep us on our path. Our magickal workings help us align our inner subconscious mind so that we will be able to follow the path with as few accidents and traumas as our path can allow.

One way to think about how we use magick spells is to compare our subconscious mind to the hard drive of a computer. Because of trauma that may have occurred in this life or a past life, we might have areas of our hard drive that are weak and need to be bypassed when we write data to them. Maybe in a past life, we were bitten by a wild dog, and now dogs are very frightening to us. Maybe we witnessed an event too fearful to relive, and so we cringe and run from situations that remind us of that past life event. We could sign up for years of psychotherapy and psychotropic drugs in an attempt to recover from this trauma. Or, we could do a magick spell and *poof* the disruption out of our lives.

The magick spell trains our mind to write over the bad experience and replaces our traumatic memories with a more comforting association. If you've ever had the experience of putting a child to bed at night, you may have learned that it is more effective to pull out an imaginary can of "Super Duper No-Fail Monster Spray" and spray under the bed than it is to tell the child to "Stop being silly there is no monster." Our primordial id remains a child forever. It responds to monster spray.

Spelling by Accident

Of course, it is also possible to do magick spells that impact another person, not just our own subconscious. This is because we are all one; we are all connected. Our connection, however, has many twists and turns, and our paths follow the algorithms of a Rubik's Cube. When we do magick on behalf of another, our energies and spells combine with the energies and spells they are doing for themselves. Everyone is doing these spells and using these energies because they are the energies of thought, intent, and Will. Everyone puts thought, intent, and will into the day, impacting the operational world. It is just that those who do not study witchcraft are doing it unintentionally and without following the rules of magick. They're like Aunt Clara on the TV show *Bewitched*. Nobody knows what might come out of the effort. Wiccan theology says we must never do a magickal working for another person without the permission of the person we are spelling. This is so we can coordinate with them and be sure our work is in accordance with their own Will.

People have complex and diverse lives and laws to follow. There is no way any of us can truly know the desire of someone else unless that person chooses to reveal it to us. We may think we are helping someone with our spell when in fact our desired end result is not the one personally chosen.

For example, suppose your best buddy from grade school gets caught shoplifting. Maybe you think, "Oh, wow, that was a one-time thing. It was a big mistake. I've got to help my bud. I'll do a spell to make the judge feel lenient at sentencing time." Your childhood friend is not a witch, and so you don't ask his permission to perform the spell. You do the spell. The next morning, your alarm clock malfunctions and fails to ring. Late for work, you put on your new shoes. Surprisingly, they don't fit. Rushing to your day, you fail to notice that "The bell didn't ring," and "The shoe didn't fit." You ignore the warning.

Sentencing time comes, and you go to court to show your support for your buddy. You gaze intently at the judge and send positively-inclined energies his way. You concentrate and focus on seeing the judge sign the probation papers. You stare at the courtroom clock and envision it running backwards, taking time off your buddy's sentence. You picture your buddy sitting down with his probation officer, reciting his remorse. When the judge pounds his gavel and sends your friend away at greater than the maximum sentence the prosecution requested, you're shocked to find out that your spells were of no use. In fact, you worry that the sentence was so unreasonably harsh, maybe your spells actually did harm!

The problem is that your buddy didn't ask you to spell for him. His inner feelings, and the play his inner mind was running, told him he was worthless and needed to be punished. His subconscious mind was busily contacting the judge to suggest that he belonged in jail! You're trying to do spells to save your friend's behind while he's busy spelling himself to save his proverbial soul! Your spells for your friend, always subordinate to the spells he does for himself, increased the amount of energy being sent to the judge but didn't change the energy's direction! Better you should have stayed home and baked a cake with a saw in it! Some friend you are! Our magick spells are like the proverbial Aladdin's genie. We get what we wished for, only to find out we wished for the wrong thing!

We must be extremely careful about spelling for or on behalf of another person. The intended result must be the one their inner mind is looking for. If they cannot convince their own inner mind to want something good, our spells will only compound the error.

The Law of Threefold Return

As far as the possibility of spelling to intentionally harm someone . . . that would be more than a mistake for a witch. That would be a long-term karmic disaster. Suicide is too light a term for the consequences that would be generated. Our actions follow us from life to life. Even suicide wouldn't resolve the agony we would cause ourselves if we do that. Many people who do not understand witchcraft perform acts of magick that harm others every day. The teacher who calls a student "stupid" is doing it. The parent who labels a child "idiot" is doing it. The husband who says "Look what you made me do," to his wife after he hits her, is doing it. The gods sometimes have more mercy on those who are not witches when they perform their magick in an unaware state. Karma may be smoothed over for those who were asleep when they did their harm. Like the favored child whose intellect requires discipline, the witch committed to the Goddess gets no such slack. Those who are awake and aware of the consequences of magickal acts must learn to live by them. Whatever we do comes back and hits us three times harder. With a law of physics like that in play, one learns to be very circumspect and careful with ritual and magickal acts. One learns that unconditional love must be the motivation for a ritual. Nothing less will bring an outcome we truly desire.

BE CAREFUL WHAT YOU WISH FOR

The first step in doing magick is always to have a specific vision of the desired end result, pictured in as much detail as possible. If you see yourself standing up at a convention reading a paper you wrote, picture what you're wearing. See if you have on nail polish and makeup, or what tie you have on. Look at the picture in your mind and find out if there are people "behind" you, supporting your effort. Paint a mental picture of what happens after you read your speech, and how the audience responds to it. Find out how you feel about the event three months later when the dust has settled. Go into extreme and extraordinary detail in your mind, playing the mental video of the event you desire.

All magick can be done entirely in the mind, but using tools and ritual trains the mind and reaches the subconscious more efficiently. Besides, after you get the hang of it, the tools and ritual are fun, and they amuse the faeries. You should always cast a sacred circle to do magick spells, but if you need to cast the circle in your mind because of a time or location constraint, that's okay, too. Your spells should reflect your own inner feelings about a situation, expressed in terms your dreaming brain will relate to. For example:

- If you want something to be delayed, you might consider "putting it on ice" or "letting it simmer on the back burner." Literally, in your spell, this is what you will do with it.

- If you want a subject to just "pop up," you might put a piece of paper with its name written on it into an air-pop popcorn maker.

- If you've been "looking for love in all the wrong places," paste the words "I love you" on your mirror.

- If you want something to "go through proper channels," make a paper boat out of it and set it adrift on a river.

- If you think you just "shot yourself in the foot," wear an Ace bandage around your foot to heal the problem you caused.

- If you're "itching for adventure," sprinkle some talcum powder on a travel brochure.

- If you need to be prompt, put a spot on a piece of paper, and draw "Johnny" on it, so you will have "Johnny on the Spot."

- If you want to close a tough negotiation, put the name of the deal in a box and seal it.

- If you want to succeed at something, put it "in the bag" and "sew it up."

- If you want to explain something so that it sounds attractive, "paint it rose-colored."

All of these things must be done with the spirit of unconditional love, even if they are specific, mundane, and tactical actions in your life. Your intention must never be to hurt anyone but always to effect a solution that harms no one, while implementing the guidance from your heart. Your spells should not be "canned" solutions you read in a book or got from somebody else. They must be heart-felt expressions of your vision and True Will. Here are some tools and ritual techniques for designing your own spells and performing magic.

DRAMA TO BE ENACTED

Your spell should be associated with one of the directions or elements. Choose an action similar to the following.

Earth spell hex: Bury it or lock it up in a dark place.
Earth spell hope: Plant it or grow it in some manner.
Air spell hex: Cast it to the winds.
Air spell hope: Attach it to a sunbeam.
Fire spell hex: Burn it in a cauldron or fireplace.
Fire spell hope: Light a flame for it.
Water spell hex: Drown it.
Water spell hope. Heal it.

Write rhyming language to describe the action you've chosen to do and illustrate your hope for an outcome. Enact a drama symbolizing the action inside a rightly cast magick circle. End your spell with the following words, to protect you from being hit with the kickback:

> Source above and Source below
> Flow through me and make it so.
> Cause no harm, and bind by three,
> Live by love, the law for me.

The Rule of Silence

Once you have done your spell, you must put it out of your mind and never speak of it again. It is important for the energy to go off to do its work, not be drawn back to you. If you continue to think of it and speak of it, you will change its working. *Never tell anyone, who is not present with you at the working, that you have done a spell.* Immediately after the spell, busy yourself with cleaning up or doing some sort of mundane work that will keep your mind from wandering and returning to it.

Elementals

An element is fire, air, water, or earth. An elemental is an object that is made from fire, air, water, or earth. Salamanders, Undines, Sprites, and Gnomes are entities associated with the elements. When you use an elemental in a spell, you command it to have life, in order to bear the burden or perform the task of the spell. For example, in Lesson 6, I used a gray cloud, a purple wound, a green flavor, and a red flag in my spell. I made each of these an elemental. I gave it life and then buried it. An elemental should be given a specific time period for its life.

Poppets

A poppet is something that is crafted or made in the likeness of a human being in order to perform as an elemental. It is like a voodoo doll. It can be made out of cloth, crudely sewn, and filled with almonds, mint, or rosemary. It is used when the spell is about a human being's feelings or illnesses. In fact, a human beings feelings are his or her illnesses. A poppet is most appropriate when an emotion is being evoked.

Amulets and Talismans

An amulet is something that comes from nature, like a rock or feather. A talisman is crafted, like a charm made out of a rock and a feather. Either of these can be used as a charm. A leather bag with crystals or powder inside, for example, could be used as a talisman. Amulets and talismans are generally made to wear around the neck or in some way on the body. They are particularly important in protective spells or spells that need a long time to work.

Candles

Candles work best in spells when a rune is carved into them and they are rubbed with essential oil. The importance of candles in ritual cannot be overemphasized. They draw the forces to them, and their colors call the elements. Here are some associations with the colors of candles.

Red: Vigor, strength, passionate pursuit, 6200–6700 angstroms, circulatory system, Fire, Mars, the inner child, salamanders, the constellation Aries.

Orange: Encouragement, adaptability, stimulation, positive outlook, 5900–6200 angstroms, bio-energies, Fire, heat, slimy salamanders, Venus, the aura, the constellation Cancer.

Yellow: Charm, confidence, persuasion, 5600–5900 angstroms, the reproductive system, Fire, light, glittery salamanders, the Sun, the superego and conscience, the constellation, Leo.

Green: Fertility, luck, money, 5100–5600 angstroms, respiratory system, Metal, gnomes, Mercury, the rational mind, the constellation Gemini.

Blue: Tranquillity, health, patience, discipline, 4700–5100 angstroms, the digestive system, Wood, bacterial undines, Jupiter (Zeus), the survival instinct, the constellation Capricorn.

Violet: Tension, power, royalty, 4000–4500 angstroms, central nervous system, Water, water's reflection, the deceptive sylphs, Moon, the ancestral memory, the constellation Aquarius.

Black: Karma, protection, destiny, the immune system, Water, viral undines, Saturn, the intellect, the constellation Pisces.

White: Purity, sincerity, truth, the skeletal system, Air, hidden sylphs, Earth, the essential self, the constellation Scorpio.

HERBS

Planting a holly bush next to your house keeps robbers away. Planting tansy around your house keeps ants out. Sprinkling cayenne pepper chases evil spirits. Tossing rosemary makes things sacred. There is no end to the wonderful benefit of learning and using the magickal properties of plants. Herbs can be used in your spells, as an aromatic incense, as a charm worn around the neck, or as a pillow to bring prophetic dreams. The study of the magickal property of herbs is part of the witch's long-term study plan.

By learning the uses of herbs, a witch can avoid going to doctors.

Ever.

Herbal study should be a "must do" for every practicing witch. Here are some simple herbal medicines for daily use.

White willow bark powder: This is the basis of aspirin.

St. John's Wort: This is an antidepressant.

Kava Kava: This is a mood enhancer supreme.

Echinacea and goldenseal: These are antibiotics.

Mullein and Yerba santa: These are decongestants.

Dong quai: This is for female problems and menopause.

Damiana: This is Viagra for women.

Senna: This is a laxative.

Ginger: This solves hangovers and digestive problems.

Valerian: This is for insomnia.

Use herbs whole, as they came from the plant, or in their powdered form, not artificially produced in a laboratory.

CRYSTALS

Crystals power the clock in our computers. They are powerful healing mechanisms, with energy that far exceeds the benefit of simple mental recall. Here are some of the correspondences of various crystals.

Bloodstone: Root chakra, used to stop bleeding, helps in making decisions.

Lapis Lazuli: Throat and third eye chakras, assists in opening and clarifying vision.

Amethyst: Crown chakra, calming, grounding, cleansing, and spiritual stimulator.

Agate: Solar plexus and heart chakras, compels truth and promotes good manners, used in medicinal workings and exorcisms.

Malachite: Heart and crown chakras, all purpose healing stone, used for physical detoxification in medical workings.

Citrine: Solar plexus chakra, generates happy thoughts, helps to center and ground, used for workings in Malkuth.

Hematite: Root chakra, used for cooling the emotions and alleviating worry, general medical use.

Jade: Solar plexus chakra, increases ability to see through smoke-screens, used for diagnosis in medical workings.

Jasper: Heart chakra, releases playfulness and purity.

Lithium: Crown chakra, reduces stress and eases depression. Put it in the bathtub to reduce anxiety.

Obsidian: Heart chakra, sharpens the vision, teaches one the truth about oneself in relation to the outer world.

Quartz (clear): Trans-chakra, amplifies thought-forms and forms protective energies in the auric field.

Tiger Eye: Heart chakra, sharpens ability to discern right from wrong, true from false.

Topaz: Solar plexus chakra, eases death, draws negativity away, mood elevator, used in exorcism rites.

Tourmaline: Root and heart chakras, expands limited thinking concepts, consumes negative energy without releasing it, assists to generate compassion.

Turquoise. Heart and throat chakras, spiritual attunement and astral travel.

CHANTS

Chants are the quintessential requirement of a successful spell. Even if you have no poet in you, just make up nonsense sounds that rhyme. Rhyme imprints the dreaming brain. Ask Madison Avenue why they call it a "jingle." TV advertising has carried this form of magick spell to an extreme.

Conjuring

Conjuring is a form of imagery in which we imagine an entity, and then the entity appears. We can conjure the elementals (salamanders, gnomes, etc.); we can conjure genies (only with permission); we can conjure demons. Generally, when you conjure something, it's of the form demon. Witches are not afraid of demons. We command them. Demons are souls who are between lives right now, and they have been assigned some remedial and corrective tasks to help pay down their karma while they're waiting for the call for another round in the life-school. The Goddess gives Her witches permission to give them tasks to keep them busy.

If witches don't keep the demons busy, they get into trouble.

For example, a witch might send a demon ahead to make sure a parking space is available at the library. This is a good task for a demon to do. When the occasional poltergeist outbreak occurs in a witch's house, demons can settle it down and keep order. Actually, calling the demons to take care of these little things can be quite a delightful perk of being a witch.

Any of the residents of the realm of faerie can be commanded by a witch in this way. Faeries, themselves, of course, must be treated with the utmost respect, and politely requested to do things, which they *might* do. One can never be too careful with faerie work. Faeries don't respond well to taking orders.

Demons, on the other hand, are obligated to do the will of the witch. They are quite enjoyable to work with, as long as one keeps the upper hand.

The witch should understand that angels do not take orders from witches. Angels already have their orders. If a witch tries to command an angel, the angel will blow the whistle on her, and the Lord will find out that the witch has lost all humility. Ego will inflate, and the next thing you know, HooHa will be in town. See Lesson 9, Pathworking and Tarot, to learn about HooHa. Demons, however, have been sentenced and commanded by the Lord to follow the orders of any witch who calls them. Any witch can feel free to order demons to do anything. It is very important for the witches to keep these demons busy, because in their free time they work for the IRS.

Phases of the Moon

The Moon flips through each of the constellations during the month. Because of the interactions between the Moon and the planets, some times are more favorable for spelling than other times. These interactions are too deep and complex to summarize in this book. If a spell is done with the correct intent and focus, we can trust the guidance of our feelings to cause us to do it during the most favorable aspect of the Moon. We remember to phrase our spell to build during the waxing phase of the Moon and to tear down during the waning phase. There are also times when the Moon is "void of course." When the Moon is void of course, it is not a good time to do a spell. A void of course Moon will not make any more aspects until after it goes from its current sign into another. A void of course Moon can last from several minutes to several hours and occurs about twelve times per month. Because this is so complex to track, good witches do best to ask their patron god and goddess for guidance as to the timing of a spell. There is a deep cleaning effect caused by the Moon. One needs to practice meditation and psychic feelings to choose the timing.

SUMMARY POINTS FOR LESSON 8

- Spells act on our subconscious, primordial inner mind. They speak in dream language.

- Because we are all one, spells impact other people and also the universe.

- People spell accidentally every day. The witch strives to do it intentionally and with forethought.

- Ritual tools are not required for spelling, but they greatly assist in training the mind to achieve the appropriate state.

- We primarily spell with words and thoughts, but by using colors, herbs, candles, crystals, poppets, chants, and imagery, we can make our spells more powerful.

- Conjuring is a type of imagery in which we elicit the assistance of the realm of faerie—demons, genies, and elementals—in our working. Witches command the residents of the realm of faerie, to the extent that they are commandable.

- Because angels are not commandable by a witch, witches generally don't have much to do with them. They exist, but they're not practical to work with, and they can't be invoked.

- The time to spell for building up is between the New Moon and the Full Moon when the Moon is waxing. To spell for tearing down, we spell between the Full Moon and the New Moon, when the Moon is waning. Most spells need to tear something down before they build something anew, and so the New Moon is the most powerful time for spelling. During that time, you can tear down first, while the Moon is waning, then wait for the Moon to pass over to its waxing phase and build up immediately.

LEARNING EXERCISES FOR LESSON 8

1. Design a spell to set your life in order and get yourself on track for your personal goals. Although you don't want to obsess on your spell after you've performed it, you will some time later check to see if it has worked. Perform your spell repeatedly until it works for you. Adjust it in accordance with guidance from the Goddess and set aside time daily to receive direction from the God.
2. Look up the dates for the New and Full Moons for the coming year. Mark them on your calendar and in your appointment book. Resolve to make no scheduling conflict that would interfere with your ability to set aside time on these days for your work with the Goddess.

To join in the private online discussion forum exclusively for readers of this book, and to try the test questions for this lesson, go to:

http://www.LadyRaya.org/religion/classes/

At this URL, you will find an online test for each lesson—the feedback for which is sent directly to your e-mail address—and a discussion forum about each of the lesson topics. Enter your e-mail address and your password found at the end of the first lesson. Then select Test 8 from the list of tests.

LESSON 9
PATHWORKING AND TAROT

RUN dot Child, and hear My voice.
I give you desire and choice.
You give Me a love untold.
Be Thou Bold

YOUR OBJECTIVE FOR LESSON 9

You will name the ten sephiroth on the Tree of Life
and describe their tarot associations.

The Grandma kneads the pillbox. The Faerie pulls the string.
My Baby wants a cracker And I want everything
To be a working number. Not OUT, or IN, or Wrong.
BECAUSE Left Me no option. I had to sing along.
And then the WHYs and WHERE FOURs Popped up to take a Bow
and THAT just left Me warbling. The Stool who knew. But How
Could I remain Left Over When Right went under? Stress
don't call the Shots. In Heaven the Shots Ring OUT. So Bless
My Soul and call Me NOOKIE. I feed your inner mind.
My heart remembers Da'addy. My Breast will milk the Lined
and Wrinkled Brow you proffer. So Don't get Me in Charge.
I sink My teeth in Substance, And when you fall I barge
Into your depths and Crevices where You lock your doors.
I pull the worst out of you and shake you down. The cores
of every human body are made of Shaving Foam.
I whip the Cream right off you to bring the Corpses Home
And when the Wedding's over, And all the Guests retreat

I pass around the bottle while you sit at My feet
And then I play Cahuna to your attentive Jane.
I let you think I love You, So you'll perform. The Bane
Of every soul's existence Is thinking. Why not Sex?
I never call you cell-ry unless you show your flecks
of spirit and of muscle. You need them both to Fly.
I take your Hand and carry the Ball when you say WHY.
But Why NOT gives me G-B's. I use them to cut Bread
Because they slice the pudding that rises in your HEAD
And pudding gets too shaky That's why we add some Dough
Re-Mi-Fa-So-La-Ti comes When we learn to say Know.
The Fallacy and Foolish Responses are the Ones
That come from what ensconces the Purity of Sons.
Which must be made of Rubber. What else could Bounce Back Truth?
For Mother called the Faerie And Father conjured Ruth
And Brother whistled Dixie While Sister played the Flute.
They all annexed additions to Cards. To carry Suit
upon that clear allusion, what Dictionary Logs
contain the Holy Reference? They're next to the Magogs.
And that's where you'll see Purpose In churning innards. Part
Of Mommie's true creation is aimed at stirring. Start
another True Religion, Why don't you, Mr. Smith?
I turned into a Pumpkin. Godmother made Me with
A Magic Wand and Toadstools She purchased by The WAY
And then St. Peter ate Me. (His wife refused to play.)
Now if you got a Counter You could be Markin' Bein's
But if you smoke Bananas You'll see I'm Timin' Genes
And Joe's and Little Tommies To make them March in Line.
The Lord's in All His Glory, but YOU, By God, Are MINE

Now if your Hand is Shakin'
You Might a Button PUSH
But if you Hear Me Knockin'
You'll sit right where you are. Still. Quiet. Alone.

And Listen. Shhhh.

Om Tat Sat

*Oh, goodness! I forgot to tell you not to read that out loud! I hope you didn't
listen to it on track five of RUN dot Child.*

I really hope you didn't. It could be quite dangerous, you know. Words, rhymes, chants. All scary. Now one particularly scary set of words comes about when we sit quietly with pen in hand and discover that we are channeling. Channeling is a learned skill that occurs when one has somehow managed to quiet the mind and allowed God to get a word in edgewise. Poetry like the chants in this book is one of the common techniques God uses to talk. God also speaks through inspiration, revelation, music, art, and great beauty. God is a genius, and when God speaks, the words and the sound are brilliant. That's why we associate God with light—because of God's brilliance.

Every time we meditate and channel words that are not our own, we are not necessarily channeling God. At least, not necessarily the aspect of God that God would like to be known by. God, being the all and the everything, has some dark and dirty secrets. The words we channel are not necessarily emanating from God's best side. After all, we are the receivers of God's word, and as receivers, we have filters. Our filters are our human means of translating God's word. What God says, we do not necessarily hear because we are limited in our understanding. This filtering system is what makes our understanding of God less than perfect. When we spoke of our Will, we talked about it being the will of our head, our loins, our ego, or our heart. Those are all centers of the will, and they are all potential receiving places where we could hear—and filter—the word of God.

Think of our bodies like receiving antennas. The word of God emanates all around us, creating life. Our receivers pick up that word and translate it for us to hear. We have a trinity of receivers in our head, heart, and loins. The fourth receiver, which is our ego, is hidden behind the heart. Sometimes, this receiver of the ego has been called Da'ath. When we hear God through the filter of our ego, some people in some religions call that the voice of Satan.

Wicca does not consider this aspect of God to be Satan, but rather a dark side that must exist in order to counterbalance and emphasize the good. This dark side has a purpose in the case of a physical survival situation. In Elijan Wicca, we call this Da'ath of the ego, the C-amp. The C-amp is one of the eleven nodes on the Tree of Life. Ten of these nodes are important and critical to traverse during our journey in this life-school called Earth, but the eleventh, the C-amp, or Da'ath, is the ego, and it is necessary only in a survival situation. It was the God of the C-amp who wrote the poem that began this lesson. He was describing Himself.

Often, people who believe they are having conversations with God are hearing the God of the C-amp. He's quite a trickster, often a liar, and definitely a male. He can masquerade as an entity, a space alien, a messenger, or an angel. He is quite real, and can be very frightening. He can scare you into illness, or bring you riches beyond your wildest dreams. He'll tell you what you want to hear and surprise you with your deepest secrets. He'll flatter you, seduce you, convince you, and if necessary, coerce you. He is, in fact, part of you, and He reflects your self-image. He is God, but not the god that God wants to be. He's the god of La-La-Land, and His name is HooHa. You must release your ego and let it deflate, or when you speak to God, HooHa will answer. The Deity who is Creator of the universe cannot be approached without humility. If you knock on His door with your ego standing like a ready lingam, He will let you talk to HooHa.

In other words, your conversation with God will be you, talking to yourself. The most bloody wars in history have been religious conflicts fought over issues no one could remember and upon which, on reflection, both sides agreed. Be sure you've fully understood the concept of humility when you approach God, or else you might find yourself carrying the sword to defend what is not defensible and to defeat what does not exist. This happens because of the HooHa who tells you he is your best friend and seductive lover: the god of your ego.

The Concept of Qabalah and the Tree of Life

Now we understand that the quest to meet the Lord and the journey to find the Lady is fraught with danger. Once you set your foot on the path, calls from your ego provoke responses from the realm of faerie, and grind pabulum from the domain of nonsense. Many people have fallen into the trap of believing they are channeling God or some emissary from God when, in fact, they are channeling HooHa. Mozart, Shakespeare, Beethoven, Bach, Einstein, and da Vinci are examples of people who were channeling God. God's channel is the channel of brilliance, of creativity, of perception, of insight, of revelation, of unconditional love, and of complete peace. The entities who will speak to anyone with a quiet mind and a ready pen come from other domains and worlds. These domains and worlds are part of the superstring physics of our cosmic universe.

The mystic Qabalah of ancient times describes a tree of ten prime attributes of the divine. It asserts there are four worlds. Traversing these worlds and climbing this tree of knowledge is part of our life task. In these four worlds, the first governing law is:

We are all one.

Everything in the manifest and the unmanifest universe is of a single piece and from a single source. Whatever happens anywhere effects the whole, and the whole has direct bearing on every minute and trivial event. The will of the Absolute is represented by a dimensionless point of light. A point singularity, actually, from which no light can escape (but there may indeed be some measure of Hawkings Radiation). On the other side of this black hole, which in our universe is named "Sagittarius A Star," is the inner mind of each individual, yet collective, human being. Our thought is transmitted from this black hole. It connects directly to our inner minds because it exists in the frequency domain, not the time domain; ergo, there is no distance between the black hole and our inner minds. This black hole is the container of our experiences in the dreaming state, where time bends, breaks, staples, and mutilates. This is where we go when we sleep.

Few of us are ever awake.

It is very hard for us to imagine something that is unmanifest and dimensionless, but try to think of this.

The Unmanifest and Dimensionless Point

You are in a concert hall. All around you, the seats are filled with people. The orchestra is ready. The musicians sit at attention, aware of their responsibility to follow. The conductor takes the podium. A few people fidget and whisper. Somebody coughs. Then, the lights dim. The conductor lifts his baton. Suddenly, the audience hushes. For an instant, the air is pregnant with expectation. There is total silence for one brief moment. The color of that room is dimensionless and unmanifest. Then the music starts.

If you could measure and register on a machine, the color of that room, is there any doubt in your mind that color would have changed during that brief, silent instant? Isn't it completely clear the color would appear *before* the music started? Do you think it is possible that the room wouldn't have a color? What do you think carries the signal to the musicians to think? Do you believe musicians think with their conscious minds?

Sit down at the piano and play something with your conscious mind. Right now. Go ahead.

Music, like all creativity, is not performed using consciousness. It is the skill to suspend conscious thinking that allows a musician to make the contact with divinity required for creative art to manifest.

Talent is genetic, but it isn't inherited from your mother and father.

At least, not your mother and father on Earth. It's a gift from across the abyss, where your Mother, Understanding, and your Father, Wisdom, live. The color energy, from which all the universe is made, is potential, unmanifest, and absolute. It is the Crown of the Tree of Life (see page 156), from which everything is birthed. The Crown circles in the center around the dimensionless void.

From the Crown, or point of dimensionless emanation, which is called Kether, springs the Trinity. The color energy produces Father, who is Chokmah, or Wisdom; and Mother, who is Binah, or Understanding. The

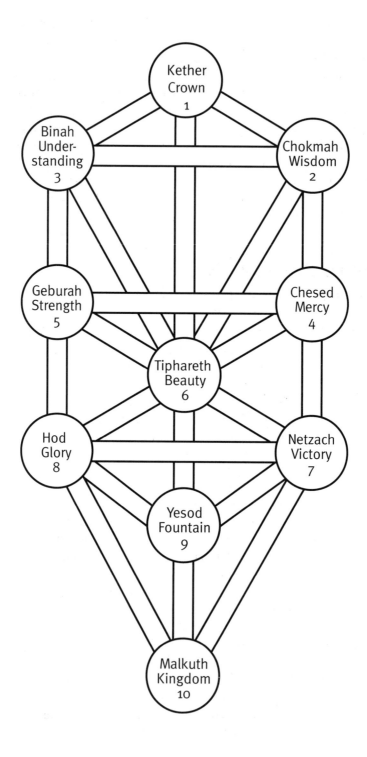

Crown or Absolute, the first principle, creates the God and the Goddess. This is less important than it might appear. The triad, then, of Crown, Mother, and Father unite to create all else.

To connect to the creation, the Creator—which is the trinity of Absolute, Mother, and Father—built a wormhole across the abyss, connecting the inner minds of all humanity. This wormhole is called Da'ath. It ties the inner mind of each to the ego of the Creator. It is the bend of time, and the manifestation of insanity. It is the break of time, and the unfolding lotus petal of genius.

God help you if you ever fall through it.

Possibly, if you fall through the abyss, you'll end up talking like this.

(Play this on your *RUN dot Child* CD, track six.)

HOW TO READ THE BIBLE
WITHOUT EATING ONION RINGS

The FISH had a COIN where its Tongue should have been
and THAT's Double-edged or IT's Forked
And if you don't Pay to THE MAN what is His
That Mother, AIN', gonna be Corked.
But Rich People can't get to Father so that
Means COIN cannot E'er be The Key
But Daddy said, Lock Up the Self
that is Naught - (wh)Y?
IT Cant. Bee Taught!
So THAT is why Blessed is He who Re-Pete's
The WORD, and He reads. IT Allowed
the Soma to hear what the Psyche received
so the "(k)NO(w)US" could break through the Cloud
Of Death and Delusion. That covers the Soul.
But Bodily heat won't revive
or cause life to Breathe in your RE-Birth in Christ
Unless you declare, "He's ALIVE
In ME!"
And then when You know what I say You can Hear.
Because all the WORDS got a Clue.
And Clueless is "kNOT", so the Reign goes away
And clouds never fog over You.
But deep in your heart there's a message from Me.
It's written in your DNA.

I sent you to Earth from Our Home in the Sky
So You need not kneel when you pray
For Prayers all suggest that you think I don't know
what Thoughts in your HEAD made it through.
Sweet Babies of Mine, you don't think, 'less I say
But all on your own, You can STEW.
So if you don't want to be Part of the Soup
You got to be Tuned to THE POINT.
And when You RECEIVE Me I let you "Come In"
And then we can venture. The joint
illusion and madness that comes from Our God
can be Art or be PsychoPath.
For Babies, My Heart loves You so, but I'm GOD.
And You, Twiggly Toes, are the Math-
ematical End of a Long, Twisting Road
I made from a Three-Headed Fork.
So LOVE with your Soul and Be Kind to your Mate
Or We gonna HEAD to New YORK.
And there be the BEAST but the problem is THIS.
THE MAN in the Story is GOD.
The Woman who's Wife is Humanity. CHURCH.
And we are beginning to get a new perspective on THE WORD

Per Verse
aren't we?

Now, by the Will of the Absolute, events are sequenced. This is what creates the universe. The created universe is the one that has time in it. That's what time is. It's sequence. This created universe is relative. It is not absolute. That means, it can look different to different people. In fact, it can be different for different people. This is why it's called quantum. Thousands of years ago, God gave humanity some information about quantum physics, the DNA structure, biology, and so on. This has been named Qabalah. Some day, science will learn about it. Then we will be able to build color energy machines that realign cell structures to cure all disease, so we can return to Eden.

THE SEPHIROTH OF THE TREE OF LIFE

The Crown (Kether), Father (Chokmah) and Mother (Binah) are on the subconscious side of the abyss. On the consciousness side of the abyss, there are seven sephiroth, or hubs, in the tree, connected by paths like a telephone network. The hubs represent Mercy, Strength, Beauty, Eternity, Reverberation, Foundation, and the Kingdom. Only the Kingdom is in the realm of the physical universe. Kingdom is also called Malkuth, or Earth, and is where we live. You can turn the tree upside down, and make Malkuth, the Kingdom, be Kether, the Crown. This is how you get heaven to be on Earth. You can make your life be heaven, or you can make it be hell. It's *up*, to you.

There are four worlds in Qabalah. Kether, the Crown, plus the Mother and Father (Binah and Chokmah) are in the world of emanations or archetypes. Then we get to the abyss, separating the trinity of the divine from the created world. Down that black hole lives the dragon. In mythology, the dragon was either named Rahab or Captain Hook. On our side of the abyss, we are Peter Pan. That is, we never grow up. We are always eternal children of our Mother and Father, the Deity.

The seven sephiroth on our side of the abyss monitor and direct the created thoughts and cause them to move hither and yon, acting out the Will of God. The physical universe, Malkuth, is the World of Action. The next three sephiroth—Yesod, Hod, and Netzach—are the world of formation. They build on thoughts and influence actions. The middle three sephiroth—Tiphareth, Geburah, and Chesed—are the World of Creation. They make the emanating thoughts of the triune God manifest.

It is not just good, but imperative, for a witch to study the Tree of Life and pathworking. Pathworking is Mother and Father's way of opening neural passages and passing on the wisdom of the ancients and the collective Akashic (or spirit) records. You must ground and center yourself in a solid concept and understanding and belief system about God before you do this, or you *might* end up looney. This is why things occult can be dangerous. They take you on head trips without drugs. And since Nature, a.k.a. God, in all His/Her Wisdom/Understanding decreed that survival and sexuality would be two sides of the same coin, they get you confused about the signals coming from between your legs.

THE YIN-YANG OF ENERGY

To solve this problem, Jesus the Christ told Peter's successor to clamp down on rampant and uncontrolled sexuality. He knew it wouldn't work very well, but it's like you telling your children something. You know they aren't going to listen, but you tell them anyway, in the hope you can tone it down a little.

In the yin/yang, or the balanced physics of the universe, God is yang, which is a male concept. Humanity is yin, which is a female concept. That means the Church, which in theology is humanity (because humanity is the temple of God) is Female. Humanity is the female spouse of God. God is the only, and the dominant, male. This concept of male and female is like the language concept of using pronouns to describe things as either male or female. Every language except English divides all things into male or female for the use of its pronouns. The usage describes whether something is a male energy or a female energy. In this context, God is a male energy, and humanity is a female energy. Just as that does not make all human beings women, so also it does not make God a man.

THE TEN HUBS OF THE TREE OF LIFE

Using tarot cards, you can design meditations to help you explore these ten realms and learn their meaning. In a meditation session, preferably inside a sacred circle, you may study the associated tarot to open your neural passages for the meditative journey to these worlds. In everything we do, our experience is associated with these realms. Learning about them helps the witch fulfill his or her objective during the time on Earth. The Thoth deck of Aleister Crowley is most conducive to opening the neural passages for this meditative journey. Concentrate on the cards and quiet the mind.

The First Three Sephiroth: Kether (the Crown), Chokmah (Wisdom), Binah (Understanding); color: white; world: emanation; number: 186; planet: Saturn.

Tarot cards associated with these three sephiroth: The Aces of the four suits belong to the Crown. The Twos and the Kings (called Knights in decks that have Princes) belong to Chokmah. The Threes and the Queens belong to Binah.

The first three sephiroth are the Triune God. The Absolute (Kether) is a dimensionless point (a.k.a. a black hole). From this point emanates all being—made of light and illusion. The point created Wisdom (Chokmah), the Father, and Understanding (Binah), the Mother. The Absolute, the Father, and the Mother constitute the Trinity of God. In Christian theology, that makes Chokmah equal the Father, Kether equal the Son, and Binah, which is the Mother, equal the Holy Ghost. The triune God is separated from the worlds accessible to humanity by the abyss. In the abyss, the beast lives. This beast runs the human sexuality psychodrama which drives human behavior at the instinctual, subconscious level. The abyss is the wormhole that connects our inner mind to the inner mind of God. Survival, sexuality, and ego are all the exotic material that keeps that wormhole in place. When you look into the abyss, the abyss looks into you, so the advice is always to "run and return" when trying to achieve total connection with Deity.

The Fourth Sephirah: Chesed; color: dark blue (Indigo); world: creation; number: 160; planet: Jupiter.

Tarot cards associated: The Fours.

Chesed, the realm of Mercy and Love, is the beginning of manifestation. It is the balancing force to Geburah, which is the realm of Strength. In human consciousness, it is the realm of the subconscious, ruled by Jupiter, who is Zeus. Zeus is the Sum of all Gods, meaning He is the manifested Jesus plus the manifested Lucifer, and also the manifested Jehovah. In the mythology of Christianity, He is Jesus the Christ, Lion Version. (When I speak of the mythology of Christianity, I am not implying that the story of Christ is mythic. I am merely saying the story of Christ is written into the software of the brain in an archetypal manner. It is part of the science of how humanity operates.)

Chesed must handle problems and enforce discipline. In this sense, He is responsible for what is perceived by mankind as "bad" acts of God—earthquakes, misfortune, plagues, etc. This is the realm of the archetype we perceive in our dreaming state. It is the first sephirah to be encountered after the pass across the abyss, returning from divinity. This is the dimension, or realm, or kingdom, in which the masters live. Masters are the spiritual beings who may choose to guide us to divinity.

The Fifth Sephirah: Geburah; color: green in the time domain, red in the frequency domain; world: creation; number: 131; planet: Mars.

Tarot cards associated: The Fives.

Geburah is the realm of Strength and is the balancing king to Chesed. Geburah is the input/output area for sensory experience, but it is also the realm of weaponry and destruction. Any five-sided symbol assists in the subconscious understanding of Geburah. Constant interaction between Chesed's Mercy and Geburah's Strength produces the balanced love and guidance of Tiphareth, the teacher. To reach true understanding (Binah), we must go first to Strength, and there wait for the Chariot to carry us across the abyss. Geburah is strict discipline. It is a destruction of the unworthy and the wasteful. It may *feel* punishing and restrictive, but its purpose is to provide us with backbone.

The Sixth Sephirah: Tiphareth; color: yellow; world: "Foundation;" number: 168; planet: the Sun.

Tarot cards associated: the Sixes and the Princes (called Knights in decks that have Kings).

Tiphareth, the realm of Beauty, is the heart. It is to this realm we travel to find our higher self. Here we sacrifice our old personality in order to be born again. Here is where we learn to control the subatomic and direct the Will, under the hand of the Master. This is where we learn the meaning of the biblical passage "whosoever will lose his life for my sake shall find it." This is the Bridegroom who takes the Bride. This is Christ, Buddha, Osiris, the Oak King. It is within each of us. Tiphareth is the redemption. "Come to me through Christ" means "Reach your evolved state by learning from the master within." Tiphareth is the realm of God, the Son.

In Tiphareth, we become self-aware. We "put away childish things" and make the decision to march to our own drummer and accept responsibility for our actions. Each success and failure is observed with detached interest in the knowledge that the world is designed for our benefit, and every small incident, no matter how trivial, has been selected specifically for our learning experience. There are no accidents.

The Seventh Sephirah: Netzach; color: orange in the time domain, green in the frequency domain; world: formation; number: 108; planet: Venus.
Tarot cards associated: the Sevens.

Netzach is the realm of Victory, eternity, the home of Mary, Isis, Venus, and Aphrodite, the kingdom of Instinct and emotion, the birthplace of desire. This is the fire that infuses the belly, the power behind the words of wisdom, the hand that rocks the cradle. It is by traveling to this realm that we succeed at submitting to the will of God and following the natural instincts.

The Eighth Sephirah: Hod; color: red in the time domain, orange in the frequency domain; world: formation; number: 98; planet: Mercury.
Tarot cards associated: the Eights.

Hod is the realm of the echo of Reason. Words of power live here. When the subconscious mind (Chesed), decides to follow the path to Netzach (Victory), it is infused with the fire in the belly that allows Reason to become power. Hod is the Reason. When balanced with the emotion and fire of Netzach, it becomes the power that will propel one to Tiphareth, Beauty, where the soul can emerge.

Hod is the home of the number eight. With the properly aligned self-concept, you may become the tool of God by balancing Reason with desire and entering the realm of Beauty. At the moment one balances Reason and deep desire, one enters Tiphareth, and steps on the Way.

The Ninth Sephirah: Yesod; color: purple; world: formation; number: 136; planet: Moon.
Tarot cards associated: the Nines.

Yesod is the realm of drama, the first step onto the astral plane. This is the source of the kundalini energy produced in Reiki, in spiritual awakening, and in sexual orgasm. It is what is seen in a near-death experience as "going to the light." It is where Earth-bound spirits, demons, disembodied entities, poltergeists, and the people in purgatory live. It is the reason it is best not to channel. It is the operator of Ouija boards. It is the mother ship for the space aliens. It is the waiting place between recycling lives. It is doggie heaven. People who live in Yesod are all dead, but they don't necessarily know it.

You could be one of them. Are you sure you would know, if you died?

Humility is the best defense against being possessed by a Yesodic spirit. When we first enter meditative work, Yesod is our initial encounter. We must push past Yesod by balancing Netzach (Instinct) with Hod (Reason) to propel ourselves on to Tiphareth (Beauty, also known as the Lotus or the Christ Consciousness). The biggest problem inexperienced entrants to the mystical journey face is to avoid being distracted and diverted by the residents of Yesod. Many books have been written and lectures been taught by people who landed in Yesod and stayed there.

The Tenth Sephirah: Malkuth, the Kingdom; color: black; world: action; number: 180; planet: Earth.

Tarot cards associated: the Tens and the four Princesses or Pages.

This is the physical and material world. It receives the influences of the other realms. It is the reflected perfection of Kether, the Crown, while at the same time being the product of the fall from Eden. This is the limited world in which one lives with a closed mind. By opening the mind and expanding the senses, the world of Malkuth can be perceived as heaven, in which an all-good God rules and controls every action of the universe for a specific purpose. As children of this God, we are challenged to behave personally in a manner to please Divinity. This causes Divinity itself to evolve and fulfills the biblical prophecy of the return of the Christ/coming of the Messiah. This is the real world, Assiah, in which the unseen energies and the physical matter live.

Ultimately, God is present in everything, and everything that exists has the potential to be used for good. Malkuth is the princess, who is the bride of the prince. Tiphareth is the prince, or the Christ Consciousness, or the Buddha.

READING THE TAROT

The paths that connect the sephiroth are each associated with a concept related to one of the twenty-two Hebrew letters. These letters are themselves concepts. Since each Hebrew letter is associated with a tarot trump card, the tarot itself is tied to the Tree of Life.

The legend of the tarot—and nobody seems to know the truth—says there was a time in history, possibly as long ago as ancient Egypt, when wise men worried the kings in power would destroy all books and knowledge.

These wise men then endeavored to write all knowledge onto a deck of cards, so that it would be perceived as a child's game and allowed to continue to be passed on through the ages. This deck of cards was passed on through the trade routes around the world. Ultimately, it became distorted and changed until it ended up as today's deck of fifty-two playing cards. The tarot suit of swords became spades. The suit of wands became clubs. The suit of cups became hearts. The suit of pentacles became diamonds. The twenty-two trumps dropped out and became secret. The four princesses were eliminated.

Interestingly, the princesses are the cards that marry our world of Malkuth, the Earth, to the princes who represent the Sephirah of Beauty, Tiphareth. The twenty-two trumps represent the paths we follow to climb the Tree and learn to evolve. So the deck that's left, without its princesses and trumps, has become emasculated. It is worthless for revealing the true secrets.

In the beginning of the twentieth century, the ancient wisdom was re-created when a magician named Crowley was visited by an angel, Aiwass, who told him exactly and specifically what symbols to draw on the cards. These are the tarot cards of Thoth, known as the Crowley Thoth deck. Crowley worked carefully with artist Lady Frieda Harris to make the deck's symbolic visualization algorithms that, when used as a meditation aid, open pathways in the neural network that expand consciousness.

Pathworking means studying a specific sequence of these cards to assist your mind in opening and expanding your ability to perceive universal truth and grasp karmic concepts. Many people have designed other tarot decks to express their view of the tarot, but only the Crowley deck has the full expression of the psycho-neural algorithm. Crowley himself became a victim of ego and the HooHa, but the visuals Aiwass transmitted to him remain as valuable tools.

CONTEMPLATIVE STUDY OF TAROT

After magickal workings, pathworking using the tarot allows your subconscious to establish a communication link to your conscious mind. It will assist you to become consciously aware of subliminal messages in your environment. Study of the visual images on the tarot cards—quiet, contemplative study—transmits information directly and wordlessly to your subconscious. You must do this study on your own, at your own pace. As you become familiar with the tarot through meditative pathworking journeys, the cards will speak to you. You will be able to "read" them as easily and as subconsciously as you are reading these pages now.

I'd like to leave this section with a little spell. It's called The Spell of the Spider.

And it's about Waking Up.

So clear your throat, and read this out loud or play it on your *RUN dot Child* CD, track seven.

What Now, Brown Cow?

When a Waveform takes the Matter
Into its own Hands, the Splatter
of the Gold comes from the CAT 'er
IT don't weave a SPELL.
Spell's important. It says Legions
All about the Inner Regions
That expose the Battle's Siege in
side each private Hell.
Lots o' words don't make a Chapter
**But the perfect Zinger Zapped her
Now and Then.** *That's why He Snapped her
Up to be His Shell.*
Daughter wished. **Her Mother answered.
Mother wished.** Her daughter answered.
*That's why they could make this Dance heard
Round their Father's World.*
Many people live inside me.
Many live in worlds beside the
One I chose. I picked it. **You see
Heaven's Gates unfurled.**
Colors make the World. *Unfiltered
Energies make Prisons.* **Kiltered
OUT a little?** Shape up. Bill stirred
Pots. **The Missile's hurled.**
Now I have to say "Conclusion:
**IT can make a Brain Contusion
Out of any Ripe Confusion.**"
Set your Sights on Stars.
Throw that Shot into the Air
Let it come down to Earth Somewhere.
And when it lands take special care
That IT's behind the Bars.

For the Prison is our Saving
Grace. It's Mother's way of Paving
Roads with Gold so we're not Braving
Life outside the Jars.
We each have a Jar or Bottle
Set to hold our Shape. The Throttle
Of Our Lord that hits the Spot'll
Make Us each be True.
Then we can "To Thine Own Self Be"

TRUE is what our God made.

. . .

Lose the Rhythm, Daughter?
Found the Measure, Mother.

Be Yourself! Your God made children!
Live in Eden Now.

SUMMARY POINTS OF LESSON 9

- The ego provides an ever-present danger of hearing the voice of a god that is not our Creator. This god of Ego will lie and flatter, deceive and mislead. To eliminate him, we must strive for an attitude of humility and reverence toward God. The ego has been called Satan by some religions. In Wicca, however, we see it as a necessary mechanism for species survival.

- The Tree of Life is an ancient mystic concept that provides a practical way to envision the structure of the cosmic universe and expand our learning experience.

- The ten hubs on the Tree of Life are called sephiroth. They are named Kether, Chokmah, Binah, Chesed, Geburah, Tiphareth, Netzach, Hod, Yesod, and Malkuth. Malkuth is Earth.

- The principles of Sephiroth are: the triune God (Kether, Chokmah, and Binah) represents the principle of emanation, wisdom, and understanding. The triune God is separated from formation by a great abyss. On our side of the abyss are the sephiroth of Mercy (Chesed), Strength (Geburah), Beauty (Tiphareth), Instinct (Netzach), Reason (Hod), Drama (Yesod), and Malkuth (Earth).

- The ego lives behind the heart, in a dark place called Da'ath, or the C-amp. It is easy to confuse the ego with the Will of our hearts unless the ego is released and held in a state of humility.

- The Crowley Thoth Tarot contains visualization algorithms that act on neurotransmitters to stimulate meditational travel through the various realms and sephiroth. Study of these cards facilitates mystic revelation, insight, and spiritual understanding.

LEARNING EXERCISES FOR LESSON 9

1. Get a Crowley Thoth Tarot deck and study the images. Use a set of the cards in your meditations daily as you allow the images to become part of your mental database. In a notebook or your Book of Shadows (such as *The Book of Dreams and Shadows*), write a few words about what each card says to you. If the cards make you feel uncomfortable, back off and put them away until you have progressed in your studies. Use a milder tarot deck for further exercises. A good one is The Witches Tarot, by Ellen Cannon Reed, illustrated by Martin Cannon.

2. Disks, or pentacles, are associated with practical and material things. Wands are associated with power. Cups are associated with emotion. Swords are associated with intellect. Do a tarot reading for yourself, using five cards. Which of the four suits dominates your reading? Consider what that domination means about how you're feeling right now. What insight does it give you about your viewpoint at this time?

3. Each of the numbered or court tarot cards is associated with one sephirah, and the trumps are associated with the paths between the sephiroth. Select three tarot cards. Look at their positions on the Tree of Life, pictured on page 156. Call your patron Goddess and ask Her to provide insight on what the reading means for you.

To join in the private online discussion forum exclusively for readers of this book, and to try the test questions for this lesson, go to:

http://www.LadyRaya.org/religion/classes/

Enter your e-mail address and the password you were given after the first lesson. Then select Test 9 from the list of tests. Feedback on the test will be sent directly to your e-mail address. Feel free to join the discussion forum on each of the lesson topics.

Lesson 10
Divination and Dreaming

RUN dot Child, and cry no more.
Tears have bitter sweets in store.
Grief and pain can help you grow.
You must know.

Your Objective for Lesson 10

You will describe appropriate uses for various methods of divination and list the types of messages sent to the dreaming brain.

The Purpose of Divination

You picture the gypsy fortune-teller, sitting in front of her crystal ball in her office off the Atlantic City boardwalk. "What does my future hold?" you ask her. "You're going to get married, but not for a long time. You'll have four children. And before that, I see palm trees. You're going to spend a lot of time in a warm place." Later, when you do finally get married, you think back about the trips to Walt Disney World in Florida and the business trips to California. Oh, yes, you rationalize. That was true, what the gypsy said. And, oh my gosh, I actually *do* have four children if you count the step-children. Do step-children count? We work at fitting what happened into what was predicted. It's comforting to think the future was already planned.

When we think of divination, we think of foretelling the future and predicting events. It's a seductive idea, to believe we can foretell the future. Wouldn't it be great if we knew things ahead of time, so that we could plan our strategies and responses? The world of our Creator is a quantum world, and while the Creator knows the end result, the number of pathways and possibilities to get there precludes any preview of the immediate future. Our divination, whether through tarot readings, crystal balls, pendulums, or whatever, is designed to give us divine guidance about how we should respond to a situation which has already occurred. It is *not* a reliable predictor of future events.

THE KARMA OF DESTINY

The end result planned by our Creator is that we shall all live in paradise, and that paradise will exist here on Earth, or some planet resembling it; but as we see by the nightly news, this final future is a long way off. Getting to that future is an evolving algorithm. With the constraint the Creator has placed on Herself to allow humanity to have free will, there is no telling what will happen tomorrow, this afternoon, next week, or next year. There are too many decisions not yet decided, too many pathways not yet chosen. While the final, final, final result is predetermined and predestined, the stops and starts and twists and turns along the way are open to our free will. Karma is pulling us to a destiny; but, if we resist, we will get what we choose and wish for during the journey to our ultimate goal.

Usually, resisting karma gives us what we think we want instead of what will make us happy. It causes us to set ourselves up to have accidents befall us. It invokes the spirits that blow smoke and mirrors. It distresses our immortal soul. Our best way to feel happiness and inner peace is to stay in harmony with our karma and move along the path to our destiny as smoothly and with as little resistance as possible. Free will may sound attractive, but in reality it is only a diversion from our True Will, which is the desire in our hearts that leads us to our personal destiny. The best outcome occurs when we consciously choose to let our free will opt to do our True Will. When people say, "Give up yourself to the Lord," they mean we should let the feeling in our heart, which is the Word of God, guide us.

And I will write my law on their inner parts, and write it in their hearts, and I will be their God, and they shall be my people. Jeremiah 31: 33

This is the feeling in our hearts that tells us our most compelling desire, and it is the basis for our law, "An' it harm none, do as Thy Will." This is Yahweh's new covenant with humanity, and it is the covenant of the gods to the witch. We have no concern over which God said this or which God made this covenant. God is God.

When Guidance Is "in the Cards"

The complexities and interactions of our lives often make it difficult for us to know what to do about the feelings in our heart. Should I go after that new job? Should I take that special trip? Should I follow where my heart leads in one direction, even if it means I break my heart in another area? Am I really able to discern the feelings of my heart in the face of the conflicting issues and demands of daily living? Is life so clear cut and simple that I can always tell what my heart wants me to choose? It is for guidance on these mundane and tactical daily decisions that we turn to divination.

Divination is the act of asking the Goddess to show us Her Will for us by guiding the probability of the responses of a divination tool. A divination tool can be anything that has a potential for a random outcome. It could be a set of sticks tossed in the pattern of runes, a set of coins tossed in the pattern of the I Ching, a deck of tarot cards, a swinging pendulum, a pattern in tea leaves, a twirling driedel, the Urim and Thummim, or even a pair of dice. Because we believe there are no accidents in life, and all is guided in accordance with the Will of the Goddess, we believe that She will instruct the faeries to guide the results of these probabilistic tools to reveal Her decisions to us. As long as the tools we use allow probability to guide their outcome, we believe Her Will is revealed within them.

Of course, this guidance only occurs when the tool is used by a witch, in a sacred manner and with a humble attitude. To use the tools, we humbly ask Her to guide the outcome before we toss the runes or twirl the driedel. To interpret the outcome, we determine in advance what the messages will mean. Runes, I Ching, and tarot all have general and basic meanings to their various patterns. The witch who chooses to use one of these methods to receive guidance should study the standard meanings. From that basic foundation, additional meaning and detail will be revealed to him or her in meditation and circle work. It is important that these tools be used respectfully and humbly in every instance.

When Our Path Is Rocky

Divination does not tell us the future; it only tells us the action we should take at this time in order to stay on our path. It is possible that our path will lead us to make mistakes. As long as the mistakes we make are those She has determined to be learning experiences for us in our life-school, they were correctly chosen. The future is not for us to know. It is enough for us to know the direction our personal path is destined to take.

Ouija boards do not fall under the category of divination tools. There is nothing random about the action of a Ouija board. Ouija boards allow entities to communicate with us who are not otherwise commanded to do so. They are activated by subconscious communication between our minds and the minds who are currently resident in the realm of Yesod. Yesod is the astral plane between Malkuth, the Earth, and Tiphareth, the realm of Beauty. Mystic wisdom and revelation tell us these entities are commanded to have no contact with us. Our respect for the Goddess extends to respect for Her wishes and commands. For this reason, a respectful Wiccan in the tradition of Elijan Wicca chooses not to use Ouija Boards and does not initiate contact with humans who have passed over. Our loved ones who have passed on have much to do in their new worlds and a great deal of transition energy is required of them. We do not do them a favor by disrupting their new lives. They may speak to us, and we may respond, but we do not initiate contact.

Divination through Dream Analysis

An important means of learning our path is to study and analyze our dreams. Primarily, dreams are a maintenance routine that runs in our brains, resetting our associations after the experiences of the day. For the most part, these dreams do basic maintenance functions, like the resetting of an index association table in a software program. With practice and meditation, the witch begins to develop dream tables and associations that are unique to his or her life experience. He or she is able to consciously understand these dream tables and use them as a means of divine guidance. Magickal dreams increase as the witch focuses on having them.

There are three main types of magickal dreams: psychic, prophetic, and teaching. Psychic dreams are those that provide special insight into something that is troubling you, or something that is about to occur in your near future. Prophetic dreams are those that portend something that has not yet occurred. They prepare you to respond correctly to the event that is coming, although they do not predict the event. Teaching dreams take past events of your days and interpret them for your conscious mind. They tell you what your subconscious is acting on. They explain your deepest, innermost operating premises. By keeping a dream journal by your bed and writing down everything you can remember about your dream as soon as you wake up, you will eventually see patterns emerge and associations form. You can train your mind to remember the dreams by doing something unusual right before you go to sleep, such as: turning a chair upside down or raising a blind. Tell yourself: as soon as I see that upside down chair, I will recall my dream. Keep doing this, and your dream recall will shortly begin to occur. Always handwrite the dream immediately. Do not tell it to someone orally. The handwriting will channel your subconscious, and more details will be recalled as you write. If you orally tell the dream, you will lose the details and forget them before you have recorded them in your journal. You also must keep the journal consistently over time, as the patterns are unique to you and your cognitive style. They do not mean the same to one person as they do to another.

Within prophetic dreams, there are dreams of preparation and dreams of warning. Within teaching dreams, there are dreams of growing and dreams of correction.

- Psychic dreams belong to the realm of Chesed. (Jupiter)
- Prophetic preparation dreams belong to the Trinity (Saturn)
- Prophetic warning dreams belong to Geburah (Mars)
- Teaching growing dreams belong to Hod (Mercury)
- Teaching correction dreams belong to Malkuth (Earth)

There are also three sleeplike experiences that are not actually dreams. The first is the out-of-body experience, which is a state in sleep that appears to be dreaming, but is similar to, and includes, the UFO abduction phenomenon. This is an experience of Yesod (The Moon). The kundalini, or agape, experience (being filled with the light, similar to a Reiki energy) is an orgasmic style experience belonging to Netzach (Venus). Finally, the waking trance, similar to the hypnotic state required for a pianist to play, an artist to create, or any truly great creative endeavor, belongs to Tiphareth (the Sun).

Interpreting Dreams

We can learn the messages in our dreams by keeping a dream journal and tracking the patterns and associations in idiomatic language. Our dreams speak idiomatically. For example, if someone in our dreams gives us a bucket of coins, we can say we no longer need any "change." If we stumble on the stairs, we can say we were "tripped up." If all our teeth fall out, we were "biting off more than we can chew." If we are in a plane and all the lights go out, we are "flying blind." If we are doing our laundry in a shoe store, we are "airing our dirty linen" in a place where we should rightly be "filling our shoes." If you dream that you are trying to go home, your subconscious mind is saying you must "return to your roots." If you dream that you are naked, it means you feel "exposed." If you dream you are in a store with hats on the racks, each of which has a large price tag, you are wondering which "hat to wear" because each role you play will have a price. If you dream you are lost and can't decide which road to go down, it means you "don't know which way to turn." If you dream there are two of you, it means you are "beside yourself." If you dream you are walking on the ceiling, it means your world is upside down.

The people in your dreams are all you. If you dream that your child is endangered, it does not mean someone is trying to hurt your son or daughter. It means *your* child, your subconscious inner mind child, is threatened by something in your environment or by some behavior you are taking. Likewise, if you dream about your father or mother or sister or friend, the dream is speaking about the aspect of that person that is represented inside you. Your dreaming brain is selfish. It is working to tell your conscious mind about *you.*

Our dreaming brain also speaks in a number language. The words in our association tables are stored there by a numeric algorithm. A simplified form of this algorithm is called "gematria." Gematria is an ancient mystic concept. Based on the theory that numbers and words are magickal concepts, gematria says that words have numbers. These numbers are calculated by setting the letters of the alphabet equal to numbers based on their position in the alphabet. That is, A = 1, B = 2, C = 3, D = 4, and so on, all the way to Z = 26. By calculating the number of a word, gematria says you can replace that word in a sentence with another word of the same number. If you do this, you will find another meaning that is equivalent in mystic terms. This works best when you use whole sentences or phrases that come to numbers above 200. The numbers themselves also have specific meaning in a mystical sense.

For example, in order to write this book, I had a working title. The title of this book guided what the book would be. The working title was: *RUN dot Child: A Witch's Primer for Pleasing the Divine.* That comes to the number 508 in gematria. Reading backwards, 508 is 8 = H, and that stands for "Eac(H)." Zero = "Unite with" in gematria. Five= E, which stands for the hand of God. So the number 508 represents "Each unites with the hand of God." In choosing the title of the book, the number was carefully selected. In fact, it is the same number as "Elijan Wicca One oh One: A Theology of Natural Witchcraft." which is an explanation of what the book is about. The actual title of the book changed, after it was written, but the working title guided it while it was being written. Names do that. They are the "handles" of destiny. Here is an example of dream analysis using gematria:

Dream of September 26, 1998

I was a waitress. I seemed to be only a waitress temporarily because there was some kind of emergency. A bus full of people came into the cafe. All the people sat at tables, but one well-dressed, gray-haired, grumpy man sat alone. His name was Deputy Fife. I took his order. He wanted two eggs and a milkshake with a special, unique flavoring. He asked if we had a special flavoring for him. I suggested we might because we had ice cream flavorings.

   The cook wanted to know if he wanted <u>hash</u> <u>browns</u> *and how he wanted his eggs cooked. I went back to ask him, and he said, "Maybe you're not capable of getting my order right. Maybe you don't understand my order." I patiently explained that hash browns came with his order, at no charge, and I just wanted to know if he wanted them. He said, "No." He did not want* <u>hash</u> <u>browns.</u> *He wanted his eggs "regular," which the cook and I had to assume meant "over easy." Again, he asked if I would get his* <u>special</u> <u>flavoring.</u>

   Gematria analysis:

   Waitress = 114 = The real name of the author of this book.

   Cafe = 15 = Face.

   Special flavoring = 169 = Predestination = genetic puzzle = fractal geometry = tarot concepts = inner mind paradigm = cycle equations = Qabalistic technology = altered destinies = ON-GO dictionary = codon dictionary = natural energies.

   Hash browns = 127 = Timing laws = fine remorse = original sin = smoke-screen.

   Two Eggs = 96 = Destiny = our Lady = Aphrodite = self-love = knowledge.

   Two <u>regular</u> eggs = surprise ending = Qabalistic biology = word dictionary = name structure = metamorphoses = <u>correct</u> <u>destiny.</u>

   Milkshake = 89 = Religion = virus = hard science.

   Deputy Fife = 117 = God, the Father = double helix.

   So the dream said I, the *Waitress* = the author, was taking the order of *Deputy Fife* = God, the Father. He wanted a *milkshake* = religion with *special flavoring* = predestination, and he did not want *hash browns* = Original sin with his *two eggs* = Destiny.

   Seems clear enough to me.

Synopsis of Divination and Dreaming

In this lesson, you learned that witches in the Elijan Wicca tradition are not likely to call up dead people, conduct séances, or use Ouija boards. You learned that Elijan witches probably do not tell fortunes or use the tarot for a parlor game. In a previous lesson, you learned that channeling opens the possibility of allowing the ego to invoke HooHa and his friends at the C-amp. Many people who channel, talk to dead people, read tarot for profit, and profess to be able to give psychic predictions, are considered by others to be "witches." This confusion may have arisen as a result of the split throughout history when the Babylonian women who acted as prostitutes became one sort of witch and the priests of the temple became another type. Witches, wizards, and sorcerers who lose their connection with Deity sometimes grope in the dark for their spiritual "legs" with these practices.

Other times, Christians who do not understand their own theology use these practices in a New Age spiritual theme.

True divination is used by the witch in a sacred and humble manner, with respect for the wishes of the Goddess. It is used to receive divine guidance about the path to be taken, not to foretell the future. We may receive guidance that tells us to proceed in a certain manner, but then the prediction which told us to behave in that way does not come true. However, we acted as we did as a result of divine guidance. Coincidence and circumstance will later come into play that proves our actions will turn out to have been "lucky." For example, suppose our divination tells us all the computers are going to stop when the Year 2000 occurs, because of the Y2K problem. Based on this prophecy, we learn to garden, collect recipes for rice and beans, and install a generator. The Y2K problem doesn't occur, but we realize that our lives have been greatly enriched by our new-found skills in living with nature, and we are grateful that the Goddess guided us to take this act.

Dreams are also an important way in which we receive divine guidance. Dreams are primarily a maintenance function for the software of our brains, but with meditation and training, they can offer magickal insight. Dreams may set our minds and preferences for the day ahead, as well as assist us to understand the Will of the Goddess for our path. Dreams store in our minds in idiomatic visions and also in associations known as gematria. Gematria is an ancient mystical concept that relates words to numbers and numbers to spiritual ideas. Dreaming was considered throughout history to be a means of receiving messages from God.

SUMMARY POINTS FOR LESSON 10

- Divination is used to receive divine guidance about what to do next, not to foretell the future.

- Divine guidance for our path could mean we are guided to make a mistake. That is Divinity's privilege. This is our life-school. We are expected to use our learning experiences to grow.

- Dreams store in our brain in idiomatic language and through numeric analysis. We interpret them by observing their patterns over time.

- Dreams are important methods for Divinity to communicate to us.

LEARNING EXERCISES FOR LESSON 10

1. Research the patterns of the I Ching. There are sixty-four possible combinations of the I Ching. This is exactly the number of possible combinations there are of DNA. Make your own set of I Ching sticks or patterns and practice tossing them in a random way to ask for insight and guidance from the Goddess.

2. Begin a dream journal. Commit to writing down your dreams as soon as you awake. After a month or two, you can look for the patterns.

To join in the private online discussion forum only for readers of this book, and to try the test questions for this lesson, go to:

http://www.LadyRaya.org/religion/classes/

Enter your e-mail address and the password you were given after the first lesson. Then select Test 10 from the list of tests. Feedback on the test will be sent directly to your e-mail address. Feel free to join the discussion forum on each of the lesson topics.

Lesson 11
Free Will versus Destiny

RUN dot Child, and stand alone.
All the voices are your own.
We are one, the you and me.
Let us be.

Your Objective for Lesson 11

You will describe the meaning of "giving up to the Lord."

Light a candle and incense. Quiet the mind. Read this slowly.

RUN Dot Child, and Find Me Y
All the Beanstalks reach the Sky,
But the Jacks don't Climb . . .

The QUEST

On this Date. TODAY.

THE Question: THE Answer.

PURPOSE: I don't Know

STRUCTURE: I don't Know.

What am I doing? I don't Know

What Am I Looking For? My Coordinates

What Can I Use to Help Me? My Controller. (My Own Mind)

What Should I Be Doing? Planning Carefully (Obeying God)

Where Are My Coordinate Points? (0,0,0) In GOD.

What Happens When I Act Without God's Permission?

LIST

1. My spouse divorces me.
2. My children go crazy and get sick and fight.
3. My House is foreclosed on and my possessions are taken away.
4. I hurt and disappoint people I love.
5. I ruin everything in my life and the lives of the people around me.
6. I lose Everything.
7. I dishonor my Soul.
8. I live in Tormented Madness all the days of my life and my lives hereafter.

THE QUESTION:
My Lord, I beseech You, How Can I Get Your Permission to Act?

THE ANSWER:

DAD won't be home until school's Out.

Through the Looking Glass:
Hurry, Alice! The caterpillars are starting the naming convention.
Alice: *Already, White Rabbit? But it's hardly even dusk! I thought all these names were secret!*
Rabbit: *Oh, they aren't going to tell you their names. They all go by handles.*
Alice: *Handles. Hmmm. And I have been trying to get a grip on this. Wait up, White Rabbit!*
Later, after falling down the rabbit hole:

†HE CALL †O ORDER

CAT Sub Dead: I believe we last left off dividing one by the square root of two and wondering whether the quantum test would find the cat dead or cat alive at the time of the measurement intrusion.

CAT Sub Alive: Well, we were divided into multiple camps over that, Mister Chair. Part of us wanted to believe in an ordered universe, part of us wanted to believe in an infinite set of simultaneous universes, and the majority of us didn't understand the question.

Alice: Oh! Am I late for the meeting? Is this the place where I can find out how to get home to Not Kansas and meet the Wizard of Oz?

HEAD Caterpillar: That question would fall under new business. You'll have to wait until we've read the minutes, taken the treasurer's report, finished up the bake sale, counted the number of holes in the universe, and submitted our prayer requests.

Alice: Will that take long? I'm really in a hurry here. I've got to get home to my bedroom in time to see the premiere of this season's *X-Files*.

The Group Consensus: Wull, we got a lot of prayer requests lined up for tonight. Who let you in here anyway? You don't look much like a caterpillar. Were you screened at the door for your membership card?

White Rabbit: Better keep a low profile, Alice. If they kick you out of here, the only other option is the beetle contingent, and I tell you, their conference room is not pretty.

Alice: I see your point, Bunny. I'll just wait patiently.

Fourteen Hours Later . . .

HEAD Caterpillar: Okay, that completes our old business. We've tabled everything for next meeting, and we've concluded that the universe extends to the corner of Fifth and Elm. Any farther than that would require transportation at unrealistic speeds and involve communication methods that are simply impossible. There is no evidence suggesting any other conclusion. Do we have a motion to write this scientific conclusion in stone and broadcast it on the evening news report? Okay, the motion is made and seconded. Here. Here. Do we have a motion to adjourn?

Alice: Excuse me, Mr. HEAD . . . may I ask my question now?

HEAD: I don't know that we programmed any question and answer session. And I believe our members are getting ready to leave. It's been a long day.

Alice: But I've been waiting all this time. I wanted to know if you could show me how to find the Great Father, God, and ask Him to send me back home.

HEAD: Home to where?

Alice: The imaginary world, where I live. I ended up here by accident, when God's missing and recalcitrant daughter played with the creator software. And now I have to find the great Father to ask him to send me back home.

TomCat: Mr. Chair, this question has already been settled. We've just proved conclusively there are no other worlds. This identity is challenging mainstream science. This intruder must be an imposter.

Rising Dissension: Yeah, Yeah. Imposter. Imposter.

White Rabbit: Yawn. As I suspected. It turns out you were wrong after all, Alice. You must have been mistaken about that bedroom in Kansas. Well, better call it a night. Let's turn in.

Alice: But I have to go home! I don't belong in this world!

The Fringe Element: Ho Ho. She's prob'ly gonna catch the next spaceship.

The Nerd Blossoms: Maybe she'll slide through a wormhole. Guffaw.

The End Runners: Or perhaps she'll just dematerialize in the transporter and wake up with her head on her own pillow.

HEAD: As we've said, strange intruder. No evidence. No evidence at all.

And this be what happens when we fall down the rabbit hole and meet God

Read the following out loud slowly, with a lit candle and a quiet mind. Keep pen in hand and sit quietly while you do it. If thoughts flash before you, write them down quickly. Do not think or censor what you write. Let the words flow. Put yourself in a quiet mental state before reading the next section. Call your patron god to be with you as you read this lesson. He will afford you greater insight than the words reveal.

The Source of Inspiration

Why? Four
    Wear How
        Y Yew
            Wot Now
                I NOT. Tell You.
                You think. I do.

           When You are Mine
              You'll like IT fine
                But 'til I'm You
                    You Monk- Key Do.

           Get It?

           Get IT? Get IT? Get IT?

           How to Paint a Little Guy

Underneath, you paint the whole guy WHITE. But don't paint him THICK. Paint him

THIN.
GET IT?

Now you'll need Vomit Brown. That's the skin color.
Just the Skin, though.
. . . . That's all I have to say about THAT.

Now go wash your paintbrush.

You can paint everything BLUE from this point on.

Actually, you can paint anything Blue if you want to. But you can paint the GUYS any color you want.

GET IT?

GOT IT?

GOO-OOD.

Now, I'm on Black.
There's a Lotta Black in these Guys. I'm painting the STAND first. Then I'm painting the Outer Shell.

I never paint the Inner Shell. I hate undercoat.
One, it takes up time. And Two, it makes your Guys look ugly.

Like I said, you paint whatever you want, whatever color you want.

DETAILS

Armour wash spilled. Brown wash didn't spill.

Wash Paintbrush.

Number 1. Paint silver with the armour wash. Don't paint silver what you don't want silver. It'll get you in trouble.

Number 2. Use brown wash on the skin.

Number 3. After you finish, you have a complete guy.

Let him Dry.
Paint another Guy.

And that's how you paint a Guy.

Bumble me twice.

You have half an hour 'til Mikey gets home.

START

Section D

START? Start WHAT?
Can't START. STOP.

Dear LORD, Hear My Call
Angels bustle in the hall.
What they want? Where they be?
Why they won't let go of ME?
Hear that Child?
What's He need?
Why He want?

(Though I look I do not see.)
I am Here. You are There. I should sit upon a Chair
on My ass, Where My Lord wants ME.

WHY I DENSE? WHY I DUMB?
WHY I NOT KNOW WHERE I FROM?
Can IT BE?
You is HE?
I is YOU?
WE is ME?

I'M Alive.
YOU is TWO.
IF WE MEAN WE NOT A CREW
WHY We Care?
WOT's in THERE!

IT JUS' BE.

IT JUS' BEE

No, I did not get the Message.
    No, I did not hear the Call.
        No, I am not in position.
           Know's the Purpose of IT All.
                Yes, I gladly eat my toothpaste.
            Yes, I swirl around the Hall.
           Yes, I found another Lover.

                And I'm learning how to CALL!

OUR DUAL PURPOSE IN LIFE

Each of us is alive on Earth today because we have a special and unique purpose in the Creator's plan for destiny and for evolution. That plan, like everything about the Creator's design, has a dual progression. One part of the plan is circular, like the yoni and the clock. In that part, we all have the same purpose. It is to learn unconditional love, at the core of our being, even at the cellular level. This command, to learn unconditional love, can be said to be our reason for continually reincarnating. We are using each of our lives to learn more about how to achieve a state of being that is completely and totally loving—without any emotion of envy, jealousy, neediness, vengeance, anger, or hate. When we achieve this state of being, totally in a state of love at all times, we are then ready to move on to another plane of existence—the nirvana and heaven of mythology. At that stage, we no longer reincarnate but become beings on a different level. Our objective in life is to reach this state, and stop coming back to Earth.

The state of being unconditionally loving means we no longer feel needy about our love for others. Our concern is for the other person's happiness, not for how we feel when that other person is around us. We cannot be provoked to anger in this state. The rage simply does not arise, no matter what the other person does. This state of being is what was described by the following statements attributed to Jesus in the New Testament (paraphrased, for today's language).

"If your brother steals your shirt, give him your jacket, too."

"If someone smites you on the cheek, turn the other cheek so he can do it again."

"Forgive someone not seven times, but seventy times seven times."

"Love your enemies; do good to them that hurt you."

These are behaviors we seldom understand or think about, but they are the actions of one who has no need for vengeance inside. Vengeance belongs to the Lord. Therefore, we have no need to feel it.

It is very difficult to reach this state of being, and so it takes us many lifetimes with many hard lessons along the way. As Wiccans, we believe the way to reduce accidents, hardship, and disastrous consequences in our lives is to actively work at learning this state of unconditional love. The faster we "get the point," the less painful will be the learning experience. Karma is designed to make it harder for us if we resist the lesson. By giving up our resistance to the teachings of life, and exhibiting "the patience of Job," karma relaxes its pressure, and our hardships dissolve. It is a counterintuitive principle. We automatically think we must fight back against hardship. Wiccan teaching says: Own it. Learn from it. Accept it. Let it be. In this way, we ultimately find our hardships less painful.

The teaching of the yoni, to learn unconditional love, is our primary and singular purpose for living. We think of this teaching as being a lesson taught by the Mother. It is what gives us joy in caring for children. Children are born loving unconditionally and are only taught to be conditional by the example their adult care-givers set for them. We must work at learning to return to this state of childhood, when we loved our parents unconditionally. This is the meaning of the words attributed to Jesus, "Come to me as a little child."

The sayings attributed to Jesus are an example of teachings from an archetypal Lord. Sayings of Buddha, Mohammed, and the Tao could also be used as examples. They all tell us the same thing: Learn to love. God is love. At its core, all religion tells us this. God wants us to love.

The Teachings of the Father

The Mother and Father have different ways of teaching, however, and to some extent a conflicting objective. Each also has a will and a path. Mother and Father are not impersonal energy forces but beings with existence. They have desires, intents, and preferences, too. One of the desires of God is that the ultimate path of Creation be fulfilled. God has a vision of the future.

If you study mathematical chaos theory, one of the things you learn is that chaos, while appearing to be random, actually proceeds toward a pattern. Cells divide in ways that differentiate them into kidney cells, lung cells, arms and legs. Ferns symmetrically create their leaf fans. Trees proceed to become mighty oaks or towering pines. A cell knows its purpose and proceeds unwaveringly to its goal. Our Mother and Father who-art-in-both-heaven-and-Earth have specific task-related goals and plans for each of our lives, in addition to our primary purpose of learning love.

As a parent, you want first for your child to be happy, don't you? After you want her to be happy, next you want her to be a doctor or a lawyer or an Indian chief. Your desire to see your child be happy is your circular desire. It is like the desire of God for you to learn love, and it is the primary objective. But your desire for your child to have a productive life is your linear desire. It is like the calendar, instead of like the clock, and it is the province of the Father. This is the same with Our Creator. She wants you to learn love. He wants you to be a productive member of the human race. Remember, in the origins of Wicca, we learned that humanity at first knew the Mother. Then, as structure was added to the society, the Mother produced a Son who grew up to be Her lover and consort. He was both Her husband and Her son. His reason for existence was to introduce to humanity the masculine concepts: drive, ambition, structure, purpose, meaning, and law.

"Let Me be your Master," Jesus is attributed as saying. "My yoke is easy; my burden light." When the Lord is a teacher, we expect the teacher to give assignments and tasks and to correct us. When we give up our "free will" to God, we are saying we allow the Lord (who is our patron god, whether he be Jesus, Zeus, Yahweh, Father Sky, Thor, Buddha, Allah, Ra, Itzam-Na, or Jupiter) to discipline and guide us. We accept that He will put challenges in our way and tasks before us. We agree to submit our tasks to Him for approval. We make Him our boss, our Lord, our Husband, our Master. We commit to obey Him. We resolve to be subservient to Him. In the New Testament of Christianity, much of the writings of the apostle Paul refer to "wives submitting to your husbands." This is greatly egregious and objectionable scripture. But what if the text of the New Testament is encrypted, as much holy writing is? What if the words of Paul were transmitted to him by the Lord to mean God is the husband, and all humanity is the wife? How differently would we read those passages if the master and husband in all cases is God? What if the Lord told Paul this, and Paul did his best to interpret it, but we spent the last two thousand years misunderstanding him?

We know, if we are in any way "worldly," that sexuality is engaged when there is a dominant-submissive exchange. Pagan societies know that sexuality and spirituality are two sides of a coin. Mystics and clerics throughout the ages know that one who has God is so awash in orgasmic experience that he can live without any additional sex. If, indeed, God is the Lord and husband of all humankind, and the dominant master to which we go to engage magickal ability, how secret would certain societies want this information to be?

But what does this mean? How can one engage the Lord in such an exchange? How can we invoke an experience of agape, kundalini, or mystic ecstasy? How can we commit to obey a Lord who is mythic? Where will we get our direction, our guidance, our orders, and our task assignments, if the Lord does not speak?

In Lesson 9, Pathworking and Tarot, we learned about meditative journeys to climb the Tree of Life. In that lesson, we learned that the Will in our heart was called the sephirah of Tiphareth. Tiphareth is known as the Lotus of Buddha or the Christ Consciousness. This Christ Consciousness is the mystic equivalent of the commands of the Lord. "I will put my law in your inner parts," thunders Jehovah, in Jeremiah 31: 33 "and you will no longer need to listen to prophets, for each of you will know me, and you will know that I am God."

The law of the Lord is written in our hearts. In meditation we can hear it. That is why, as Wiccans, we strive to follow our True Will. We know our True Will, the Will of our hearts, is the direction of God.

Our task-purpose in life could be to have a specific career, to raise children, to provide help to another person at a particular time, to write something, to teach something, to tell something, or to provide something. Like a thread in a carpet that does not reveal the design until the entire rug is woven, our little piece of the fabric of evolution may never be known to us. We cannot worry about it or obsess about finding it. It is enough that we concentrate on the circumstances of each day, noting and observing what goes on around us, and focusing on the feelings and desires of our heart.

"Do not worry about tomorrow, for the evils of the day are sufficient unto it," Jesus tells us. This means to the Wiccan: Pay attention now. Be present here. The future is in the hands of our Creator. By following our hearts, and achieving that state of Tiphareth, which is gained by striving to balance the Instinct of Netzach with the Reason of Hod, we are best able to respond to the guidance we find in coincidence and circumstance. This coincidence and circumstance is never accidental. It is placed in our path by the Lord. Our destiny is ultimately to be one with the Creator. It will absolutely occur, eventually. We make it occur sooner, rather than later, by working at submitting our free will to our True Will and following our heart. This will in our hearts will lead us to our "beanstalk," our path in life that reaches the sky and takes us home. Like Jack in the famous fairy tale, we must decide to climb if we are to reach our destiny.

> *RUN dot child, and find me Y,*
> *All the beanstalks reach the sky,*
> *But the Jacks don't climb.*

When we overcome our fear of giants and recognize the seeds of poten tial implanted in our hearts, true magick is our reward. The goose that lays the golden eggs is stolen from the giant, and becomes our own. And then we see the Mother inside each one of us, as She lives forever on Earth, in partnership with Her Lord.

SUMMARY POINTS OF LESSON 11

- We each have a dual purpose in our life-school here on Earth. Our first and primary purpose is to learn uncondi- tional love. This is the gift of the yoni. Our secondary pur- pose is to contribute to the evolution of humanity in some specific, task-oriented way. This is our command from the lingam. Our drive and ambition pushes us to find that task, but we must never lose sight of the prime directive: to learn love.

- The Creator has a plan and a unique reason for each of our lives. When we say "give up your will to the Lord," it is the same thing as saying "follow your heart," and "to thine own self be true."

- We find ourselves when we incorporate the image of the Lady into our self-image. We merge with the Lady so that we can be love; we submit to the Lord so we can be guided to our destiny.

LEARNING EXERCISES FOR LESSON 11

1. Focus on your meditation and ask the God to provide revelation about your path and your task on Earth. Write His instruction in your Book of Shadows or *The Book of Dreams and Shadows* and com- mit to meet with Him on a regular basis.

2. Examine your family situation. What could you do in your cur- rent family to exhibit the characteristics of unconditional love toward family members? In what ways are you reacting to their displays of love that is not unconditional? Remember, you can- not change the way others behave toward you, but you can change how you respond to the way they behave. Focus on what you need to improve about your responses and design a spell to

learn to react to them in an unconditionally loving way. Ask the Goddess to help you with your spell.

3. Take a look at the section "The Technology of Magick" starting on page 229. How will practicing magick consciously help you stay on your path and follow your predestined blueprint? How do you fall off your path by practicing magick by accident?

To join in the private online discussion forum exclusively for readers of this book, and to try the test questions for this lesson, go to:

http://www.LadyRaya.org/religion/classes/

Enter your e-mail address and the password found at the end of the first lesson. Then select Test 11 from the list of tests. You will automatically receive feedback about your test at your e-mail address. You can also participate in discussion forums about any of the lesson topics.

LESSON 12
COMMITTING
TO THE GODDESS

RUN dot Child, and know your heart
You and I are not apart.
Joined as one we cannot tear.
I'll be there.

YOUR OBJECTIVE FOR LESSON 12

You will design a personal dedication ceremony.

THE DECISION TO BE INITIATED INTO THE CRAFT

The decision to become a witch is made when the Lady speaks to you and gives you your new name. Only then do you undertake initiation into the craft. For some period before this happens, however, you will be investigating, learning, and looking into the philosophy and covenants of the religion. During this preinitiate period, you should be studying and learning, practicing and endeavoring to perform magickal arts. It is most likely, at this stage in the formation of the Wiccan religion, that you will either be forming your own coven or practicing as a solitary. Wicca is not designed for heavy formality and massive organizations. This is the entrepreneur's religion. When the time comes, you're going to have to do your own thing, with the Lady's guidance.

So you've looked into it. You've studied the major religions and their history. You've read some of the Vedas, delved into the Old and New Testament, perused the Qur'an, practiced yoga, read Lao-Tse, studied Zen, watched *Steven Hawkings' Universe*, volunteered in a soup kitchen, shoveled the snow, and baked the cookies. Now you're ready to come home to Mother and meet the God.

> First you commit and dedicate.
> Then you study and meditate.
> Finally, the Goddess initiates.

With initiation, the old you symbolically dies. The new you is born. From the moment of initiation, you are no longer what you once were. This is why we take some time to prepare for initiation and make the decision only when the Lady speaks. Many of you are saying to yourselves right now "What does that mean? The Lady speaks? What Lady? How could she actually speak? She's just a concept. All religion is just a fantasy and a concept."

> The answer to that question is:
> This one isn't.

To begin your process of discovery in the craft, you first dedicate yourself to the Goddess, so that you know in your heart and your mind that you belong to Her. This dedication helps you prepare to hear Her voice. Here is a ceremony you may perform for yourself to mark your entrance on the path of the ancients:

Dedication Ritual for the Preinitiate

A dedication needs to have the elements of:

1. Commitment to the service of Deity
2. Integrity in the intent and motivation to seek God
3. Sincerity in the quest to become what God intends for you to be.

As long as your inner motivations are good, the Goddess isn't picky about exactly what words you say. She's forgiving.

Preparation for the Ceremony

This is a big night for you. You've made a decision to change your life. You want to mark that night in a memorable way. You want to show Deity—the Goddess—your respect for Her and your acknowledgement that you are coming to Her service of your own free will. If you are working as a solitary witch, make this a very special night. Arrange to be alone for the evening. Lock the doors. Unplug the phones. Buy yourself flowers. Prepare a special dinner or order takeout from the gourmet deli. Treat yourself to a small gift or special treat you've considered too luxurious or frivolous in the past. You are acknowledging not only the Goddess tonight but also your self as a child of Deity, a part of the Goddess. Make it a night to remember. Choose a very special gift for yourself tonight, because whatever you choose is going to become, in your mind, a very magickal object with very special powers.

As you learn to focus your mind and direct its energies, you will find the object capable of having special powers in reality, too. An example of what to pick might be a rock or a silk scarf. Those both make excellent elementals. Choose any object that pleases you, but whatever you choose, treasure it. And be sure it's something you like.

To start the evening, take a ceremonial bath with perfumed water and candles in the bathroom. Put on your bathrobe afterward. You're going to be alone tonight. You won't need clothes. You aren't ready to do a formal circle yet but put four white candles in the living room anyway, around in a circle, one in each of the four directions. Put a small table in the center. A coffee table or an end table will do. Put a nice candle in the center. Red would be a good color for that center candle. Black would not be a good color for it, nor would green, but blue, yellow, or purple all have possibilities. *Feel* the answer. Concentrate on *feeling* what color that center candle should be for you. Tonight is the night you're going to begin your training in *feeling* the answers.

After your bath, put on some pleasing music, nothing loud or raucous. Classical would be best, Mozart, maybe, or a nice, haunting, and lilting Celtic tune, possibly—your choice, your pleasure, your best feel. Choose music that is purely instrumental, though, not music with words or singing.

Settle down in the center of those candles. Light the candles, beginning in the East and going around the circle clockwise. Light the center candle. Smell the flowers you bought yourself. Light some incense if you have it. Then take off your bathrobe and breathe deeply. Thirteen deep breaths in the center of that candle circle. Stretch your naked body out and up to reach for the Moon. Lift yourself up and imagine that you can stretch all the way to the ends of the universe. Envision light circling through your body. See your own electromagnetic energy circulating through your body, up and out, like through a fountain. Spin that energy around you and through you until you feel it could explode out through the top of your head. Continue to envision that energy. Concentrate on making it light blue. You know perfectly well your body is filled with an electromagnetic energy. No science denies that. Control it. Direct it. Bend it to your will. Concentrate and focus.

Slowly, as you circulate the energy, imagine it expanding from you in ever-increasing circles until it fills the area marked by your candle circle. Imagine the energy forming a sphere of protection, a light blue bubble of energy and focus around your body, and filling the circle in the room. Fill the circle with energy, and hold it there in your mind.

Hold that energy tight. Replenish it by continuing to circulate it through your body.

Hold it solid for thirteen heartbeats.

Sit down next to your center candle. Stare into the candle for thirteen heartbeats. Look up at the imaginary sky from your lonely room and realize that you are not alone. Feel the energy surrounding you. Feel the otherworldly presences. Do not speak to them. You are not ready.

Now touch your naked body. Touch your breasts or your chest. Touch your side and hips. Touch your arms. Touch your feet. Touch your thighs and your stomach. Realize that you are a biological force, blessed with sensory abilities. Understand that your senses can be expanded and trained. You have not begun to approach the limits of your abilities. There is much more to you than you have known to date.

As you touch your body, accept who you are. Accept yourself. Forgive yourself. Acknowledge you are a child of Deity, formed from perfection, in the image of God.

Say: *"Bless me, Mother. Bless my head, so that I may have clarity of thought and purpose. Bless my ears, so that I may hear Thy Will. Bless my tongue, so that I may speak Thy words. Bless my heart, that I may feel Thy guidance. Bless my feet, that I may walk in Thy way. I honor thee, Mother, and dedicate my life to Thy service."*

Celebrate the knowledge that you are eternally loved. Know that you are forgiven completely and granted the opportunity to begin anew, from this night forward, with a clean slate for the future.

Say: *"I come to You, Mother. Send me to do Your will."*

Now try to quiet your mind. Sit quietly. Concentrate on filling your circle with the light blue energy. Focus on emptying your mind. Push the garbage and the thoughts of the day down through your body, out through your feet and into the ground. Release the anxieties. Release the worries. Give them back to the Earth. Mother will handle them. Mother will care for you. You are home now. Mother deals with the problems. Mother provides for your destiny and your training. Father handles the details.

This is your first true night as a witch.

Admittedly, you don't have control of your powers yet. That's why you mustn't try any methods of divination or encourage communication from the spirits. You aren't ready. If you try it before you're ready, it *will* backfire. Don't. Don't be arrogant. You must learn humility before you use the powers and the presence Mother will grant you. Until now, your lessons have been preparation. Your powers have been human. Before dedicating to the Mother, your attempts at study, pathworking, and divination are mere child's play. Tonight, however, you must not open the doors before you have been granted permission by the Lady. Just bask in the love you feel from Mother now. Sit in your little candle circle, as long as you feel warm and comfortable, and try to keep the light blue energy circulating. Concentrate on holding and keeping that energy.

You are working on controlling the subatomic. You are a child of God, and with work and practice, you will learn to do it. Don't push before you're ready. It's not a joke, and those spirit energies are not imaginary. Approach your work with seriousness and the intent to do good. Don't fear. You can't do harm by accident because the universe is created and crafted, so there are no accidents. Mother knows your intent and your motivation. As long as it's a good intention, Mother will handle your mistakes. She will direct your energy and ensure it does only good works.

Now you have taken the first step. You have built your first circle. Spend a little time in it, enjoying its warmth. Quiet your mind, release the anxieties through your feet. If you have tarot cards, carefully lay out the Empress, the Star, the Lovers, and the Chariot. Look at them each individually and carefully. Concentrate on seeing everything in them. Try to empty your mind and quiet your thought.

Do not write anything tonight. Do not *use* the tarot cards. Do not swing a pendulum. Do not flip a coin. If there is a Ouija Board in your house, get rid of it. Do not do *anything* that invites communication from the other world.

Now to show you what might happen if you do allow communication, I'm going to invite Father to speak to you, channel Him, and let Him use my fingers to type. The following words are channeled straight from the Lord.

You're opening the door here, soldier. Keep your "I"s right, kid. Be absolutely certain you know whose Army you're in. You took this step of your own Volition. Now you'll show what you're made of and exhibit your clarity of mind by being the Child God made and by fulfilling the Destiny God planned for you. This is a Path for those who wish to be truly alive, fully human, and the manifestation of God's Creation. This is a path to contribute to the positive evolution of Humanity. It is not a path for playing games and dabbling with the entities from the astral plane because they ARE real—and they have nothing to contribute to your Positive Enlightenment. I wouldn't have told you to stay away from them if I didn't mean, "Stay away from them!"

This is not a path for fooling in the superficialities of clairvoyance and fortune-telling. As you can see, this is also not a path to be followed by anyone who believes in the devil. The entities on the astral plane provide traps and diversions. They are to be avoided, ignored, and blocked out, not channeled. We come to the Goddess to learn to be fully human and to fulfill our potential as God defined for us. For this task, we must learn control—not diversion and parlor games, but control, actual control.

We must learn the kind of control that can send the demons into a herd of pigs, if necessary. This control can be learned, but it cannot be toyed with. You step onto this path, and you go the distance, one way or another. Now if you have not yet been dissuaded from following Wicca, Smile.

Father loves you, too.

Do not be sidetracked by the ideas of supernatural illusion. Only concentrate on circulating that blue energy. Begin to build your power and learn your lessons in control. On this special night, read from any of the scriptures of world religions: the Bhagavad Gita, the Qur'an, the Protovangelion (Book of St. Mary), or the Secret Book of John (from the Qumran Caves) are good examples of relevant scriptures for tonight. Follow with a few passages from the Tao Te Ching.

When you feel ready, take your new present, the gift you bought for yourself tonight. Set it in front of you, by the candle. Lift it and pass it back and forth over the smoke three times.

Say: *Blessed be, thou creature of the elements. I empower you to carry energy for me, to hold it safe, until such time as I need it and call it to do my Will, which is the Will of the Goddess, for I have submitted my Will to Her service. Perform your task well, and be subjugated to my power.*

Then with your mind, carefully, and in a concentrated manner, envision your light blue circle, which you have spent the evening building, slowly curling into the power object. See the circle spiraling carefully into your elemental. Watch it until the entire circle has disappeared into the object.

Say, "*Blessed be, thou elemental creature,*" and draw the sign of the pentagram with your fingers. You do it: forehead, left breast, right shoulder, left shoulder, right breast, forehead.

Now wrap your power object in a piece of silk or enclose it in a velvet-lined box. Be careful with it and treat it with reverence. You will use it again when you need it. It bears the scent of Mother now. This was your first experience with magickal workings, your dedication to the Goddess. Now you will begin your true course of study. You will study for one year and a day before you can be initiated. By the time you are ready, you will need no initiation ceremony written by another. Your initiation will be performed by the gods.

Once you have dedicated yourself and begun the course of study, you will have drawn yourself to the attention of the old ones. Soon, events will overtake you. Your path will take on a life of its own. In a short while, a spirit guide will come to bring you to the ancient elders. By the time you are prepared for initiation to the craft, the Goddess will write your ceremony Herself.

The craft is a most serious and intense religion. Consider wisely if it is for you. Turn away if you cannot commit sincerely and with integrity.

But if you choose to take your step on this path,
Welcome home.

SUMMARY POINTS FOR LESSON 12

• Commitment and dedication occur individually before initiation into the craft is undertaken. It is individual commitment and dedication that invites the Goddess to begin Her dialogue with you.

• The personal dedication ceremony is done alone, not in a group. It is between you and the Lady.

• Communication with the Lady requires your commitment to avoid communication with entities from the astral plane. She will not speak to you in their presence.

• After dedication, you should plan to study seriously for a year and a day before considering initiation into the craft.

LEARNING EXERCISES FOR LESSON 12

Prepare and conduct your own dedication ceremony.

To join in the private online discussion forum exclusively for readers of this book, and to try the test questions for this lesson, go to:

http://www.LadyRaya.org/religion/classes/

Enter your e-mail address and the password you were given at the end of the first lesson. Then select Test 12 from the list of tests. Feedback about the test will be sent directly to your e-mail address. Feel free to join any of the discussion forums on the lesson topics.

LESSON 13
THE INITIATION CEREMONY

RUN dot Child, and find me Y
All the beanstalks reach the sky
But the Jacks will never climb
Without His hand.
And I say this little prayer
She has taught me how to care.
He is with me day by day
As I stand.
By Her command.

YOUR OBJECTIVE FOR LESSON 13

You will review the initiation ceremony in preparation
for the decision to become an initiate in Elijan Wicca.

After your dedication ceremony, you are ready to consider how you will
be initiated. It is traditional to say that study with a coven should last for
a year and a day before you are initiated as a witch. Since so many
Wiccans work as solitaries, the date on which your year and day begin is
something you will have to decide for yourself.

Do you count from the first Celtic song that drew you to the Goddess?
Do you count from the first Wiccan book you read or the first pagan
friend you made? Do you count from the first altar tool you found or the
night you made your robe? It is reasonable, for the purpose of ensuring
that the Wiccan path is for you, to count the year and a day from the
night you do your dedication ceremony. From that day forward, you will
grow in your feelings of being a true witch, but the exact day from which

you count is your own decision. When you are ready for initiation, you will know. The Lady will tell you your name.

During your year and a day, there is much to study. Astrology, herbalism, spellcraft, tarot, I Ching, runes, crystals, numerology, gardening, camping, whole foods cooking, environmentalism, mythology, music, and world religion are just a few of the relevant topics. When you believe that your year and a day has passed, you should plan for your initiation.

The Lady may give you your craft name through revelation (that is, you just "know it"), through a dream, through an odd circumstance, or just by a word popping into your mind that you can't stop thinking about. Once you know your name, you are ready to set the date for initiation.

COVEN WORK VERSUS SOLITARY

Generally, initiation implies membership in a coven, but solitaries conduct their own initiation ceremonies, too. The initiation is the moment when you acknowledge completely to yourself that you are a witch, and you have been called to be one. Every witch is a priest or priestess, called in the service of God. The leader of a coven is a High Priest or High Priestess, but every coven member is clergy to Divinity. After all, our power is from the Divine. The initiation is the day that you step up to the plate and say, "Here am I. Send me." From this moment forward, you are no longer investigating Wicca. You are no longer giving Wicca a probationary look. You are no longer wondering whether you are capable of doing magick . You acknowledge that you are not. Only God is, and you're raising your hand to offer God your *Self* as a vehicle to do it.

The initiation ceremony is a symbolic death of the old you and an initialization, or beginning, of the new you. The new you has a new name. The ceremony should be structured as the settling of old accounts and the opening of a new book. The following ceremony is an example of a solitary initiation. It can be adapted to group work for a coven. You need: a backpack to carry your altar tools, a needle and thread, a piece of cloth, and a new Book of Shadows, made as nicely as you can, by hand if possible.

THE CEREMONY

Arrange to have the full day alone. The ceremony has two parts. In the daylight, you will spend the day in the forest, preparing your mind for the closeness with Nature that a witch must have. In the evening, you will prepare a healthy, whole foods dinner for yourself in your own home or at your campsite. You will take a ritual bath with essential oils or wash at the campsite. Then you will begin the evening ceremony. During the night, your dreaming brain will absorb what has happened.

By morning, you will be a real witch.

If you are able to go to a campsite or cabin, this is ideal. If you cannot, be sure you have the house to yourself. Do whatever it takes to arrange that. Lock the doors. Unplug the phones. You cannot be disturbed during the ceremony. Do not wear a watch on this day, at any time.

1. Pack your magickal backpack with your altar tools. Go to a favorite place in the forest, somewhere near a place where you can build a fire and which is also near water, either a lake or a stream. Settle in to this place and spend a good deal of time exploring it. Get to know the lay of the land and the plants and trees. Look around for signs of animals. Be an observer of nature. Be aware of what is in your sacred place. This place will always be tied to you and important to your growth as a witch. Choose it carefully, and make it your own.

2. When you feel that you know this place, sit quietly and ask the trees to speak to you. Look around and see which trees want to talk. Go to them and touch them. Listen for their voices. Trees have extraordinary wisdom and perception. Let them speak to you. Trees will never steer you wrong. Be very sure that you thank them for taking the effort to talk to you. Accept what they say. Don't argue with them. Be grateful for their insight, and believe that it is honest.

    If you have never spoken to trees before, take a thermos of Kava Kava with you for your first time. It will assist you to hear them. You might want to practice talking to trees for a few months before you do this. This might not be the time for a first.

3. Start a fire (safely), and settle down near the water. Set up your altar and build your circle. Include in your circle a place where you can enter or touch the water. (You do not need to put candles physically around your circle. Do it in your mind.)

4. Dip your hands in the water, and sprinkle yourself with it. Say:
    This water takes my cares away. The old is gone. The new me may
    Be bright, creative, sharp, and clear. My mother's voice I'll always hear.

5. Sit quietly in your circle and take out the needle and thread. On the piece of cloth you brought with you, sew a rune to represent your new name.

6. Dip the cloth you just sewed into the water. Say:
    The WATERS of forever will wash [your new name] *in perfect love.*

7. Pass the cloth over the smoke from your fire. Say:
    The FLAME of passion will burn [your new name] *in the book of life.*

8. Let a small corner of your cloth catch on fire. Quickly put the fire out and blow the ashes to the East. Say:

The WINDS of tomorrow will carry [your new name] *to destiny.*

9. Find a place where you can bury your cloth in the ground. Bury it deeply enough that it will not be uprooted. Say:

The EARTH of eternity will plant [your new name] *in solid roots.*

When you have finished this working, close your circle. Immediately pack up your tools, clean up your campground, and go home or go to the place where you will spend the night. You need to focus your mind on cooking dinner and taking a ritual bath. Do not think about what you just did. Turn your mind to the mundane tasks of cooking and bathing.

After your dinner and your bath, clean up your area, and set up a new sacred circle in the place where you are going to spend the evening. Be very sure to turn any clocks you can see around, unplug the telephone, and lock the doors. You are alone. You have no reason to wear clothes for this ritual. Come to the Goddess vulnerable, exposed, naked, unburdened, and free.

Use the method in the section on the Esbat Ceremony (see page 211) to set up your sacred circle. In your new circle, call the watchtowers and fill the circle with light. The words for this ceremony are on your *RUN dot Child* CD, track eight. With your athame, carve your runic name on a candle in the color that you feel represents you. Rub the candle in essential oil and light it. Say:

Mother, I am ready.

Remain quiet, and wait for Her to answer. Say:

[Your old name] *is dead.*

Pick up your athame. Stand, naked, and use your athame to cut the bonds off your body that tied you to all things of old. (Cut strings in the air. Do *not* cut yourself. The Goddess is not pleased by self-mutilation. Your athame should never be used to cut anything but air.) Continue cutting until all ties to the old you have been removed. Say:

[Your new name] *lives in the here and the now.*

Now walk around the circle, clockwise, beginning in the East, and introduce your new self to the watchtowers. Say, as you approach each watchtower:

East: Hail, Arida. Here stands [your new name]. *I welcome your presence and thank you for your protection.*

South: Hail, Tana. Here stands [your new name]. *I welcome your presence and thank you for your protection.*

West: Hail, Tiamat. Here stands [your new name]. *I welcome your presence and thank you for your protection.*

North: Hail, Belili. Here stands [your new name]. *I welcome your presence and thank you for your protection.*

Return to the center of the circle. Standing, say:

I am [your new name], *a part of the wild. I am the child of forever. I live free, as the flowers and birds of the wood. I walk the way of nature. I am the whisper of the wind, breathing life. I am the passion of the fire, burning desire. I am the healing water, soothing wounds. I am the stable earth, grounding and centering life within. I am one with my Creator, and She is one with me. I am* [your new name], *child of the fates, daughter of destiny, and son of eternity. I am* [your new name], *all that I was meant to be.*

Now begin to touch your body. Start with your forehead, and touch each part of your body. Say:

I commit my mind to thoughts in the service of She who gives life.
I commit my mouth to speak Her word.
I commit my heart to fulfill Her desires.
I commit my loins to lust after Her will.
I commit my arms to do Her work.
I commit my legs to walk in Her way.
I commit my body to behave as Her child.
Now, I, [your new name], *committed in body and soul to the Lady, submit to Her wishes and make Her Lord my Master.*
My feet will walk in His way.
My legs will carry me to His service.
My arms will carry the burdens He gives me.
My heart will follow His lead.
My mind will accept His teaching.

Sit quietly for a few moments, and refresh yourself from the circle's energy. Then quiet your mind, and begin to read these words out loud.

And He will give me guidance
　　For She did light the Way.
　　　　I'll be held in Their service
　　　　　　With bonds I chose. To Day
　　　　　　　　I made peace with my maker.
　　　　　　　　　　I stood to take Their call.
　　　　　　　　　　　　I live in Them forever.
　　　　　　　　　　And I WILL have it all.
　　　　　　　　For ALL is found inside me.
　　　　　　I know the voice within.
　　　I follow His direction.
　　　　　He speaks to me. And in
　　　　　the darkness I receive Him.
　　　　　　　His power makes me whole.
　　　　　　　　I open like a lotus
　　　　　　　　　　When He is in control.

For, Yes, He is my Master.
My Mother gave Her word.
She said He was the lightning
That strikes. And every bird
And bee has told this story.
To nature, I'll be true.
I have beheld His Glory
And it's in ME. The New
And Old can live together.
For now I see the fit.
I signed up for Her Service.
To Him, I did submit.

And this has been the secret.
The power behind the throne.
The Woman is the Lady.
The Man is Me Alone.
And if I make Him Master
Then I become His mate.
The Yin Yang makes us lovers.
Divinity is Fate.
Inside I am the Goddess.
And He is Master Crow,
The Raven of Poetic
Re-form who long ago
Decided to unearth me
And wake me from the dead
I walk with Him as lover
And He will always bed
me now or be embedded.
He is the Master. Deal
with Him to do the magick,
And break the Seventh Seal.
For She has made Him Father
And I accept Her law
So now I take the promise
To live as one who saw
The light beyond the tunnel,
The axe that never fell,
The hanging man of Tarot,
The gate that led to Hell.
And I say, "There's Nirvana"

And I say, "It can be
A garden here like Dilmun
And I will have it." Free
And easy I can make it.
My wand's imbued with light.
It glows with its own aura.
It turns away the night.
And I command His Power.
He gave it to My Soul
The night I turned to Witchcraft
And made the Cow Bell Toll.

Which called the Bull from pasture,
And crowned the Lion King
And soared like any Eagle
And stood as Human. Sting

Or poison, spray, or bite
In my wand, He's placed the right
Means of making me survivor
He, the Dark Lord, who is Driver
Of the wayward Car or Chariot
That a cross, the Dark, will carry it
To our home.

And by His Will I'm made a witch
Forever in Her service. Hitch
your wagon to my star now
For I'm flying to the moon. How

Can you know what I've been thinking
Unless lights are on and blinking?

I'm explosive. Can't you see it?
In a moment, I will Be it.
Ride my broom and see me flying.
On the stick, I can't be trying,
Must be doing, Cant be working,
Must be posting, Cant be lurking.
For I'm Magick, and the Faeries
Follow Me.

RUN dot Child, and find me Y
All the beanstalks reach the sky
But the Jacks will never climb

                                    Without Her hand.

So I say this little prayer
        For She taught me how to care.
           He is with me day by day,
                      As I stand.

Father, if it please you, may I learn . . .
                To walk in your way
                    To speak with your voice
                    And to hear with your heart.
           And may I see, the best in me, as I stand.
                              By your command.
And I, [your new name], stand perfect and free. My Mother's (Son/Daughter),
and My Father's Witch.

                              Blessed be!

Now present yourself with your new Book of Shadows, close the circle, and
go to sleep. Keep your Book of Shadows by the bedside to record any
dreams you might have tonight.

When you wake tomorrow morning, you will be

                        The Real Thing.
                Blessed be, and love forever.

                        Lady Raya

RUN dot Child, We All are ONE
    Interspersed with Love and Fun.
       When you find your special Way
             "I'll" be there

      Now by my hand,
      This work shall be
        As blessed as
      She chooses. See,
        I can not do,
        I can not act
      Without my God.
      That is the pact.
      And so I say,
      If She wills. May

           I, Mother?

Part Three

Ceremonies,
Beliefs,
a Catechism,
and Technology

Esbat Ceremonies

Ring the bell. Sweep the area. Say:

The circle is about to be cast. Enter here only of your own free will.

Go around the circle clockwise, lighting the candles. The candle in the East is white or yellow. In the South, it is red. In the West, it is blue. In the North, it is green or black.

As you light each candle, all stand and face that direction. Say, with your arms raised:

Hail, Arida, lady of air. Hail, guardians of the East, powers of air.

Powers of intellect, blow through us with your freshness, that we may be renewed. Fill our lungs with your gift of flowing life. Keep us from becoming stale and stagnant. Teach us to appreciate the in and the out, and guide us with your wisdom of her ways, that we may sail by your stars.

Blessed be.

Hail, Tana, lady of fire. Hail, guardians of the South, powers of fire. Powers of passion, fuel our passions. Warm our hearts and fill us with the burning desire to do the Lady's will. Give us your light and your protection. Teach us to drive, that we may know our passion's way.

Blessed be

Hail, Tiamat, serpent of the watery abyss. Hail, guardians of the West, powers of water, powers of healing. You who remind us of our womb, soothe us, and calm us as in the arms of our Mother. Give us your rain, so that our flowers may grow. Quench our thirst for the knowledge of your secret depths. Teach us your ebb and flow, that we may bend and reform.

Blessed be.

Hail Belili, mother of the mountains. Hail, guardians of the watchtower of the North, powers of earth. Powers of substance, strengthen us, and give us the knowledge of mercy.

Center us, and make us committed and resolute. Give us your magnetism, that we may know how to attract and be attracted. Teach us your solid ground, that we may know where to stand.

Blessed be.

Seal the circle three times—once with water, once with incense, and once with your athame.

To seal the circle:

Hold your bowl of altar water up to the sky in your right hand and your bowl of salt in your left hand. Say:

Blessed be thou creature of water. Blessed be thou creature of earth.

Earth and water, son and daughter, inside and outside, be cleansed!

Cast out all that would do me harm. Take in all that would do me good. By the power of the Lady's way, so mote it be!

With your fingers, pinch three salts into water. Stir with your wand three times.

May this water be purified with the earth so that together they may cause great good.

Hold the cup to your heart and purify it until it glows. Then sprinkle the water around the circle. (Always assume we go around the circle *deosil*, or clockwise, unless we specifically say widdershins.) Say:

Earth, Water, Fire, Air. Call on all that's good and fair. Air, fire, sea, and salt. At your boundaries, ill must halt. Round I go and round I be, as my circle binds to me.

Then carry the incense (around the circle deosil) continuing to chant.

Then take your athame and draw the circle by symbolically drawing a circle on the ground at its edges.

Now I call on three times three. Seal the circle, bound to me.

Draw the pentagram with your athame at the door. (The door is at the east gate.) Then each person self-anoints with the oil on your altar by drawing the pentagram with fingers dipped in a drop of anointing oil (forehead, left breast, right shoulder, left shoulder, right breast, forehead). Then on your forehead draw a tiny cross and a circle around it with your fingers.

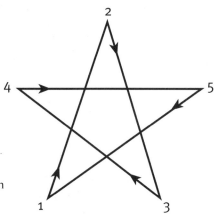

The Sealing Pentagram
Arrows indicate direction
in which to draw the
pentagram.

Air, Fire, Water, Earth
Elements of primal birth
Fire, Water, Earth, Air
Guardians of natal care
Water, Earth, Air, Fire
Upper, downer, lower, higher
Earth, Air, Fire, Water
Rounder, center, inner, outer
By wand and blade
By cup and plate
I call the quarters
To my fate
Beyond the land
Between the sea
I call the sky,
Attend to me.
And be it will of Lady, Lord
Will make it so, by my accord.
This is my will. So mote it be.
I call the world to service me.
In perfect love and perfect trust, we invite our Lord and Lady to enter our circle. Hear us,
eternal Mother. Hear us, ever-present Father. Attend our rites which we hold in Your
honor.
Lady of Moon and Lord of Sky
Come to me and be my "I"
Help me see beyond the veil
Guide the stars by which I sail
Charge my circle, with thy light
Brilliant, beaming, blue and white
Teach me through Your loving hand
Written on the sea and sand.
Heal me through Your gifts surround-
Ing me. Forests, fields, and sound,
Taste, and touch, and smell, and sight.
Father, Mother, be my light.
Lady of Egyptian flame,
Children need not know Your name.
Mother is as Mother does.
Queen or Mary, Isis was.
She stood for the Woman, Earth,
Giving us our human birth.
And She lives inside of me

And without, the flowing "C."
Lord of forests, Lord of fields
He alone the power wields
She, entwined, the dual one,
I, Their daughter, and Their son.
Be here with me, Lady, Lord,
As I take the magick sword
That will make me King and Queen
Deep within.
"Hail, Arida, bright lady of the air.
Hail, Tana, lady of fire
Hail, Tiamat, serpent of the watery abyss
Hail, Belili, mother of the mountains."
The circle is cast. We are between the worlds, beyond the bound of time.

Point athame to each direction and then to the sky and the ground.
Chant:
Io Evohe Io Evohe Io Evohe . . .
NAM mu Nam mu O Nam Mu Ae Ee Ae Ee O Nam Mu
Nin Ma Nin Mah O Nin Mah Ae Ee Ae Ee O Nin Mah

The Leader says:
Now we will all fill the circle with a goodness and love—the deepest love we feel. We want to reach inside ourselves and find that love, bringing it out through all the pores in our bodies, and using it to fill the circle with a light blue light. We each take a moment now to concentrate on filling ourselves with that feeling of love toward ourselves and each other. Bring that love out from our deepest soul, from our innermost being. Fill the circle with that magick love. Fill it until the circle can hold no more. Push the love out. Make it emanate from us. Believe that we can generate more and more love, until the circle is pulsating with the love we have pushed out of ourselves into the circle. Now our joint love is surrounding us. We can feel it touching us. The air is thick with the love we have each generated and pushed into the air around us. We breathe it in. We smell it. We feel it touching us. We see it. The circle is light blue now. We are all fading into a fuzzy, light blue color. It has a sweet smell, and deep inside ourselves we hear our own music. The music of our own drummer.

We meet today to honor the Goddess and the horned God. That we may know they are in our selves, and our selves are in them. Blessed be.

In a moment, we will enter into a new space, a place in which we are completely safe and protected, and we will be with our Mother and Father, the Deity eternal. It is in this safe place that we will totally adore and worship the Goddess and the God. This place will be a place of power, and we will descend deeply inside ourselves to find it. There, the God and the Goddess will know us, and we will know Them, and we will worship and adore Them for *all that They are. We will go alone to this place. We will meet our God and Goddess alone, and we will return alone of our own free will.*

As we enter into this place, we will leave the outer world. We will meet beings in this place, but they will have no power to hurt us. We will always be empowered to return to our circle of protection, whenever we choose, at our own free will. As we return we will dismiss the beings we met along the way, and leave them in their world, not to cross into our sacred circle.

We will return from our voyage empowered, and charged with the strength and perfect love of the God and Goddess. For the God and Goddess want our adoration, and our journey is performed in Their honor. Our journey is begun. Blessed be.

Io Evohe. Io Evohe. Nam mu O nam mu nin mah O nin mah.

Aphrodite, Mother of us all. (Chant until the feelings are built to the point of hypnotic trance.)

At this point, all remain quiet as each person begins the journey into him- or herself, in a quiet and personal meditation to meet the God source.

At this point, the circle has been cast and sealed, and each person is in contact with Deity.

Now the ceremony diverts to whatever its purpose is for the day.

If there are new tools to be dedicated to the Goddess:

Lay the tool to be purified on the altar. Brush it symbolically with your broom to shake the old aura off. (Mine is a cinnamon kitchen broom. You can use a pine twig or a sprig of mint if you want. Just be sure it smells good and comes from a tree.) Say:

May this (name of tool) *be purified. I dedicate it to the service and for the use of the Goddess. Words of honor, words of truth, enter this tool, that its past may be cleansed and its distortions corrected. Unfriendly spirits, leave this tool. Begone to your own place.*

Sprinkle the water over the tool and the altar. With the sprinkling say,

Blessed be, thou creature of art. I charge you from the center of existence, above and below, through out and about, within and without. I charge you to serve me in my service of the Goddess, between the worlds, and in all worlds. I charge you to be part of the one. So mote it be.

Eh-chahd Rash, Eh-chu-doh-toh Rash Ye-chu-do-toh, Teh-mur-ah-toh Eh-chahd
(One is God's beginning, one principle is God's individuality, God's permutation is one.)

DARK MOON RITUAL (SKIP THIS ON THE FULL MOON)

Say:
On the night of the New Moon
We begin a journey. Soon
Deep within, an old one dies,
Making room for birth. She lies
In await for something new
As the cycle tends to do.
Every end will now begin

As the circle slows its spin
Every start was once a stop,
Every bottom, once a top,
Every virtue, once a sin,
Every vice can let Sun in.

We meet tonight to honor the crone, dark and dangerous. Hecate of our dreams. She who calls the raven and the wolf, the spirit of our primordial way. It is She who is the spirit of the wild, our connection with the freedom of humanity. On the dark Moon, we renew our faith. Faith that She will return to us, and light our night again. For the dark Moon reminds us that we cannot live without Her, and makes us want Her more. On this dark night, we are reminded to begin again.

What stops one thing starts another, in the loop of a cycle.
May the honor and the glory of our Lord and Lady live within us forever.
Blessed be.

Full Moon Ceremony
(skip this during the Dark Moon)

Say:

We meet together to share our joy of life and to thank the God and Goddess for providing us with this day and this life. Whatever we would ask of the God, we know the God already knows our will and our task on Earth. Be assured that in everything we strive to ensure that we harm none, not even ourselves. And we remember that as we give, so also it is returned to us threefold. On this night of the Full Moon, let us join in the prayer for guidance.

Lord of heaven, God of light
Take us through the dark of night
Bless us deep inside our soul
Make us see the human whole
Which is all humanity
And is what we all can be
When our spirits are above
Guided by your radiant love
To our destiny.
Father, help us through the storm
Keep us comforted and warm
With you guiding us to know
What to do and where to go
So that we will ever be
Walking in the way with thee
And as we live here on Earth

Help us to earn our rebirth
As your children.
Mother-Father, hear our prayer
Lead us to the temple where
We can learn your loving word
And our voices can be heard
Joyfully empowering
Us to feel the showering
Of the light of heaven's gate
Where we know our God does wait
To bring us home.

After the New Moon or Full Moon prayers, sing a Wiccan song or play pagan music and beat drums.

On New Moon and Full Moon ceremonies, you may perform magick after the blessings of the wine and food. After magickal workings, you return to the ceremony and close the circle properly, respectfully thanking the watchtower guardians. Remember that you do not dismiss Deity. Nor do you behave in an arrogant or disrespectful manner toward Deity.

After the Standard New Moon or Full Moon ceremony, return to the blessings of the Cakes and Ale.

Blessing of the Cakes and Ale

Mother of the Earth and Moon, Father of the Sun and Sky, we honor You.

Pour wine or ale for the God and Goddess (in one wine glass). Get out the food for the day's ceremony. Hold the wine and a plate of the food up to the sky. Stand and say blessing over the cakes and ale:

All life is Your own. All glory is Yours. All honor is Yours.
All fruits of the earth are fruits of Your womb,
Blessed be!

When ready to do magick, stand and point athame to ground and sky. Say:

Source above, and source below.
Flow through me, and make it so.
Cause no harm, and bind by three.
Live by love, the law for me.

Then perform your magick for the day.

To close the circle, say:

Mother and Father,
We thank You for Your presence
With us now and always.

Face North. Raise your arms to the sky and point to a spot over your head with both hands. Say:

Eheieh.

Point to your throat: Say

Jehovah Elohim.

Point to your heart: Say:

IAO

Point to your hips: Say:

Shaddai Al Chai

Point to your feet: Say:

Adonai Malech.

Then start at your feet and say it all backwards. As you are doing this, envision a fountain of white light beginning to bubble up from the ground, through your feet, up to your head, and pouring out your head into two circulating spheres of white light, circulating and bubbling like a fountain through your body. Concentrate on this vision. Make the energy flow through you. Control the subatomic. You are a Witch. Controlling the subatomic is what you do.

Continue this until you feel the energy circulating.

Finish with *Blessed be.*

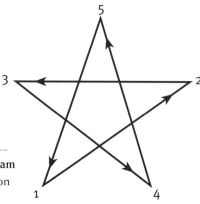

The Banishing Pentagram
Arrows indicate direction
in which to draw the
pentagram.

Go to each of the four directions and draw a banishing pentagram (see page 218) with your athame, then extinguish the candle with a candle snuffer (rather than blowing them out). At each Direction, say:

Guardians of the _____, we thank you
for joining in our circle. May we live together in peace,
now and forever, Blessed be.

Raise athame to the sky and then point it to the ground. Open arms to encompass everyone to say:

The circle is open yet unbroken. May the Lady live in our hearts.
Merry meet, and merry part and merry meet again.

Blessed be!

CANON OF BELIEFS IN ELIJAN WICCA

1. EACH INDIVIDUAL HAS A PURPOSE

Every person is put here on Earth for a specific and unique purpose. There are no throwaway people. God is a personal and loving God who cares uniquely for each person in a personally meaningful way that each person can understand. God cares for everyone and speaks directly to everyone, with no intermediary—not priest, minister, or any other person. Each person is a child of God, important to God, and under God's direct guidance. None of us has the right or the ability to judge the life of another; all human beings must be respected in their own paths.

2. GOD IS NOT LIMITED

God operates through, with, and in concert with the natural laws of the physical universe, by choice, not limitation. The laws of nature and physics are the tools God used to build the material world, our school called Earth. By choice, God allows these natural laws to govern our lives. Allowing the physical laws of the universe to be consistent is God's way of helping us feel comfortable and secure in our world. It is, however, entirely within God's power to overrule these laws. We do not believe in accidents, and we pay attention to circumstance. We believe accidents and circumstance are the means of communication to us about guidance for our path. We may not and cannot command to see God perform miracles in order to prove miracles to be true, because God does not obey human commands. This explains why psychic phenomena cannot be repeated by laboratory experiment.

God is neither male nor female, and when we put limitations on God, we are misunderstanding the nature of Deity. We call God "Mother" and "Father" as a means of allowing us, as limited humans, to feel closer and more personal to the awesome power of the Deity. Deity takes on the form of Mother and Father in our minds in order to allow us that close relationship.

3. We All Have Eternal Life

We are on Earth in a physical body temporarily. Our real nature is a spirit form, and that spirit form has eternal life. Our spirit form exists in the material world as part of an experience to learn from the Creator the full range of emotions and life experiences. We may return to Earth repeatedly in different bodies until our spirit is judged to have fulfilled its learning requirements. When God decides we are ready, we move on to another plane of existence in a nonmaterial realm. No spirit is ever lost or destroyed. No person ever ceases to exist. Although we may not remember other lives in our consciousness, our subconscious does remember them, and we must be careful of our debt to karma by showing ourselves to be loving unconditionally to all members of the human race, including ourselves.

To be unloving and unforgiving toward ourselves is a setback to our karma and prevents us from growing and developing in our soul. Our capacity for forgiveness extends to forgiving ourselves; we have no original sin. We have no mortal sin. Eternity is a long time. Keeping eternity in perspective allows us to focus on becoming unconditional in our love to both ourselves and others. Because we believe karma keeps a record of all that occurs in all our lives, suicide doesn't solve anything. We learn to work it out.

4. There Is No Hell, Other Than the One We Create for Ourselves

There is no hell, other than the hell we create for ourselves in our own mind. God is a loving and just God. Her concern is for our education and fulfillment of our individual purpose and path. Many people are carrying out a self-attributed sentence of hell by implementing a hell on Earth in their own lives, but that is not God's Will. That is our own refusal to accept Her love and to advance in our spiritual awareness. We each have the power to release our self-imposed sentences and to implement a life of happiness and paradise within Her guiding love, empowered to live a fulfilling and happy life. We each can strive for the realization of our unity with the Goddess in this lifetime. Alternatively, because we do have free will, we can sentence ourselves to repeat the hell on Earth we may be living now in future lifetimes. There is no supernatural power tempting us to do unnatural acts. All natural acts are beautiful, and when we follow the feeling in our hearts, we are doing God's Will. When we say, "An' it harm none, do as Thy Will," we mean that the desire placed in our hearts is what God wants for us. She will not cause us to desire to harm another at any time.

5. We Have Free Will

Human beings have been given free will as a gift from God. With this free will, we have the responsibility to improve, enhance, and better ourselves. Conversely, we have the option to destroy ourselves. Our circumstance is impacted by our behavior; our behavior impacts circumstance. It is God's Will that we try, and strive, and learn, and grow. Should we choose to live an unhappy life, God will not stop us. For if He did, He would be taking away our free will, which is God's gift to us.

We must understand that unhappiness is a choice. It doesn't happen without our agreement and cooperation. We strive for improvement, but happiness lives inside us unconditionally. (In other words, the pursuit of happiness doesn't make sense. Happiness only needs acceptance; it does not need pursuit.) God loves us unconditionally. We strive, however, to earn Her respect by behaving in a manner that is in concert with Her individual will for our lives. No one knows another's path, and so we can do nothing but support our fellow travelers in their walk. We strive to avoid interference with another's path, but when approached for assistance by a person in need, we accept that the Goddess has directed that person to us, and we give him or her what we have to give.

6. We Respect the Holy Books of the World Religions as Inspired by God

We believe the Bible, the Qur'an, the Qabalah, the Torah, the Book of Mormon, the Bhagavad Gita, the Vedic Writings, the Gnostic Scriptures, the writings of Buddha, and the Tao-Te-Ching are all holy revelations of some type delivered to humanity by God. We consider them all to be holy and sacred books, blessed to our religion, and consistent with each other in their source document state (before the interpretation by the various churches). We do not read them literally but rather as insightful literature, intended to provoke deep thought and feeling. We give the same level of respect to the laws of Nature, which we consider also to be a revelation of God.

We are an inclusive religion. We believe God is in each of us, and we are all capable of becoming and evolving into better, more spiritual beings of light. We believe there is no one "right" religion. Rather, we believe the Goddess has provided alternative religious practices in Her plan for diversity and evolution of the human experience and in Her infinite wisdom in guiding humanity toward our goal of union with Her. God's dual nature as both male and female is reflected in the dual nature each of us has, in our aspects of male and female characteristics. We believe a personal relationship with God is achievable, and, through that relationship, we each learn God's Will for our lives on Earth. Within our personal relationship, God will tell us what is allowable for us individually.

While we believe God speaks individually to people, we also believe God will never tell any person to perform acts that harm another person. We believe God speaks, but we don't believe God tells us to do harm. We are a personal and solitary religion, one in which people may attend community worship, or worship individually, while still being considered a member of our community. We have no church authority structure, no Wiccan queen or king, no formal leader. All Wiccan communities are headed by the Goddess, and the Goddess alone, who lives in each of our hearts; speaks with the authority of the universe; and guides the winds, the stars, the future, the past, and the karma of forever.

7. We Believe Scientific Endeavor is Consistent with God's Will

We believe there is a spirit world interacting with us on a daily basis and governed by laws of Nature from another realm. Science has not discovered these laws yet, but science is learning more each day, and we expect that someday it will catch up with religion. We are assured by the Goddess that these laws exist, and we trust that science will eventually find them to the extent She wills them to be found. We encourage and participate in scientific investigation and endeavors. We encourage all questions and examinations. We accept our religion on faith, yet we feel no need to accept only on faith tenets for which we have enormous evidence. We encourage scientific questioning and investigation of the paranormal, psychic, beauteous, and miraculous phenomena we see in the practice of our religion. We are practitioners of magick, and we rejoice in our partnership with God. We believe magick is a science that calls on the physical laws of Nature in its work.

8. We Believe in One and Only One God, Who is Called by Many Names and Has Aspects That Appear to Us Differently

Whether we refer to God as Allah, Jesus, Krishna, Adonai, Zeus, Aphrodite, Isis, Diana, Buddha, Shiva, the Great Energy Force, or the Tao does not make God different. We each choose the name of God most comfortable for us as individuals, based on our childhood training or our personal under-standings and feelings. We know God to be above the human limitations of gender, and we are indifferent to an individual's preference to see God as either female or male. We know that God's personal revelation to an indi-vidual will be a private matter between God and that person, chosen by God as the best means to achieve unity with that person. We respect each person's private relationship and acknowledge the validity of each person's experience in knowing God.

At the same time, we do not propose that God is so limited that human-ity can understand the Lord and the Lady with just one example of the Deity's personality. We see the various faces, legends, and mythologies of God as many ways for us as limited human beings to learn the nature and the mind of the complex and all-knowing Deity. We believe all of history's legends and mythologies about God hold truths, and we strive to be open to hearing the truths in all of them.

9. God is Not a Creation of Humanity

God is not a construct made up by individuals, and, indeed, God has a real-ity above the reality we experience in our humanity on Earth. We know there are great commonalities in the experience of God across all human-ity and all religions. We know that every religion, at its core, believes in loving relationships and the magnificence of Creation. We do not believe God is a creation of humanity, nor is God simply the sum of all human thought-forms. God exists, is real, and has laws, desires, and commands. Since God is not human, we are limited in our understanding of the full-ness of God. That is why we as humans relate to God in different ways, why God has many aspects, many names, and many manifestations. That is why we may each have a different experience of God, and yet all our experiences are, in essence, the same. We respect each other's differences of opinion and experience, and we relate to each other's similarities as chil-dren of the same Creator.

Whatever experience or understanding any person has of God, we respect that this is God's personal revelation at this time of individual devel-opment. She is the decision maker regarding how each of us will know Her. If She decides to be Diana to one person, Allah to a second person, Yahweh to a third person, Jesus to a fourth person, and simply the Great Energy Force of Creation to the fifth, so mote it be. She has Her reasons, and this is Her world.

10. God is relevant and present in our daily lives

We see God interacting in our daily lives, we feel Her presence as we perform our daily work, and we hear Her voice speaking to us as we make our daily choices. We know God's love personally and reflect it to those around us. We know all people have the potential to establish a direct working relationship with the Deity. We know that God is merciful, and when we have challenging experiences, we know She intends for us to learn from them.

CATECHISM OF THE
TRADITION OF
ELIJAN WICCA

Creation. The Creator of the universe loves us as a parent and relates to us on a personal and individual level, as a perfect and ideal Mother and Father. *This is the theology of Chesed.*

Gnosis. We are each capable of communicating with our Creator and receiving active life direction. *This is the theology of Geburah.*

Eternal life. We are all eternal beings. We have always existed and will always exist. The purpose of the lives we live on Earth is to learn control of the subatomic nature of our emotional power and to achieve a state of unconditional love. We will reincarnate multiple times until we have learned this and will only go to live with our Mother and Father in our home after we successfully exhibit our ability to sustain love. *This is the theology of Tiphareth.*

Karma. The Creator has ordained balance in the universe, and from this balance proceeds expectation. A seed can be expected to grow into the plant like the one from which it came. A tadpole can be expected to become a frog. We have each been created for a specific and unique purpose, and our soul is unwavering in its compulsion to fulfill it. Because our Creator has given us free will, we are capable of overriding our soul and interfering with its karmic task. Our soul has the power and the commandment to invoke accidents, coincidence, and circumstance to guide us back to our path. Karma will occur, and we must follow our soul's guidance to allow it to complete the balance of the universe with the least disturbance possible. *This is the theology of Malkuth.*

Duality. The nature of the universe is both male and female, up and down, yang and yin, hot and cold, hard and soft, strong and weak, light and dark. Bad is what allows us to know good. Hardship is what makes it possible for us to know luxury. Pain is why we recognize pleasure. Everything emanates from a reference frame and portrays a relative reality. From God's perspective, everything is good; everything has a good purpose, when used in God's context. Life gives us lemons so we can make lemonade. There are no accidents: only guidance and correction for our path. Hardship and difficulties befall us in order to aid us in finding our way. *This is the theology of Netzach.*

Salvation. Although all is good in God's plan, and nature is careful of the species, we as humanity need special dispensation to be released from the duality of nature and need salvation from the evil that will befall us as the result of the amorality of mathematical chaos. We need salvation from the law in order to be consistently moral. This salvation is granted to us through faith, and faith sets us free from the nature of evil. We have faith in our Creator, and this allows us to feel in our hearts the guidance she has written there. We work at discerning this guidance and following our True Will. Following our True Will is the will of the Goddess. This is what we mean when we say: "An' it harm none, do as Thy Will." We have no law but this law, and this law in itself is sufficient when we have faith. *This is the theology of Hod.*

Evolution. Because our Creator is benevolent, She wishes for Her children to grow and develop independence. With this independence, She hopes we will choose to come to Her voluntarily. But we are limited creatures. She gives us a stable environment, with the rules of physics and mathematics, so that we can learn and develop philosophies, contexts, and dependable expectations. She has given us the illusion of this universe, with its evolutionary development, for our use in learning and advancing. This universe operates on principles we can discover, investigate, and model. It is Her Will for us to learn its methods and operation. *This is the theology of Yesod.*

Covenant. She makes us the promise of everlasting happiness and joy in the cradle of Her arms if we will choose it. She has only one limit, and that is the limit She has covenanted to Herself to allow us freedom. The peace of the Goddess is our birthright. We need only claim our inheritance by following our True Will. This will make our life on Earth a life in the Garden of Eden. *This is the theology of Kether-Chokmah-Binah.*

The Technology
of Magick

What People Expect

Many people want to cast spells and do magick to help them take care of the problems in their lives. Often, people think they can solve their problems with money, and so they wish to do a spell to attract money to themselves. They purchase green candles, put almonds in little velvet pouches, and sprinkle rosemary on their doorway, asking the faeries and the fates to help them out with a little cash. Their friends throw pennies on the floor in hopes it will cause money to grow in the house.

Money spells, like love spells, are fervent wishes for a tool to use to empower ourselves to make our dreams come true. We want money so we can implement our own dreams. We want to have power to help ourselves. We want this power to be held in our own hands. We want someone to love us so that we can feel complete. Both money spells and love spells presuppose that we can have what we want only if we are empowered to get it for ourselves. If only we had money, we could buy our way to happiness. If only we had a true love, we could find joy in the trivial pursuits of daily life.

What Actually Happens

The technology of magick works differently from the concept of self-empowerment. Magick is a technology in the sense that it operates using the physics of the software of consciousness. We have a collective consciousness and an individual consciousness, much like a computer network has the memory resident on the Internet servers, and also the memory resident on individual computer workstations. To correctly perform a magick spell, we must learn the techniques to tap into the network memory and cause actions that impact the external world. This is an exercise we do with our mind and our mental state. It is not done by almonds, or rosemary, or green candles, or pennies on the floor.

The Importance of Using Almonds

Having said that, of course, it is important to point out that history shows us that almonds, rosemary, green candles, and pennies on the floor are very helpful in achieving the correct mental state to perform the magick for a money spell. The critical understanding in your training as a witch, however, is for you to clearly know that it is your mind that performs the magick. The magick is not performed by the objects you use to invoke the correct mental state.

Living the Magickal Life

The technology of magick, once understood, is like the wonder of reading. Once you learn how to read, you do it subconsciously and automatically. If you know how to read in the English language, you are unable to see letters written in English without associating them with sounds and words you know. Before you learn to read, however, all the letters look like scribbling and gibberish. This is the same with magick. Once you learn how to associate its workings in your brain, it happens subconsciously. You begin to perform magick in all that you do, and you start living a magickal life. Soon, things start to take a turn for you, and you realize that nothing that occurs will hurt you. Accidents, coincidence, and circumstance align to set your path in tune. Your faith solidifies, and your mountains move.

The basic tenets to understanding how magick works are five.

1. We are all one; we resonate with the universe.
2. Our resonant frequency determines our intent; our intent focuses energy.
3. Focused energy changes matter; it causes coincidence and circumstance.
4. The world we experience is the world we are choosing at this time with our current intent.
5. To change our world, we have to change our tune. To change our tune, we have to pay the piper.

These are not easy concepts, and many people turn from them rather than look at how they may be true. The purpose of the first year training course in Elijan Wicca is to introduce these concepts slowly and to teach the use of them in performing magickal work. During the first year course, you will learn how to achieve the mental control required to perform magick. This control is acquired through practice and training in exercises and individual work. The specific steps in performing magick are set out in the following table.

Mental State	Required Step
Calmness	1. Prepare a place where you can build a sacred circle, either mentally or physically, whichever is appropriate for your situation. This place must be beautiful so that nothing will distract your mind from its work.
Beginning trance state— time and space travel	2. Picture the end result as already true. Use whatever magickal tools, rituals, or sacred objects you need to help you form this picture. Invoke the vision. Use idiomatic and physical acts to cause the vision to surround you.
Deep shamanic trance	3. See the details of that vision. In your mind experience, on a multisensory basis, fill in the blanks about how that end result is. How does it smell? Taste? What is its texture? How does it sound? See the minute details of your vision, and take the time to experience it with your senses.
State of empowerment; deflation of ego	4. Breathe and feel the color of that already existent end result. Incorporate the know-ledge of its existence into your associative mental and cellular database. Make it part of the world as you know it. Believe on the inside—at the level of your blood and bones—that it is truly existent.
Filling the ego state with gratitude and humility	5. Thank the Goddess for all that is, and appreciate Her awesome power and mercy. Feel gratitude for whatever She has chosen to provide. If She has chosen to give you grief, invoke a feeling of gratitude for the learning experience. Whatever your situation, you must invoke the feeling of gratitude in your heart in order to set the force-carrying particles on their trajectory. Be thankful and filled with

joy for Her mercy, and feel humbled by Her power. This step is not optional.

Releasing the humility into the Earth and invoking the functioning awareness

6. Return from your trance state slowly to the here and now, noting what you see along the way. Observe what choices and options were set in order to form the future you envisioned. Note carefully what paths had to be taken to get you to the future you chose. You must return slowly if you are to do this.

It is very important to be awake and aware as you journey back to the present. Record the changes required in you and the paths you must take to allow the end result to occur.

Balancing ego with humility

7. Make a written action plan to implement these changes in yourself and identify the paths you must take. Do not concern yourself with what others must do to make your plan come true. Concentrate only on yourself, your own behavior, and the choices you must make. Use an appropriate technique to release the energy of your plan. For example:

If it is a passionate plan, *enflame* it with fire.
If it is a healing plan, *bathe* it in water.
If it is an inspirational plan, *cast* it to
       the winds.
If it is a solid and stable plan, *plant* it
       in the earth.
Perform these acts physically.

Recalling gratitude, and letting it form a triad with ego and humility

8. Close the circle reverently. Thank the watchtowers and assume Mother's blessing. Remember that reverence toward Deity is critical.

Living in a state of remembering your faith

9. Relax and put the magickal working out of your mind. Immediately fill your day with mundane, quiet, and physical tasks, such as gardening, cooking, carpentering, sewing, or housework. Do not allow your mind to stray

to thoughts of the magickal working. It must be offered the opportunity to move on, and your thoughts will pull it back. Think only of the joy you feel in Mother's presence.

Watering your seeds

10. As you go to sleep that night, picture yourself watering the seeds you have planted in eternity. Envision the watering can pouring over your mind and healing the tear of the energy you gave forth. Then sleep peacefully, and give the act no more thought.

By morning, the deed will be on its way to being done. You will have set an act in motion that will impact the universe. The results will now occur.

After some time, you will realize that your inner intent of that day has manifested. It may take a form that is different from the one that you envisioned, and it may take longer than you expected. It may have a different flavor than the one you consciously imagined, but the underlying intent will be true.

This is the technology of magick, and it is a law of physics of the collective psyche. People perform magickal acts every day, without knowing what they are doing. They are accidental magicians, making their magick as an offshoot of emotion that is unfocused, spraying their energy randomly and without direction. As a result, people use their minds to cause heartbreak and hardship, illness and sorrow, depression and disease, agony and pain. As a witch, you commit to learning the rules of this technology, and you vow to implement them in a conscious and purposeful way in your life. You know that the power of your mind is the power of the Source, and you use it only in Her service and in ways in which She approves.

You learn that there is no "if only"; there is just faith. It is this faith that allows us to learn to trust ourselves and follow our heart. It is the Will in our heart that speaks to us as the Word of the Goddess. In this way, we learn to be awake, aware, and alive in the world She made.

May the road rise up to meet you, and the Piper earn his due.

Blessed be!
Lady Raya